MW00879543

EASY

BOOK FOUR

BURNOUT SERIES

DAHLIA WEST

TABLE OF CONTENTS

CHAPTER ONE

Daisy Cutter opened her wallet even though she already knew what she'd find. She counted out the $52 as though by some miracle more bills would appear. When they didn't, she sighed and looked up at the Arrival/Departure screen on the monitor in front of her. She didn't have enough for a bus ticket back to Nebraska, just as she hadn't eight months ago.

She stuffed her wallet back into her jeans pocket and pulled out her cell phone. She frowned as she looked down at it. Matt's number was first on the list. If she loathed calling her mama at this moment, she absolutely refused to call Matt. He was the whole reason she was here in the first place. She scrolled down and chose her mama's number. Daisy tapped her foot as she listened to it ring, wondering what kind of mood the woman would be in as though she had any other kind of mood aside from 'irritated'.

"Yeah," came Sue Cutter's perpetually haggard voice. Daisy's frown deepened. It was, apparently, impossible to catch the woman in a good mood. Daisy wondered, briefly, if her mama had even bothered to look at the Caller ID before answering.

"Mama," she said, keeping her voice light. It wouldn't do to sass someone when you were about to beg for money. It wasn't like Sue needed to be reminded that she and her daughter didn't see eye-to-eye on anything.

Daisy's mama was quiet for a moment, and Daisy wondered if

she was simply going to hang up on her. Instead, she said, "Got your phone back."

Daisy grimaced and glanced around at the other people in the terminal, people who *had* enough money to get where they were going.

"Yeah," Daisy confirmed. "Thanks for keeping up the bill."

Sue snorted, and Daisy realized that her mother had more or less simply forgotten about the phone. Sue Cutter wasn't the type to throw money away, as she was about to remind her wayward daughter.

"Don't got no cash," she informed Daisy, "if that's why you're calling." The story had been the same when Daisy called way back in August. She bristled, feeling both irritated and embarrassed. She was calling for money, but it wasn't as though Daisy wouldn't pay it back- eventually.

"Well, I'm not," she lied and kicked a bench with her cowboy boot. She winced as her big toe throbbed.

"So, when are you coming back?" There was no mistaking the underlying tone in her voice.

Last August, Daisy had announced that she was finally, *finally* getting out of their shithole town. She told her mother, and anyone else who would listen, that she and Matt were headed to Sturgis, and if Daisy liked what she saw, well then maybe she'd move there.

Sue Cutter had not been impressed.

She'd told Daisy that Matt was nearly as useless as Daisy herself, and the sooner Daisy Mae put down the crayons and started focusing on a real job, the better off they'd all be.

Daisy adjusted her backpack and heard the *colored pencils* -thank you very damn much- clack together in the front pocket. Her mother had never found Daisy useful for anything- and her drawing even less so.

"Don't see no point in spending money on something that don't come to nothing," Sue Cutter would repeat, often and loudly.

Daisy always resisted the urge to point out that stocking your fridge with beer for a guy who only stopped by a few times a month was just as pointless. If Earl Minor hadn't rescued them from the Vista Valley Trailer Court by now, he wasn't going to.

"I'm not coming back," Daisy said in as firm a tone as she could muster considering she was flat broke and stuck in an unfamiliar city.

"Oh, really? Got your new *career* all worked out?"

Daisy wasn't sure if her mother meant her art or something else. She spun on her heel and walked out of the bus terminal through the double doors that led out to the sidewalk. "Anyway," she said loudly into the phone. "I was just calling to let you know I'm staying."

Sue snorted. "What's your new man's name?" she asked sarcastically. "Cause Matt Clawson's too busy with Steph Newtown to bother with you, not that he was ever any kind of catch to begin with. Boy, you sure can pick 'em."

Daisy also resisted the urge to point out just where she'd gotten her unfortunate taste in men. She sighed and shielded her eyes from the harsh morning sunlight. "Bye, mama. I'll call you again when I get settled."

Not wanting to go yet another round with the older woman, Daisy disconnected the call. She looked around and decided for no good reason to take a left. She headed up the block, following the chain link fence until it gave way to a railroad track. Beyond it was a place called the "Rainbow Motel," or the "Rain ow," as it were, seeing as how one light bulb was burned out. Daisy smirked as she headed for the rat trap. She could relate. She might have one bulb burned out, but she wasn't worried. She could still shine.

The lobby smelled like stale cigarette smoke. If she closed her eyes, she could almost convince herself she was standing in the middle of the double-wide with the orange shag carpet and the lumpy, brown couch pushed up against the wall, but the lobby of the motel had a dingy tile floor and a counter instead, and it was marred with deep-set scratches.

An old woman sat perched on a stool and gave Daisy a cool-eyed assessment as she stepped through the door. Daisy straightened her shoulders. She was no stranger to that look. Though, frankly, what the old woman had to feel superior about was anyone's guess with her stained shirt and her leathered face. The woman looked like she'd been rode hard and put away wet a few too many times. Daisy was only 24, and though she was aware of what people often thought of her appearance, she had a clean shirt on and a smooth face.

Daisy slid half of her only remaining cash across the counter.

"Do much entertaining?" the woman asked.

Daisy bristled at her tone. At first, she was a mixture of embarrassed and incensed, but then she remembered she was new in town. This woman didn't know shit about shit and had no basis to form such a low opinion of Daisy.

The woman sighed and eyed the TV she'd obviously rather be watching. "You bring any johns back to your room," she told Daisy, "I get ten bucks."

Daisy glared at her. For a moment she almost reached out and cracked the woman's jaw. The woman turned back to her and eyeballed her again. "Don't imagine you'd have that many takers, what with all that ink and that nail in your nose."

Daisy, irritated but not cowed, put her tattooed arms on the counter, leaned in close enough so the woman could see it was a stud and not a nail. "I'm not a whore," she seethed.

The woman merely shrugged. "Don't care what you call yourself, if you *sell* yourself, I get a cut."

Daisy snatched the room key off the counter and walked away. It wasn't until she was safely in her room that she threw her backpack at the wall. It thudded and then bounced onto the bed. She looked around the room with a grimace, but shrugged it off. It was just temporary. Things would get better; they always did.

She checked to see that her pencils hadn't broken and laid them gingerly on the small, wobbly table alongside her sketchbook. She had a little more than twenty bucks and three changes of clothes. It wasn't much to build a life on, but you had to start somewhere.

CHAPTER TWO

Jimmy "Easy" Turnbull walked into the one-bedroom house he rented from his former lieutenant, now boss, Chris "Shooter" Sullivan. He shed his grease-stained shirt, tossed it directly into the washing machine, and headed down the hall. In the small bathroom, he unzipped his black cargo pants and yanked them down his hips as he settled onto the crapper. He was practically vibrating from excitement; he had business to take care of, and it had nothing to do with the porcelain throne. He slid off the work boot on his right and tossed it onto the floor, but still within reach.

He pressed the pin on the ankle of his prosthetic and detached it. A year and a half ago, he could barely get it on and off, mostly because he'd refused to try. In the VA hospital, he'd been surrounded by artificially cheerful physical therapists who never stopped telling him how lucky he was that he survived and how quickly he'd learn to walk again if he gave it some effort. But Easy hadn't wanted to learn how to walk again. He hadn't even wanted to be alive, and he definitely could not see how getting ambushed by a roadside bomb in Iraq was in any way 'lucky.' A slightly-above-the-knee amputation was nothing to celebrate.

He rolled down the neoprene sleeve and the comfort sock around his thigh and tossed them into the sink. The redness and swelling had taken over a year to go away as he'd struggled with learning how to negotiate what he still thought of as the bane of his existence. It was still a temporary prosthesis. He'd gone through three different socket types already in an attempt to find the right fit. Once they had it figured out, he could get a custom leg made, but having a leg made seemed so... permanent... so accepting, like losing another battle, the *biggest* battle. He could learn to live as an amputee, but he didn't have to fucking *like* it.

He heaved himself up and reached into the shower to turn on the water. He frowned as he negotiated his way into the stall and lowered himself onto the small, white, plastic stool. He'd forgotten about the shower. He'd cleaned the place up from top to bottom, but he hadn't thought about the stupid stool. He cursed himself as he lathered up with the soap. The bedroom was fine. He could leave the lights off, and with Brenda a little bit tipsy she'd barely notice his leg-hopefully. However, the bathroom was a problem he hadn't thought of. If she spent the night, and he actually was hoping she would, she'd need to use the shower. Though Easy had come to terms with the fact that his life would never be what he envisioned, he'd be damned if he'd hang out a huge fucking banner that said "Handicapped" on it.

They'd go to her place, he decided, as he shampooed his short, blonde hair. She had two roommates, but surely she had her own room. He could deal with that. In his other life, before the IED, he'd have fucked *all three* of them, all night long, and, if they were any fun, he might call one or two of them the next week. He'd had more than his share of women but none in the last three years since he'd lost his leg. He hadn't even come close, always backing out at the last second before closing the deal.

At first he wasn't sure how he'd manage it; his balance hadn't been exactly perfect. He had enough trouble maneuvering himself into bed, let alone with anyone else. Plus, in the back of his mind he always knew he looked like a freak with the leg off. The stump, though healed, was something out of a horror movie, not that Brenda would have to look at it. He'd leave on the neoprene sock, but there would be no denying the missing limb.

Brenda knew, though. Everyone did. It was no secret that Easy, Shooter, Hawk, Tex, and Caleb were the only remaining members of an Army Ranger unit that had served both in Iraq and Afghanistan. It was also no secret that some of them had not come back in the same condition in which they'd enlisted. Shooter had scars across his torso that looked like ground chuck. He always kept his shirt on for that reason. Easy never wore anything but pants or jeans and did everything he could to hide his limp, which was usually only a problem toward the end of a long day when his muscles could take no more. He couldn't get underneath the cars at the garage quite as easily as the others, but he still did it. He was determined to pull his own weight on the job.

As he sat on the toilet once more and dried himself off with a towel, he was surprised to notice his hands were shaking just a bit. Three years was a long time to go without. Brenda was perfect though, with long, brown hair and a great ass. She was cute and flirty without being too obvious. She was exactly the type of girl he'd thought he'd be married to by now. Without the bomb, he'd have been an Army Officer with a beautiful wife, adorable kids, and a house with a yard that didn't take him four fucking hours to mow because he kept slipping in the wet grass.

He couldn't have the uniform; he'd long since given up on that. He could, however, have the wife and kids. He'd only been hanging out with Brenda at Maria's bar for a few weeks now, far too early to be thinking about family life. Right now, he just had to concentrate on getting the fucking right. It could work, though. It *would* work.

He reattached the leg and pulled on a fresh pair of blue jeans from the bottom dresser drawer. He pulled a tight, grey t-shirt over his head and his large biceps stretched the fabric. He was probably overcompensating with the wardrobe, but he didn't want to think about that too hard. As he reached for his cell on top of his dresser, his hand passed over a tiny silver box. He smirked at it as he picked up the phone and dialed. It had been a long time since he'd even glanced at that box. In fact, he might throw that box away.

Brenda answered on the third ring, giggling into the phone. He couldn't help but smile.

"Hey!" she greeted him, in a sing-song voice.

"Hey," he replied, picking up his keys and pocketing them. He had the truck, but she'd probably rather take his bike. So far he hadn't taken anyone for a ride, but he figured if it was going to be a night of firsts, he could just add that to the list. "You gonna meet me tonight?"

More giggling. "Of course," she replied, and that had him smiling all over again. He couldn't help that he was born with an Angel's looks and a Devil's grin. He may have lost a lot of things, but he'd never lost his ability to charm women's panties off.

"You gonna have breakfast with me, too?" he drawled and closed the dresser drawer.

Brenda gasped and he chuckled to himself.

"God," she breathed into the phone.

"Is that a yes?" he prompted, checking his hair in the mirror hanging on the back of the bathroom door. He kept it short, a remnant from his Army days. It looked fairly dry.

"God, yes!"

"See you tonight, baby," Easy told her.

"Bye!"

He caught sight of his shirt in the mirror, looking slightly disheveled on one side. He tugged at it to straighten it. Over his phone he heard a clatter and then "Was that him?"

"Oh, it was totally him!" Brenda told either Roommate 1 or Roommate 2. Easy didn't actually remember their names. Brenda was the most attractive of the three, and he'd been monopolizing her since the first night he'd spotted her at the bar.

"Yeah, and... ?" nameless Roommate asked.

Easy cleared his throat and opened his mouth. Brenda clearly thought her phone was disconnected. He was about to call out to get her attention, when another voice, Roommate 2, he guessed, said, "The cop or the other one?"

Caleb had spent a fair bit of time schmoozing the trio of women as well, though that would never go anywhere. Caleb had a steady thing in Sioux Falls. He wasn't above the occasional flirting on a Friday or Saturday night, but it always ended there.

"The other one," Brenda replied. "He wants to get *breakfast!*"

Roommate 1 (or was it 2?) squealed and then devolved into a fit of laughter. "You gonna *hop* into bed with him?"

Easy closed his mouth.

"Anna!" Brenda scolded, but to his chagrin, she laughed, too.

"No," said Roommate 2. "She's gonna play Pirates and draw him a treasure map to her booty!"

"Stop!" Brenda cried, laughing hard.

Easy's jaw twitched.

"He's got the peg leg," Roommate 1 declared. "All he needs is an eye patch."

Easy quietly hit the End Call button on his phone and stared at it for a moment. It didn't matter, he told himself. It wasn't like Brenda was *The One*. It wasn't like she was anything at all. He slid the phone into his pocket but couldn't manage to do any more than that. His anger slowly boiled over into rage as he looked at himself in the mirror across the room. He looked fine- fine God damn it! But he didn't *feel* fine. He had never felt fine since the day he woke up in a hospital bed two years ago, missing so much more than just his lower right leg. In fact, he might never feel fine again. That thought scared him so badly that, without thinking, he suddenly reached out to the dresser.

He grabbed it with both hands and, with a shout, pulled the whole thing down. It landed with a loud crash on the floor at the foot of the bed. The tiny, silver box went flying, and Easy's eyes tracked it. He stared at it as it landed on the carpet. A moment of white hot rage solidified into something halfway between resolve and despair. He took a step toward it. He was halfway across the room when he heard a familiar voice calling his name.

Easy took a deep, steadying breath, shocked at himself. "Y-yeah," he called out to Hawk, as he heard the large man's boots coming down the hall. Hawk and his girl Tildy had moved into the house next door, which had also belonged to Shooter before they bought it from him. It was mostly nice to have a brother living next door, and Easy really liked Tildy, but there was a distinct lack of privacy. It had been a bad idea to bring Brenda here anyway, stool or no stool, because it would bring on too many questions.

Hawk entered the bedroom and eyed the dresser on the floor. Easy wiped his palms on his jeans. "Redecorating?" Hawk asked, cautiously.

"My damn leg," Easy said with a shrug, and his belly twisted at his own words. His damn leg, wasn't it always his damn leg? "Gave out on me," Easy lied, stepping toward the middle of the room. "I grabbed the dresser, but it went down."

Hawk nodded and helped Easy put the room back to rights. His large hand swept over the silver box and plucked it off the carpet. Easy reached out and snatched it from him. "Thanks, man," he told Hawk, tossing the box back on top of the dresser and gesturing toward the door.

Easy skipped a jacket, because it was May and not necessary. He locked the front door and followed Hawk down the porch steps. "Tildy coming tonight?" he asked, for lack of anything better to say.

Hawk shook his head. "Nah. She's staying with Slick."

Slick's real name was Sarah, and she was Chris' wife. She was also a new mother and often spent her Friday and Saturday nights at home. Chris still made an occasional appearance at the bar to remind the clientele that Maria's was under his protection, but he preferred more and more to be home with his family.

Easy didn't think it was his business to ask how long it would be before Tildy ended up pregnant and took Hawk out of rotation as well, but the two houses were small and close together, and furniture being knocked over wasn't the only thing that could occasionally be heard.

"Thanks for the help," Easy said to Hawk and pulled his keys back out of his pocket. "Let's go." He couldn't get laid, but he could still get a drink and God he needed one right about now.

CHAPTER THREE

Daisy heard the unmistakable sound of motorcycle engines as they drifted by her hotel room. She tossed back the fireproof curtain and gazed out into the dusk. The digs might be crap, she thought, but a beer or two could take her mind off it. Plus, she was sucker for anything with two wheels.

She shimmied into a short jean skirt and pink tank top and headed out the door. She followed the Harleys like a siren's song to a low-slung building with a large parking lot and sign out front that said "Maria's." The outlaw country blaring from inside and the bikes in the lot told her this was definitely her kind of place. She paused a moment on the sidewalk as two riders turned off the main drag and into the gravel lot. One was a large guy, decked out in black, with a long, black ponytail. Daisy thought he was hot as hell until she saw his friend.

Blonde, muscled, and tanned, Daisy was pretty sure the hottest guy she'd ever laid eyes on in her life just rode into view. She tried to hustle and catch the door while he was heading inside, but the gravel and her cowboy boots were a bad match. By the time she'd gotten inside herself, the hottie was lost in the crowd. She scowled, disappointed. The place was jumping though and had more leather and studs than poor Daisy's nether regions might be able to withstand.

She took a deep breath and tried not to think about how long it'd been since she had a bike or a man between her thighs. Right now she wasn't too picky about either, and if all went well she might get both. She spotted the bar on the other side of the room and headed that way. A platinum blonde failed to notice her as she mixed drinks and then stacked them onto a tray. She skirted out from behind the bar to deliver them to one of the many tables.

"Hey!" called an old man perched on a stool. "What about my beer?" he asked.

"Stuff it, Milo," the blonde replied, muttering something about being two girls down and some other obscenities having to do with impatience.

The old man gave Daisy a disgruntled look as she took the stool next to him.

"Busy," Daisy observed, nodding at the crowd.

Milo grunted. "She's pouring *and* serving," he said, jerking his head at the blonde. "Should just be pouring. She knows I like a steady supply to wash down the fries."

He had a huge basket of chili cheese fries in front of him that set Daisy's stomach rumbling. Lucky for her, the juke box was loud and the crowd even louder.

"You come here a lot?" she asked him. "Is it always busy like this?"

Milo nodded and grabbed his glass. "Always," he told her. "I'm always here and it's always like this." He tipped the glass, then remembered it was empty, and slammed it back down on the counter.

Daisy glanced around and only spotted one other waitress in the whole bar. She herself had waited tabled from time to time for cash. Delay, Nebraska had a serious lack of employment opportunities. It was the Silver Spoon or the gas station or the packing plant, and at least you got free meals at the Spoon- such as they were. Working at the packing plant meant you might seriously never eat again after seeing what went into a hot dog.

The blonde looked exhausted and it wasn't even midnight.

"Damn people," Milo groused, glancing around furtively. "Come to my place, so's I can't get my beer for my fries."

"Oh, Lord," Daisy replied, already sick of the conversation. She

12

took the glass, put one knee on the stool, and reached over the bar. She filled it with Bud as the guy watched.

"Adams," he protested. "Adams!"

Daisy glared at him over her shoulder then slammed the glass down in front of him, froth splashing over the edge.

"Take what I give you, old man."

At that moment, the blonde came around behind the bar. She gave Milo, then Daisy, the stink eye.

"Sorry," Daisy said, shrinking a little on her stool. "You're pretty slammed. I was... I was just... "

The blonde kept her pinned with a withering look.

"I could take your next tray," Daisy offered, sensing an opportunity.

The blonde raised an eyebrow.

"I schlep the trays and keep the tips?" Daisy suggested. "You don't have to pay me extra."

The older woman looked her up and down. "Got ID?" she finally asked. Daisy produced it. "You ever wait tables, Delilah?" she asked, studying the card.

"It's Daisy. And yeah, I have."

"Not that it matters," said the blonde while handing the license back across the bar. "I'll take anyone with two arms and pulse. You got yourself a deal." She stacked more drinks onto the now empty tray and pushed it over. "Goes to that table over there," she said, jerking her head.

Daisy turned to look, and her stomach gave another kick -but from a different kind of hunger- as she spotted the hot blonde.

"Don't gawk," the woman scolded. "Just serve."

"Yes, ma'am," Daisy replied, not taking her eyes off the man.

"It's not ma'am. It's Maria. Get moving."

Daisy took the tray and wove her way through the crowd. She had three beers and three shots. Balancing all of them, she arrived at the table and tried to catch Blondie's eye.

"Hi!" she gushed at them, setting the drinks onto the table.

The large Sioux nodded politely and took up a shot. The dark haired guy who hadn't arrived with them gave her quick smile but looked away. Blondie, so far, wasn't budging. Daisy took the last shot in one hand, the last beer in the other, and leaned across the table. "Here you go, honey," she drawled, pushing them in front of him. He finally looked up at her. Daisy sucked in a breath. He had gorgeous green eyes.

"Can I get you anything else?" she asked him with a sly smile.

"I'm good," he told her.

"You're definitely that," Daisy replied. The guy with the short, dark hair snorted. Blondie wasn't interested, though. Daisy picked up the empty tray and hustled back to the bar, disappointed. She didn't have much time to dwell on it though, because Maria refilled her tray and sent her packing again.

This time she ventured to the other side of the bar's pool tables, to another table full of hot guys. God, but this place was full of them! They weren't sporting cuts but still looked appropriately badass. Daisy flashed them a smile and passed out the rounds.

"Nice tats," one of them said.

Surprised, Daisy's eyes drifted down the front of her shirt. She looked back up at the guy, who laughed and glanced deliberately at her arms.

"Oh!" she said, giggling. "Right. Thanks." The guy himself was tatted up as well, one full sleeve on his right arm. "They're mine," she told him.

His eyebrow raised. "Did you-?"

Just then a sharp whistle pierced the air, louder than the jukebox. Daisy looked across the bar at her temporary boss, who was getting antsy.

"Sorry," Daisy told him. "It's packed. Gotta go!"

As she made her way back to the bar, she passed a brunette who ended up at- wouldn't you know it- Blondie's table. She draped an arm over his shoulders and leaned into him.

Well, there you go, Daisy thought to herself. Disappointing indeed, but the one thing Daisy needed more than a roll in the hay was cold hard cash, and there was a blonde of a different sort across the room who was willing to let her earn some.

CHAPTER FOUR

Easy took another sip of his beer and still couldn't find a way out, at least not written on the bottom of the bottle. He couldn't tell her he'd heard her comments. It was bad enough having to listen to them, to admit that they'd *hurt* him. He didn't want her to know that the opinions of some chicks he didn't even know had absolutely gutted him. That was unacceptable.

Brenda was blathering on about some band she wanted to go see next week. Easy was barely listening. He glanced at the door and briefly considered walking out, but that would only raise eyebrows… and questions.

As he turned back his gaze fell upon the girl who'd brought him his drink. He'd never seen her before, didn't know Maria had hired anyone new. The girl had a thing for tats and metal, that was for sure. She wasn't his type, either. Not by a long shot. Maybe, though, that was just what he needed.

Fueled by anger instead of helplessness or even nervousness, he stood up quickly. His beer swayed and threatened to topple before he steadied it with one hand. *He* didn't sway though, and was god damned determined to make it all the way across the bar without so much as a shuffle.

"Gonna take a piss," he announced crudely, but crude was better than being a whiny bitch, he thought. He could feel Brenda's eyes on him as he walked away. She was no doubt wondering why he'd barely looked at her since she'd shown up. It was time to pull the pin on the whole thing, he decided. He headed into the small hallway that led to the bathrooms. He passed up the men's room and took the three steps to the ladies' room at the end of the hall, last stop before the Fire Exit.

He was feeling a few butterflies at this point, probably to be expected, but his cock wasn't paying much attention. He pole armed the bathroom door and stepped inside. The tiny blonde waitress was at the sink sweeping her hair back behind her ears. Easy's eyes traveled the length of her to her firm, round ass, and his dick jerked in approval. For some odd reason, he found himself wondering if her penchant for piercings extended to any other parts of her.

She caught his gaze in the mirror and grinned. "You lost?" she teased.

He didn't answer; he didn't know what to say, anyway. Weeks of talking to Brenda hadn't led anywhere. This wasn't a relationship, he reminded himself. This was purely mercenary. As his body filled with lust, his mind became surprisingly calm. He'd obviously put too much pressure on himself to find a girl who'd overlook his handicap. All along he should've just been looking for girls who didn't need to know.

He strode up to her and wrapped one arm around her waist, pulling her back into him. If she had any doubts about why he was there, surely his hard on pressing into her ass made it clear. With his free hand, he swept her long, blonde hair off her shoulder and pressed his lips to the side of her neck. She giggled and pushed back against him. "Nice to meet you, too," she said.

Easy's hands skimmed over her tank top and he cupped her breasts in both hands. The material was thin, so was her bra and her nipples jutted into his palms.

"Oh, God," she whispered as he pinched them, gently rolling them between his fingers. He bit her neck, just enough to sting, and she arched her back, filling his hands.

"You smell good," he lied. She smelled like onions and fries, which made sense. She did feel good, though, and he figured that was all that really mattered. And she was into him, which was the other catch. She'd certainly do, he thought to himself and let go of one

breast. Slowly he ran his hand back down her stomach, making it
clear where he was headed next. If she was going to object, she might
as well do it now, so he could give up and find someone else.

He felt her take a deep breath, but the command to stop hadn't
come yet. Ever the gentleman his mother raised, he refrained from
shoving his hand straight into her shorts. Instead he cupped her pussy
through the denim and started rubbing. She was warm and obviously
not inclined to stop him since she was now grinding on his hand. In
the mirror he saw that her eyes were closed, lips slightly parted and
cheeks flushed pink to match her shirt. Easy smiled to himself in the
polished glass- like shooting fish in a barrel.

He popped the button on her shorts and ran one finger under
the waistband of her cotton panties. They were cheap, and the elastic
was worn. He ignored it and tugged on them. As he pushed her
shorts down over her hips, she paused. For a moment, he thought she
was finally going to stop him, but instead she said, "Is the door
locked?"

"It's fine," he replied. Not quite a lie, he figured. It was fine as
far as *he* was concerned.

He ran his fingers down her ass, which was as smooth, white,
and tattoo free as the day she was born. He pushed his hand between
her legs from behind and felt her soft curls. He squeezed and pinched
and rubbed her folds, slicking up her entrance with his fingertips with
one hand as he unbuttoned his own fly with the other. His cock was
pulsing behind his zipper.

She wiggled against his hand while clasping the sides of the
cracked porcelain sink with her own. He took a condom out of his
pocket and nearly dropped it onto the gritty floor. He was glad she
was facing away and couldn't see how badly his hands were shaking
now. He preferred to think it was pure need that had him feeling
light-headed and jangly. He wasn't afraid of a piece of pussy in a dirty
bathroom; that was for sure.

He rolled the condom down his shaft, wincing at the tight feel.
It had been a long time since he'd worn one. He moved behind her,
spanned one of her bare hips with his hand, and guided his cock to
her entrance with the other. Fuck, she was wet, seeping juice onto his
fingertips as he parted her. With one thrust of his hips, he buried

himself deep.

They both cried out at the same time, he from desperation and she because, well fuck, he realized, she was tight as hell and clamped down around him like a velvet fist. Her cunt fought the sudden invasion despite being well-prepared. He withdrew and shoved in it in, losing control of himself and the situation. He already felt the familiar heaviness in his lower belly, the tingle in his sac.

"Damn," he half-cursed, half-gasped as he erupted into the latex that separated them. Even before the last of his cum spilled, he staggered back into the wall behind him. There was a sheen of sweat on his palms and his brow as he fought to catch his breath.

The girl looked bewildered and disappointed. He glanced away from her accusing glare. Just then, the door opened and Brenda stood gaping at the two of them, her mouth opening and closing like a goldfish. Easy fought off a wave panic at being caught; after all, this was what he wanted. Except he'd envisioned a lusty barmaid, swooning from post-orgasmic bliss and himself standing tall over her, rock hard cock ready to impale the next willing female, provided of course it wasn't his now-ex.

Instead Brenda had walked in on a disaster of a quickie that had left him feeling drained but in no way satisfied. She couldn't know that, though, having just walked in on them, and if he could keep his cool and get the hell out of there, there was a small possibility that she never would.

As he stripped off the condom and tossed it into the garbage, Brenda finally found her voice. "What the hell?!" she shouted.

Easy zipped up his fly and shrugged at her.

"What the hell are you doing?!"

Easy didn't answer her, but next to him he heard the waitress curse under her breath. Easy strode past both of them and into the hallway. "Couldn't wait," he said and walked away.

"Bitch!" he heard Brenda yell behind him.

"Trust me," said the blonde. "I had no idea, nor do I care. I don't need this shit."

Easy wasn't entirely sure whether she meant the drama, the bad sex, or both. It was probably both. He winced and kept walking. She hadn't come, he knew that much. He hadn't been that inept since high school. It was probably best that he hadn't gone home with Brenda. He didn't need one more thing for her to hold over his head. He crossed the bar and headed toward his table.

"Hey, goddamn it! I am not done!" came a loud voice carrying over the music. Easy was silently grateful that it was Brenda who was shouting.

He sighed and turned, bracing himself to have a humiliating confrontation with his... ex? Almost ex? God only knew. But when he looked across the room, it wasn't Easy that Brenda was laying into. He watched, his brief moment of triumph fading. "Fuck," he muttered to himself.

Clearly, he hadn't thought this through. Lately he hadn't been thinking anything through. In the last two years, he'd gone from a careful planner to a straight up asshole who got into fistfights with his friends and kissed their women just to piss them off.

The blonde shook her head, her short hair falling down almost over her eyes. "Look, I really don't give a shit. I don't know you. I don't know *him*."

"Slut!" Brenda cried and shoved the blonde into the bar. Several patrons skittered out of the way.

"You better back up," the barmaid warned. She didn't look scared, merely irritated.

A hulking shape appeared beside Easy, but he kept watching the two women.

"What'd you do?" Hawk asked him quietly.

Easy pinched the bridge of his nose. "The blonde."

Hawk snorted and raised an eyebrow. "Oh yeah?" But his amusement faded as he looked at the feuding women. "How far you gonna let this ride?" he asked. There was an edge of rebuke in his voice.

Easy sighed. "It's my mess," he replied. "I'll clean it up." As he took a step forward, Brenda also took a step forward and brought up her fist. "God damn it," Easy muttered and surged through the crowd.

Brenda had a good arm, a little slow though. It was too slow for the blonde, who snatched an empty tray off the counter and held it up. Brenda's fist connected with it, and by the looks of it the corkboard didn't do much to soften the blow.

Brenda squealed and grabbed her hand. The blonde gripped the tray and started to bring it up, ready to swing it at Brenda's head.

"Jesus," Easy said, surprised. He was close enough now to intervene and he placed his hand on the tray, pushing the barmaid back slightly. With the other hand, he grabbed Brenda's arm. "Move," he ordered.

Brenda protested, wailing like a banshee. Easy shuffled her toward the exit.

"Come on," he said and pushed her through the door. Her roommates followed like sheep.

Brenda turned on him, her hand all but forgotten now. "Why would you do that?" she demanded.

Easy shrugged. In the end, there would be no point in telling her the truth. He'd never take her back, even if she apologized, which she might not. Then he'd just embarrass himself.

"She was there," he replied smoothly, herding her toward her car. "She was into me and she's got a great ass. Who could resist?"

Brenda's mouth opened again. "You're an asshole! You know that?"

Easy smirked at her. "You can't say you didn't know."

In the year Easy had lived in Rapid City, he'd made a name for himself charming the pants off every pretty girl within a thirty mile radius, or so the stories went. What people saw was an attractive, confident guy who hit on a lot of women. It wasn't his fault that everyone just assumed he took them home. Brenda might have almost been his first since losing his leg, but she sure as shit didn't *know* that. Neither did anyone else.

"Go home," he told her. "Maybe I'll call you if I get an itch."

"You bastard!" she shouted at his back.

He couldn't argue with that. She had a point.

CHAPTER FIVE

Daisy sat in Maria's office, her pride and her feet hurting in equal measure. With the look Maria was giving her, she suspected her nose might be hurting too, when the older woman decided to finish what the other girl had started. "Guess I didn't mention the part where you don't bang the customers in the bathroom- didn't think I had to."

Daisy felt heat creep up her face. "You don't. Usually."

"So, you just came face to face with a tall drink of water and went at him like a woman lost in the desert?"

A laugh escaped Daisy, and immediately she was sorry for it. "Um," she mumbled. "Yeah. Kind of. I mean, pretty much exactly like that, actually."

The blonde woman raised an eyebrow.

"It's... um... it's been a *while*," Daisy admitted. "And I just, whew," she said, leaning back in the chair. "I was there, and he came in, and... I lost my head. I'm sorry, Maria. And that girl, I have no clue who she is. I don't know who *he* is. I swear I'm not usually like this."

Maria sat back in her chair and gazed at the ceiling. "Well, I can't say I blame you, coming off a... *dry spell*," she said with a smirk. "And running into a guy like that."

"What's his name?"

Maria raised the same eyebrow again. Daisy thought if she kept talking, Maria's eyebrow might get stuck all the way up there.

"He mentioned it," she lied. "But I forgot."

Maria rolled her eyes. "His name's Jimmy. Goes by 'Easy'."

Daisy snorted. "That part's right."

Maria laughed. "He's from New Orleans, but yeah, the name works both ways. He gets around. But you want my advice, don't take up with him. He's got some darkness around him. He oughta work it out of his system before he drowns in it. And you know what they say about drowning men. They're likely to pull you down with them."

Daisy moved forward in the chair. "Is he... dangerous?" She frowned. She definitely did not need anything like that in her life. Never again.

But Maria shook her head. "No. Not that I've ever seen. Though he's ex-Special Forces, so he *could* be, under the right circumstances. No, he had a bad tour a few years back. Lost his leg. I didn't know him before, but I get the sense that he might've lost more than that."

Daisy blew out a hard breath. "God. I didn't even notice."

Maria shrugged. "Not much call to strip down in my bathroom. And if you want the job, by the way, you'll never do it again."

"The job?" Daisy held her breath. She needed money, and a place like this was definitely her kind of place, crazy, jealous girlfriends aside.

"We're slammed like this every weekend," Maria told her. "I lost two waitresses, and I'm in a bind. You seem to be able to handle yourself. If you can manage to keep your paws off my customers, we could work something out."

"I can," Daisy insisted. "I can definitely do that."

"You'll have to pass a drug test, too."

"Not a problem," Daisy said confidently. "The only needles I like have ink in them."

"Yeah, I see that."

"They're mine," Daisy told her, holding out her arms. "I mean, I drew them myself."

"Oh, yeah?" Maria said, duly impressed. "They're good."

"They're *damn* good," Daisy corrected.

The older woman could sense the pride in Daisy's voice and

nodded. "That they are." She reached into the desk drawer and pulled out a blank employment application. "Fill this out," she instructed and handed Daisy a pen. "I'll give you the address of the testing facility before you leave."

Daisy couldn't believe her incredible luck as she hastily filled in the empty boxes. Maria went to help her husband, Thomas, finish closing down the bar. Daisy was ecstatic. The tips she'd made tonight were far and away more than she'd ever made at the Silver Spoon. She smiled to herself as she thought things would turn out fine in Rapid City, just fine. She'd save some money, find a place. Maybe by the end of the summer she'd have enough saved up for a car. It wouldn't have to be anything fancy, just something that-

She paused. Her pen hovered just above the page as she gazed at the application.

Have you ever been convicted of a crime?

Daisy's enthusiasm faltered. She could sense all her earlier plans fading away, slipping through her fingers. She couldn't go home, no way, not back to the trailer park and that boring, old town and those boring, old towns*people,* who had always looked down on her.

Here was a job, where no one minded her tattoos or her nose stud. Here, in one night, she'd earned more money than she'd made in a *week* at the diner. She shifted in her chair. Here was Home, she decided. And that was that.

On the line, in bold, black letters, she wrote: '**No.**'

CHAPTER SIX

Easy stalked across the gravel lot, kicking up dust as he went. He skipped the coffee in the break room and went right to work, right to fucking up as well, apparently, because the torque wrench caught his thumb and peeled off some skin.

"God fucking damn it!" he shouted and threw the offending tool against the wall.

Shooter turned and looked at him from across the bay. Easy hung his head and went to retrieve the wrench, ignoring the black spot the impact had left on the wall.

"What's up?" his former lieutenant asked.

Easy didn't respond.

Hawk tossed a spark plug on the counter. "Got laid last night."

Easy glared at the larger man as he returned to the truck he was working on.

"Is that what we're calling it now?" Emilio teased. "Oh, wait. Yeah, it is," he added, somewhat deflated.

Shooter's eyebrows raised. "Really?" To Easy he said, "You know that's supposed to have the opposite effect, right?"

"Just let it go."

"The brunette that's been all over you?" Shooter asked.

"No," Easy snapped. "Just let. it. go."

"Blonde that Maria just hired," Hawk told the boss. "Cute. Plenty of sass. Good fighter, too."

"Did she fight with *him*?" he asked, nodding to Easy.

"Nah. The brunette got all riled up when she walked in on the two them going at it in the bathroom. Took a swing at the blonde."

"Oh, Christ," Shooter muttered.

"It was just a fuck up," Easy told them. "It's not a big deal. It's over."

"Well, maybe-" Shooter started.

"Over!" Easy snapped.

If Shooter was irritated at being dressed down by his employee, his considerably *younger* employee at that, he didn't show it. "Alright," he agreed. "Over."

Easy turned his attention to the engine and tried to forget about last night, the nights before it, and pretty much the last three years in general. He managed to succeed, for the most part, until lunchtime. He looked up as Sarah pulled into the lot and parked her SUV next to Shooter's bike. Tex trotted out to help her carry in the meal she'd brought for them, while she wrangled Hope's car seat.

Sarah was her usual bright self, which when he first met her, had irritated him to no end. Now it didn't bother him so much. After all she'd been through, which was considerably more than Easy himself had endured, she deserved to be happy. And the little nugget she was hauling inside was the culmination of all Sarah Sullivan's' long-fought-for hopes and dreams, so the name was actually perfect.

She dropped the baby off in the office with Shooter and made her way to the break room. Easy followed her in to wash up. The plan was to eat, get back to work as quickly as possible, get *home* as quickly as possible, and then stay there, completely avoiding Brenda, the barmaid, and his brothers who, as much he wanted them to, probably would not let this whole thing go. It was simultaneously the best thing and the most annoying thing to have people who cared that much about you.

As Sarah unpacked lunch he caught her eyeing him. Easy dried his hands, sighed, and threw the towel at the sink. It was definitely a throwing things kind of day.

"Don't," he said.

"What?" she asked innocently.

Easy shook his head, not buying it. "I know he told you. I don't want to talk about it."

Sarah scowled and turned to face him fully. "But what about Brenda?"

He tried to keep his face passive as he shrugged.

"I thought you liked her," Sarah protested.

"Well, I don't," Easy told her, growing more irritated. He walked to the table and grabbed a plate.

"You did."

"I didn't," he insisted. "I was just killing time. Then I killed time with someone else. Not a big deal."

"Do you know her? I don't remember hearing about her."

Easy turned on her and glared. "Hearing about her? Does he fucking report in to you about every fucking thing I do?" he demanded.

"I just-"

"I don't need you checking up on me."

"I don't check up on you," Sarah argued. "I just worry-"

"Well, no one asked you to," he snapped.

"Jimmy, you're my-"

"I'm nothing," he told her. "I'm just the guy who works for your old man." This was a total lie, and they both knew it. After they'd gotten over their initial wariness of each other, which culminated in an actual wrestling match on his living room floor, they'd become pretty close- as close as a guy could be, Easy figured, with his friend's woman. Right now he didn't want a friend; he just wanted to be left alone.

Sarah put her hand on her hip in that way she did when she was about unload on someone. Usually she directed her ire at her husband, which was usually pretty fun to watch, Easy had to admit. He was not a good target, and today was not a good day. "Jimmy Turnbull, if you think-"

"Mind your own god damn business!" Easy shouted at her to stop her before she got on a roll.

Before she could say anything else, if she was inclined to, the door swung open. Shooter stood in the doorway with Hope in his arms. His gentle holding of her was completely at odds with the look on his face. "You need to re-think your tone when you're talking to my wife." His tone was low, probably to keep from scaring the baby, but it only made him seem more menacing.

Easy immediately felt sorry that he'd snapped at her, but it wouldn't have happened if she'd just minded her own business, if they'd all just mind their own business. Not willing to apologize nor willing to continue to argue, Easy threw down his plate and walked past Shooter. He kept on walking right through the bay toward the open garage door.

"Where are you going?" Hawk called after him.

"To lunch!"

"Slick brought lunch."

Easy didn't dignify that with a response. He lurched into his truck, slammed the door, and cranked the engine hard. Luckily, he didn't flood it. It roared to life, and he stomped on the gas, kicking up more dust than his work boots ever could. At the entrance to the street, he instinctively turned left, because to the right was Maria's and the blonde barmaid he definitely did not want to see again. He jerked the wheel and made it home in record time. He scowled as he thought of the cold pizza still sitting in his fridge. Whatever Slick had brought, it was better than greasy pepperoni. He slammed the truck door, and his face darkened even more as he spotted Tildy sitting on her front fucking porch.

"God *damn* it!" he muttered to himself as she waved.

"Hey!" she called out.

Easy ignored her and took the steps on his own front porch two at time.

"Hey!" she said again. "Jimmy."

"I'm busy," he told her.

"Why are you home?" she asked. "Did something happen?"

He grabbed the doorknob and shoved his front door open. "Yeah!" he bellowed, because she'd hear it anyway. Or maybe she'd get up and come over, and that was the last thing he wanted right now. He turned and pinned her with a withering look. "I fucked a barmaid in the bathroom at Maria's, and *I don't need a fucking lecture about it!*"

Somewhere a dog barked, and Easy had a niggling thought that there went his neighbors' opinion of him. He stepped inside the house and slammed the door behind him. It rattled on its hinges. Whatever Tildy had thought of his outburst, she didn't come over-thank God for that. He pulled the pizza out of the fridge and threw it onto the kitchen table. He glared at it as though through sheer force of will he could turn it into a steak, a cheeseburger, or whatever Slick had made for lunch that day. When that didn't work, he picked up a slice and chewed it ruthlessly.

It served him right anyway.

CHAPTER SEVEN

Daisy wiped down the bar and tried to ignore the fact that her phone was ringing. Maria seemed content to ignore it as well, so long as Daisy didn't answer it when she was supposed to be working, but Milo was far too curious for his own good.

"Gonna answer that?" he asked around a mouthful of sandwich.

"Mind your own business, old man," Daisy told him.

Instead of being offended, he grinned at her. "Could be your boyfriend," he teased.

"Don't have one," she informed him.

The old man snorted. "Doing the bebop in the commode with a fella means he's your boyfriend."

"Doing the *what?*" Daisy snapped. "And anyway, no, it doesn't. It doesn't mean anything at all."

"Ooooh. You're one of *those girls*."

Daisy glared at him in spite of his teasing tone. "Old man, I'm about to take that damn sandwich away."

Milo recoiled.

"And it so happens, I'm not one of those girls. It was just a dry spell. I lost my head. I'm over it."

Milo nodded thoughtfully. "I'm having a dry spell," he declared. "I can relate."

Daisy rolled her eyes. "You don't say."

Milo bristled. "Hey, now! I'll have you know that I do very well with the ladies."

Daisy opened her mouth to make another sarcastic comment, but Maria interrupted her. "It's true," she told Daisy. "God knows why, but the man does pretty well with the widows in town."

Milo sniffed. "Well, I did. But I lost my mojo somewheres." He shook his head. "Got a plan to get it back, though," he told her, and preened. "Gonna grow out my hair. Go for a rocker look."

"Oh, good Lord," Maria muttered and rolled her eyes.

Daisy tried hard not to laugh. "Do you play guitar?"

He frowned. "Nope," he said and held up his hand that was missing most of a finger. "Doubt I'll be starting now."

Daisy sighed and clapped him on the shoulder. "Stick to being you, old man," she advised.

"You think?" he asked, doubtful.

"Absolutely."

At that moment, the door swung open, and Daisy watched a woman maneuver through it while hauling, of all things, a child's car seat. Two other women shuffled in behind her. Daisy liked Maria's, but even though afternoons were apparently pretty slow for lunch, it still didn't seem like the place for a ladies' luncheon.

Maria, though, skirted the bar with a wide smile on her face. "Oh!" she practically squealed, which surprised Daisy. Maria seemed like a ball buster really. "Let me see her!"

The ball buster went weak-kneed over the baby, and even Milo put down his sandwich to get a better look. Daisy squinted at them, confused. The mom-in-question had on yoga pants and a tank top. The other two were in tailored business suits. None of them looked like they had the chops to be a biker's old lady.

The mother tilted her brunette head toward Maria and spoke in hushed tones. Then she glanced meaningfully at Daisy. Daisy bristled and tossed the rag on the bar. If anyone was out of place here, it was Yoga Pants and the Uppity Yuppies. Maria made over the baby a bit more then seated the group at a nearby table. Daisy, reluctantly, grabbed a tray and stocked it with glasses and a pitcher of ice water. She headed over to the foursome.

"I'm Sarah," Yoga Pants told Daisy.

Ordinarily, Daisy would have a few choice words for someone

who eyeballed her the way these women were, but her boss was standing with them, and that seemed like a good way to get fired on her first official day.

"I'm Daisy." Daisy set the empty glasses down on the table.

"I used to work here," Sarah said.

Daisy paused and looked up at her. "Oh," she said, looking from Maria to the women and back. Sarah didn't seem like the type, but then again, maybe motherhood slowed you down a little.

"Best I ever had," Maria declared and squeezed Sarah's shoulder.

It would have been easy to feel slighted standing next to a person whom your boss clearly liked more than you, but in the short time Daisy had known Maria, the woman had not gushed over anything or anyone. Truthfully, from anyone else's mouth, this wouldn't actually be considered gushing, but from Maria, it was akin to standing next to Old Faithful.

This woman must have something about her that was worthy of such praise, despite her rather unfortunate appearance. Then again, the baby was pretty small, and Daisy had to admit that she might wear yoga pants too, after pushing a cabbage patch doll out of her hooha.

Maria left to pull drafts, and Daisy filled the water glasses. "It's pretty busy," she told Sarah. "I mean on Friday nights, anyway."

Sarah nodded. "Yeah. Rough crowd, too. I miss it, but I don't, you know? I'm home with her now," she said and tugged at the baby's blanket. "Which is the only place I want to be for a while."

Daisy glanced down at the sleeping infant and smiled. It was impossible not to. She was adorable. "What's her name?"

Sarah smiled. Daisy thought if the girl grew up to look anything like her mama, she'd already be halfway to the easy life. "Hope," Sarah told her.

Daisy smiled back. "Great name."

Sarah nodded. "She had some complications when she was born, but we're through it." She tenderly stroked Hope's cheek. Daisy didn't know what kind of complications, but the little girl looked perfect to her, if not small. Whatever they were, they must have been a hell of a trial to inspire that look from her mother. Daisy decided then and there that it was easy to like this woman.

Sarah cleared her throat. "We're friends of Jimmy's."

Or possibly I should stop making hasty judgments, Daisy thought.

It wasn't hard to see where this was going. Three uppity women who looked like they were Cosmo Models in an article entitled 'Babies, Husbands, Careers: Secrets to Having it ALL!' were not about to welcome a tattooed, pierced loud mouth into their inner circle.

"Who?" Daisy asked nonchalantly as she finished filling the glasses. Let them think what they wanted about her. A quickie in a bathroom wasn't worth all the drama. They'd see she wasn't planning on invading their garden parties like an ugly weed, and they'd leave her alone.

Sarah cleared her throat again, this time embarrassed, and looked at her friends. "Um, the guy. The guy you... from last night."

Daisy rolled her eyes. "Oh, yeah. Sir Speedy."

The youngest one choked on her water. Daisy bit back a grin and handed her a napkin.

"Wasn't very memorable," Daisy explained. "What about him?"

Sarah's face turned red, to match her friend's. "We... we just... I haven't been around lately," she announced.

Daisy quirked up an eyebrow.

"I've been home," Sarah clarified. "And Abby says," she nodded to the redhead, "she's never seen you before."

"Just started last night," Daisy replied, trying to keep the edge out of her voice.

Sarah's face turned nearly purple. "So, you don't *know* him."

"Nope," Daisy said casually. "Don't care to. He cheated on his girlfriend, right in front of her and didn't give a shit."

"She wasn't his girlfriend!" Sarah insisted.

Daisy frowned at her. "She tried to take a swing at me."

"Well," Sarah said, floundering. "We don't know her either. But she wasn't his girlfriend. We wanted her to be though." She looked back at her friends then at Daisy. "We were hoping she'd be."

Daisy crossed her arms in front of her. "Well, I didn't mess that up," she insisted. "I didn't even know about her. I was just minding my own business," she said, glossing over the flirting she'd done earlier that night. "*He* came up to *me*," Daisy told them. "And I just... went with it," she finished, for lack of any better explanation.

"She had a dry spell!" Milo chimed in from his stool a few feet away.

Daisy felt her own cheeks pinken. "Shut up, old man," she snapped.

"Just sayin'."

Daisy glared at him. "Say anything else, and I'll put you on the No Fly Cheese Fry list."

Milo shrank into his stool.

"I don't know him," Daisy repeated to the woman. "If you've got a problem-"

"He's got a problem," Sarah told her.

"Yeah, I heard. Missing a leg. And that sucks, truly, but it's not a free pass to treat people like shit."

"He doesn't do that!" Sarah argued.

"Yeah, he does," the redhead replied.

Both Daisy and Sarah looked at her.

Red shrugged. "He does."

Sarah sighed. "Not all the time. And he was getting better! You didn't know him when they released him from the VA. He was a lot worse," she said as much to her friends as to Daisy. "He was getting better. But yesterday and today, he's been... moody."

The redhead clamped her lips shut as though 'moody' didn't quite cover it.

"I just thought you might know something," Sarah told Daisy. She looked genuinely concerned.

Daisy couldn't help but feel for her. "I don't," she said quietly.

"So, he didn't say anything to you at all?"

Daisy grimaced and shook her head. "No." She lowered her voice. "To be honest, he didn't say anything at all." She sighed. "I don't know why I did what I did," she admitted.

Milo grunted behind her. Daisy clenched her fists but didn't turn around.

"I'm not after Jimmy," she told them. "It was just a crazy thing that happened. I don't know anything about him. Sorry."

Sarah sighed. "It's okay."

"Are you going to eat?" Daisy asked. "Or did you just come here for that?"

"We'll eat," Sarah said more brightly. "I'm starving."

Daisy nodded and took out her pad. "Let's start with drinks."

"Just water for me," Sarah replied. "Breastfeeding."

"Is the baby hungry? Milo asked. "You should feed her."

"Jesus Christ, Milo," Daisy snapped. "Mind your own business. And stop bein' a perv!"

Milo muttered something about MILF's and Daisy pinched the bridge of her nose. "You don't even know what that means, old man," she guessed. "And this is your last warning."

"I'm used to him," Sarah declared.

"How long did that take?" Daisy asked.

"About two weeks after I quit."

"Fabulous," Daisy replied dryly.

"I'll have a martini," the redhead told her. "I'm Abby, by the way."

Daisy nodded and jotted it down. "I'm Tildy," said the youngest one. "I'll have a club soda."

Daisy eyed her. "Are you old enough to be in here?"

Tildy giggled. "Just barely. I don't drink much." She hesitated. "I like your tattoos, though."

Daisy looked down at her arms then at the brunette, skeptically. Tildy blushed. "No, really. I want one," she said quietly.

Abby and Sarah laughed, but good-naturedly.

"I do!" Tildy insisted. "I want a hawk," she declared.

"A hawk?" Daisy asked.

"That's her fiancée's name," Abby told her.

Daisy glanced at the ring and nodded.

"You have one," Tildy shot back.

"That I do, the redhead confirmed and sipped her water.

Daisy wasn't too surprised. A lot of people had tattoos where no one could see them.

It's on her ass!" Milo said loudly.

That *was* surprising, and Daisy looked at Abby, both eyebrows raised.

Abby glowered. "I was playing pool with my boyfriend. There was a bet. I really wanted to win. That's how he knows." Her chin jutted out. "I'm not above cheating to win."

Daisy grinned. "I have a lot of tattoos," she replied, "but none on my ass. You're a braver woman than I am."

She headed to the bar to turn in the drink order while the women perused the menus on the table. Maria didn't need the order, however, and already had the drinks ready to go. Daisy reached out and snatched Milo's half-eaten sandwich off the bar and tilted the plate into the trash can.

"Hey!" he protested.

Daisy pinned him with a harsh look. "I warned you, old man."

CHAPTER EIGHT

Daisy stepped into a pair of jean shorts as she got ready for work. The week had been slow but steady and the money was great. She'd have to dip into her savings though, at some point, to buy some more clothes. When she'd first come to South Dakota eight months ago, she'd only planned to stay the weekend, not settle here permanently.

She put on a black, short sleeved t-shirt and added matching eye liner. After stuffing her nearly empty backpack into a drawer, she locked her room door behind her and headed toward the bar. From the window of the motel's lobby the woman who ran the place watched her as she smoked a menthol. She looked like Norman Bates' mother- after she'd been stuffed. Daisy gave her a shit-eating grin and strode past. The parking lot of Maria's was already filling up, and the sun hadn't even gone down yet.

She grinned to herself as she reached for the front door. She didn't mind hard work as long as she had something to show for it in the end.

The place was hopping and she quickly clocked in and tied her apron around her waist. She headed over to a group of what appeared to be one percenters and started gathering up their empties. A few of them tried to flirt with her, but she didn't return the sentiment. There was no way she'd get involved with anyone on the wrong side of the law. She'd learned that lesson the hard way.

On her way back to the bar, she spotted the redhead, Abby,

walking toward her. She smiled. "Hey, there!" Daisy called out above the din.

Abby smiled back and took up a stool next to Milo.

"Vegas," he grunted and eyed Daisy. Clearly, the thought of losing his fries was heavy on his mind.

"Milo," Abby said dryly.

Maria didn't wait for Abby's order. She just plunked a martini down in front of the woman.

"Can you make it three olives?" Abby asked.

Maria sighed. "You didn't eat today?"

Abby shrugged. "Too busy."

"Woman, you own a restaurant!"

"Doesn't mean I have time to *eat* there!" Abby shot back. "In fact owning a restaurant pretty much ensures that I'll never have time to eat again."

"You own a restaurant?" Daisy asked as she loaded up her tray again.

Abby nodded. "And a hotel."

"Nice," Daisy replied, duly impressed.

"The restaurant just opened. We're still in the red on it, but it's taking off."

Daisy dropped off another round of drinks across the bar and mulled over Abby's status as a hotel/restaurant owner. She didn't seem much older than Daisy herself. She must be loaded, smart, or both, Daisy decided. On her way back she asked, "Why're you called 'Vegas'?"

Abby chewed the last olive and swallowed. "'Cause I'm from there."

"Wow. I've never met anyone from Vegas."

"Have you ever been there?"

Daisy shook her head. "Nah. I'd like to, though. Sounds like a fun town."

"It is," Abby agreed. "Definitely." She wrinkled her nose. "I don't know when I'll ever go back though. I'd have to stay where no one knows who I am."

Daisy smirked. "Are you a wanted woman?"

"Worse. An *unwanted* woman. I'm not welcome there."

Daisy paused with a pitcher of beer in her hand. "What? Like the whole town is against you?" she snorted. "Sounds like me."

"Where're you from?"

"A tiny, little shithole called Delay in Nebraska. We've got a gas station, motel, diner, and grocery store. That's about it, though."

"Did they chase you out with pitchforks?"

Daisy laughed. "Nah. They'd never go to that much effort. They just give me the stink eye whenever they see me walking down the street. Tattoos and piercings don't exactly jive with their wholesome, small town image. Most of them think I'm a-"

"Slut."

Daisy craned her neck to look at a girl who looked vaguely familiar, but she couldn't quite place. She wasn't Easy's Crazy Not-Ex Girlfriend though, so she must have been one of her minions.

"Don't start," warned Maria. "She'll probably kick *your* ass, too."

Daisy didn't know if this was carte blanche to wail on the girl, but she figured it might be. She wasn't really in the mood to fight, but she wouldn't back down from it, either.

"You just roll into town and screw every guy you see?" the minion asked.

"She hasn't screwed me, yet!" Milo said halfway between gleeful and mournful.

Daisy shot him a look. "Hold your breath 'til that happens, old man."

"You know, Brenda's finger's broken after that stunt you pulled."

Daisy rolled her eyes. "I doubt it. She throws a weak-ass punch."

"Well, her finger's all swollen," the minion insisted.

"So's her god damn ego," Daisy shot back. "He ain't hers, leastways I didn't see her name on him anywhere *I* looked."

This was a bit disingenuous as Easy hadn't taken any of his clothes off while they'd been going at it, but the minion hadn't actually seen them. For all the minion knew, Daisy and Easy had been stripped down to their born glory and filming their own Tijuana Donkey Show. Daisy wasn't above letting them think that.

"God, you're a slut."

Daisy huffed. "Really? That's the best you've got? My mama can think up ten better insults before she's had her morning coffee." Daisy leaned forward and put her hands on the bar. "My skin's not just inked up, honey. It's *armored*, too. You're going to have to do a shit ton better'n that."

The girl's eyes narrowed and she opened her mouth. "You're a-"

At that moment, Abby lurched off her stool, swayed, and deposited her martini directly onto the front of the girl's shirt. She laughed and hiccupped at the same time. "Oh, sorry!" she slurred. "Didn't see you there!"

The girl screeched in outrage, spun on her heel, and stormed away.

Abby turned back to the bar and sat her now empty glass on the counter. "Maria, I need another," she declared, suddenly sober.

"You're wasting my gin," the blonde drawled.

Abby wrinkled her nose. "I know. Believe me. It pained me to do it. Should've been a cosmo, though. She'd never get the stain out."

As Maria poured Abby a new drink, Daisy said, "Thanks, but I can fight my own battles."

The redhead's lip curled up. "Please. That was hardly a battle. If she was going to do something, she would've done it. Nah. She was just gonna stand there all night and bitch and ain't nobody got time for that."

"Amen," said Milo. "If there's gonna be a catfight, let's get a pool of jello. Otherwise I ain't interested."

Daisy reached for his plate, but he moved it out her reached and stuffed some fries into his mouth. He chewed indignantly.

"Jesus," Daisy muttered and cleared the bar of empties. "I've never seen this much fuss about a two-minute tango."

Abby pulled an olive off her toothpick with her teeth. "Don't let them get to you," she told Daisy. "There's nothing wrong with going at it with a stranger in the bathroom."

Daisy raised an eyebrow. "You speaking from experience?"

The redhead sighed and shook her head. "Sadly, no. I never got to do it," she admitted. "Always wanted to though. But I met Tex; we got to know each other and now, no dice."

Daisy followed her gaze across the bar to the pool table closest to them. "The Sioux or the blonde?" she asked.

Abby sighed again, this time contentedly. "The blonde."

"Damn," said Daisy, approvingly. "I'd say you came out ahead on the deal if you get to have that fine hunk of man every night instead of a stranger for just one."

"You better believe it," Abby confirmed. Her fingers went to the necklace she was wearing and she stroked it lovingly.

"He gave you that?" Daisy asked.

Abby glanced at her, cheeks flushed and nodded.

Just then, Daisy's phone went off. She ignored it and wiped down the bar.

"That's her boyfriend," Milo chirped.

"You have a boyfriend?" Abby asked.

"No," Daisy growled and shot Milo a look.

Milo shrugged. "Phone's always ringing."

Daisy blew out a harsh breath. "And do I answer, old man?"

Milo's face screwed up as he considered this. "No," he decided. "What does that tell you?"

"Ex-boyfriend," Abby guessed.

"Give the lady a gold star," Daisy grumbled, her mood suddenly soured.

"I'd settle for another martini."

Daisy gaped at her. "How many can you drink?"

"Don't judge me," Abby replied.

"Oh, I'm not," Daisy assured her.

"So, your ex keeps calling."

Daisy glowered. "Don't know what he wants. We are never getting back together."

"Never, ever, ever...getting back together!"

Daisy rolled her eyes. "Knock it off! You are not Milo Cyrus!"

"Is it a sordid tale of woe?" Abby asked.

Daisy shrugged. "Not really. Girl meets asshole. Asshole leaves her in Sturgis during the rally and goes back home."

Abby's mouth dropped open. "*He left you?*"

Daisy nodded solemnly. "We had a fight, and he took off the next morning."

"Holy shit!" Abby breathed. Then her forehead wrinkled. "The rally's in August," she pointed out. "What've you been doing all this time?"

Daisy's stomach tightened. *Oh shit*, she thought. She'd managed to open her mouth and insert her whole foot inside. She was desperately trying to think up a reply when a man stepped up to the bar. He had shoulder length, brown hair and what was not really a beard but some serious five o'clock shadow. It suited him though.

His black t-shirt hugged his body. Large biceps stretched the fabric and black ink travelled the length of both arms. She recognized the face as well as the tats.

"Hey," Daisy said and smiled up at him. He returned the sentiment. "I remember you from last week," she declared. "You said I had nice tats."

"Why does *he* get to say it?" Milo whined.

"Tats!" Daisy barked at him. "Tats! Clean your ears while you cut that hair."

The guy grinned at her. "Both are nice," he told Milo loudly. Daisy blushed as her heart thudded. She was not about to take this man's chili cheese fries away, no, sir.

"I'm glad you remember me," he said in a smooth, velvet voice. "I'm Adam." He reached out to take her hand and shook it. Then he turned her wrist and inspected her ink. His thumb ran over her orange white koi on her forearm. "Traditional and Japanese, but it works," he said. "Very nice."

Daisy would've said something about Sailor Jerry but she'd momentarily misplaced her tongue.

Adam turned, looked down, and nodded. "Abby," he drawled. She blushed and nodded back.

"Holy hell," Daisy breathed as Adam walked away. She looked at Abby, who was ready to fan herself. "Have...?" Daisy asked. "Have you two...?"

"No!" Abby cried, and shook her head vehemently. "Oh, no. Worse, in a way."

Daisy stared at her. "Worse how?"

Abby wrinkled her nose. "Remember when I told you I had a tattoo of my own?"

Daisy nodded, then recalled Milo's offer of information about said tattoo's location.

"Oh," she giggled. "Yeah, that's why I don't get ink there."

She couldn't imagine lying on a chair, face down, ass in the air while Adam stared down at it, for hours, possibly, depending on the art. Rather, now she could imagine it, and it sent shivers down her spine.

Breaking the awkwardness, Abby said, "Hey, you play poker?"

Daisy was momentarily tripped up by the question. "What? Do I-? Yeah. Yeah."

Abby grinned. "Fantastic," she said and took out a pen. She scrawled an address onto a napkin. "Every Thursday, my friends and I play at Sarah's house," she told Daisy. "You should come. It's a blast."

Daisy glanced down at the address and frowned.

"Oh," Abby said quietly. "Yeah. Easy will be there. Awkward. Forget I said anything."

"No," Daisy protested. "It's not that," she insisted. And it wasn't. She was long over that mistake. "I don't have a car."

"Oh," Abby repeated and took back the napkin. "Oh, no problem. I'll pick you up. If you're sure it's cool..."

Daisy nodded. She had no friends yet and Abby and her friends seemed nice. "Totally cool," she assured Abby. "I'm so over that."

CHAPTER NINE

Daisy saw a cherry red muscle car pull up in front of her motel room and had to do a double-take to make sure it was Abby. The tall redhead opened the driver's side door and stepped out, dispelling any doubts.

"Nice ride," Daisy called out as she locked the door behind her.

Abby grinned. "Thanks," she replied, patting the hood. "This is my baby."

Daisy settled into the front seat and ran her hands over the leather. "You know, a few years ago, I'd have fallen hard for any guy who cruised around town in a ride like this."

Abby looked at her over her sunglasses and put the car in reverse. "How about now? Have you seen the error of your ways?"

Daisy laughed. "Hell no. I just traded up. Nowadays it's a hot guy on a hot bike."

Abby joined in her laughter. "Can't say I'm any better. My car- not my baby, mind you, a different car- crapped out on me on the highway on the day I came into town. Tex rolled up behind me on his huge, black Harley, and I just about wet my panties."

"A guy like that would make any girl's panties wet," Daisy teased.

Abby giggled, slapped Daisy lightly on the arm, and pulled out onto the main road. As she drove through the city, Daisy leaned her head back against the seat. "Matt doesn't have a bike. Or a muscle car. Just a beat up truck. Should've been my first clue his priorities were screwed up. You know how some guys you can look at the way they treat their cars and you can see how they'd treat you? Should've picked up on that."

Abby smiled. "I know what you mean. The way Tex goes over every inch of his Harley, polishing it, testing it, I never wanted to be a motorcycle so badly in my *life*."

"So, you're Vegas from Vegas," Daisy ventured. "I take Tex is from Texas?"

Abby nodded. "They all met in the Army. They're all ex-Rangers."

Daisy gave a low whistle. "Yikes," she muttered.

"Shooter was a sniper," Abby informed her, "as you might guess. Hawk's into computers. Tex knows about eight languages and has a psych degree on top of that. Doc, Caleb, has emergency medical training, but he's a cop now."

Daisy glanced at her. "A cop?" she asked and tried to keep the waver out of her voice.

"Yeah. I think he'd had enough of the blood and guts on tour. He's an officer now. I was surprised he's not interested in becoming a detective or anything like that. He's happy on the streets, I guess."

"So, he's pretty straight and narrow," Daisy guessed, and couldn't tell if that was a good or a bad thing.

But Abby surprised her and shook her head. "Not really," she said quietly. "I mean, he wears the badge, but... I get the impression that he's not all about the rules, you know."

Daisy scowled. Even worse was a cop who thought the rules didn't apply to him. She made a mental note to stay far away from Caleb.

"And Jimmy-" Abby glanced at Daisy to see if it was okay to talk about him. Daisy just shrugged.

"Jimmy's got a degree in mechanical engineering. I guess he loves seeing how things work and putting them back together. He's not a bad guy," she insisted. "I think he just came out of it the worst, you know? Makes sense that he'd take the longest to recover."

Daisy watched the downtown area give way to warehouses. "Maria said it was a bomb."

"Took out half their unit," Abby explained. "And they were all pretty close. They're the only ones left so they decided to stick together."

Daisy nodded to herself. "Like a family."

"It *is* a family. They think of themselves as brothers, which means they support each other through everything." She sighed. "Of course, it also means they fight like brothers, too. And they don't pull punches, literally or figuratively."

"Are they violent?" Daisy asked cautiously. She'd seen some one percenters get into it at Sturgis. Some of them were ex-military; all of them were pretty much crazy.

"No," Abby assured her. "Only with each other. And not seriously. No one's ever gotten hurt."

They pulled into a large circular driveway, and Abby parked in front of the log cabin style house. "Wow," Daisy muttered, taking in the view of the place. Her whole trailer could fit in the garage.

"It's great, isn't it?" Abby replied. "They love it."

"It's beautiful out here," Daisy commented looking at the wooded areas surrounding the house.

Abby rounded the car and headed up the front steps. "South Dakota isn't anything like the desert," she told Daisy, "but it has its own kind of beauty."

"Better than Nebraska," Daisy pointed out. "It's just corn and cows."

Abby opened the front door and ushered Daisy inside. The living room was two stories high with a large fireplace and not a stitch of shag carpeting to be seen.

"Hey!" Tildy gushed and swept Daisy into a hug.

Tildy's man sat on the couch, nursing a beer, and nodded to her. Daisy could totally see why even a girl as bambi eyed as Tildy would want a tattoo that reminded her of him. *Lord*, she thought, and wondered if he was that big all over and how a girl as small as Tildy managed to take it.

There were two she didn't recognize seated in chairs across the room. "I'm Chris," one of them told her. "This is my place."

He looked slightly older than the others, but it looked good on him. So did his jeans. Daisy was beginning to wonder if she wasn't quite out of her dry spell yet, because every man in here was mouth-wateringly delicious looking.

Tex, whom she hadn't officially met but recognized because Abby had pointed him out, gave her a warm smile as he leaned up against the wall. Daisy smiled back. She figured the dark, broody one might be Caleb, the cop, and only gave him a cursory nod before looking away quickly. He didn't seem all that interested in her anyway, which could only be a good thing.

"Something sure smells good," Daisy declared.

"I'm trying to help Sarah in the kitchen," Tildy replied.

"Well, I don't cook," Daisy announced. "But I can wash dishes. If-"

At that moment, Easy rounded the corner. Daisy had known she'd run into him here, but apparently her indignant brain had made her mental image of him uglier and far less attractive than RealEasy, who stood out as the hottest guy in a room chock full of them. The imaginary punch to the gut nearly knocked the wind out of her.

Then she realized he was holding the baby Sarah had brought into the bar earlier. Hope was snuggled against Easy's chest, taking up real estate that Daisy found herself wanting to occupy, despite it being a very, very bad idea.

"What is *she* doing here?" he demanded, dispelling any idea Daisy had of Round Two.

She narrowed her eyes at him, feeling a little embarrassed that she'd let herself fantasize, however briefly, about him. It hadn't taken long for him to remind her why it was never going to work in the first place.

Easy was an asshole.

"I was *invited*," Daisy shot back. "They like me." She indicated Abby and Tildy. "Probably because, you know, they got to *know* me. Don't worry," she sneered. "I'm not here because of us."

Easy bristled and shifted the baby a little in his arms. "There is no 'us'," he growled.

Daisy laughed. "Oh, you're right about that. It isn't a relationship by anyone's standards. Not even mine," she added, because she could practically hear him judging her.

46

It irritated her that he'd called her out like he couldn't just forget it happened and move on. He had to point out that she wasn't good enough, not only for him, but to even join their circle of friends.

"She should leave," he declared.

"*She* has a name," Daisy replied.

He sneered at her. "Yeah, sorry. I didn't care then, and I don't care now."

"Jimmy!" Abby scolded.

He shrugged. "It's not like she asked me for *my* name, either."

"Well, I *tried*," Daisy pointed out. "Earlier, if you remember. But you were too busy acting like an asshole to notice."

Easy snorted. "So, you just bone assholes on a regular basis?" he asked, trying to shift the focus back to Daisy.

"Pretty much all of them have been, yeah," Daisy responded coolly. "From the one that cheated to the one that knocked out one of my teeth and the ones in between. Yep, all assholes. You're just the one who doesn't know my name. And to be honest, that doesn't put you very high on the list. In fact," she informed him. "A two-minute schtup standing up in a bathroom where I didn't even *get off* doesn't even deserve to make the list at all. So, why don't you forget it happened? I pretty much have."

Someone whistled, but Daisy didn't look around to see who.

"I'm new in town and I don't have any friends. I'd like to make some. And right now something in the kitchen smells awfully damn good, and, seeing as how I've been living off of bar food and trashburgers for weeks, this will be the first time I've had a home cooked meal in... Well, honestly, my mama's not exactly the Nebraska Martha Stewart, so unless ravioli from a can counts as home cooking, then I've never had it. So, do you think you could find it in your too-small Grinch's heart to let me get a decent meal and talk to someone who isn't ordering a beer?"

Daisy crossed her arms and waited for him to decide. She was totally aware that everyone in the room was looking at her. Even Sarah had come out of the kitchen to see what all the fuss was about. Daisy didn't care. She'd learned long ago that you couldn't hide who you were, especially not in Delay, Nebraska. Everyone knew you were from the trailer park. Everyone knew your daddy got your mama pregnant and took off before you were even born.

No amount of church-donated clothes and shoes would let you fool anyone into thinking you were anything but Poor White Trash. Over the years, she'd also discovered that being open about it and yes, occasionally wielding it like a weapon of sorts could make things easier on herself. Now Easy had to decide if he was going to be the guy who wouldn't let a broke-ass barmaid have a meal.

It wasn't hard to be an asshole when you were surrounded by a group of them, but it was often difficult to be the only one. Easy shifted the baby in his arms and finally looked away from her. Daisy figured it was as close to a guy like him waving the white flag as she was ever going to get. She lifted her chin and walked past him toward Sarah and the kitchen beyond.

CHAPTER TEN

Easy couldn't bring himself to look at her as she walked past him. He knew that none of this was her fault, anyway. It only bothered him that he thought of Brenda when he looked at her.

Her, he realized, looking down at Hope, he didn't even know-

"Her name is Daisy," Abby told him quietly, as though she read his thoughts.

He had a vague memory of daisies tattooed on her shoulder. She had tried to talk to him, multiple times, but he'd been brooding over Brenda and hadn't responded. Then he'd cornered her in the bathroom, but she hadn't minded. *Well, she's used to assholes*, he thought. Apparently, serious assholes at that.

Now *he* was the asshole. Wasn't that always the case? Everyone was looking at him. He'd fucked up; he knew it. He didn't need a lecture from his former lieutenant, or insight from Tex, or any damn thing else. He strode to Shooter and passed the baby to him then turned and walked toward the door.

"You're leaving?" Abby asked, slightly panicked.

Easy ignored her and kept moving. He stepped out the door onto the front porch.

"He's leaving?" he heard her ask the others. "He can't just apologize? Is... is he going to make us *choose?*"

Easy didn't wait to hear the rest as he descended the steps and headed to his truck. Fuck no, he wasn't going to make them choose.

At this point, they'd choose her. *Daisy*, he corrected. And who could blame them? Then he'd lose his family- again. He stepped on the gas and shot toward the country lane that led down the foothill. It was a fairly quick drive back into town, quick enough in the truck at least. Easy still couldn't drum up the courage to ride his bike out this far.

He didn't call it fear, not out loud. He simply told them his thigh got a little numb if he rode too long, which was not a lie. The damn temporary prosthetic wasn't the greatest fit, but Easy still wasn't too comfortable even driving outside the city limits. He'd sucked it up for Slick's wedding in the Badlands, but that was it. For a while he'd had crazy visions of putting it down on the pavement and losing the other leg. That fear had now subsided until it was mostly just a nagging bad feeling in the back of his mind, but it hadn't yet gone away.

As he hit the city limits he turned onto the road that led through town. He passed Maria's, which looked slow, but then again it was only Thursday. He briefly considered stopping but really didn't feel like being surrounded by people. He passed the motel and Burnout and turned down his own street and pulled in the driveway next to his bike.

He killed the engine and hauled himself out of the front seat. It was early yet, he thought to himself as he looked up at the cloudless sky. Their poker games usually lasted half the night, a nice distraction from sitting at home, which until recently had been a perilous pastime. Inside he felt jangly, hot and intense, and recognized that he was on the edge. He stood, paralyzed, at the bottom of his own front steps.

Next to him was a bike, small and shitty as it was. It was a Harley to be sure but only just worthy of the name. Easy hadn't wanted to invest a lot of money at the time, not when he was secretly unsure he'd even be able to ride again. Beyond the front door were other options as well. Such as Jack Daniels, who a year ago had felt more like a brother than the men he'd served with. Easy had, so far, not found a problem that Jack couldn't solve, or at least make him forget about for a while.

Also waiting ever so patiently was the box, a small bit of cardboard and silver Christmas wrapping paper replete with sparkling snowflakes- a gift to himself that he hadn't yet opened. He stood on the concrete walkway with his keys digging into the palm of his hand. The booze, the box, or the bike?

He'd been off the hard booze for a while now, and he wasn't ready for the box. He turned around and strode to the BarelyHarley and swung his leg over the side. He kicked it to start and revved the engine a few times, warming it up. He backed it up out of driveway and aimed it at the street. Right about now he could probably use a helmet, he realized, but then again if he was going to wipe out, maybe it was best not to survive it.

He hit the highway at sixty and threaded through traffic until it thinned out to just a few stragglers. The night sky was littered with stars, easily visible now that the lights of city were so far behind him. He'd bought Hope a star just after she was born, one of those silly internet things with a "deed" -more or less- and her name on it. As much as he'd wanted kids of his own, he didn't know a damn thing about them. A star seemed as good a gift as anything else he could think of, which was not much given his inexpertise. He tried but couldn't pick out the one that was hers, but he'd written it down for when she got older and wanted to see it for herself.

He still wasn't sure about motorcycles in general. He'd ridden a few times before he'd enlisted. He'd liked it well enough, and the freedom was exhilarating. Then, after Iraq, he'd been almost rooted in place, fighting off panic at the thought of being trapped in a vehicle as the other members of his unit had been. He recalled the freedom of the bike, but the idea of nothing protecting him from other vehicles or the road had been equally terrifying. He could tolerate either type of vehicle at this point, but he wasn't sure he'd ever actually like them. At this point driving *anything* was just a way to get from point A to point B, not something he enjoyed the way he used to.

By the time he reached the Badlands the moon was hanging over it. He parked the bike and walked to the edge of the scrub where the ground started to get rockier and eventually gave way to canyons beyond. He didn't know how he felt about this place, the sterile wasteland that seemed both beautiful and terrifying at the same time. Slick and Shooter had gotten married here, right on this spot. Easy had never seen two people happier. Tildy had almost died near here, violently, and her smile dimmed just a bit any time they rode out here for a picnic. Easy figured the Badlands were just like life, embodying both the best moments and some fucking horrific ones.

He wondered, not for the first time, if all his best moments might be behind him.

CHAPTER ELEVEN

Daisy was in the kitchen when Abby came in behind her. "He left!" she told them.

Sarah sighed and shook her head. Daisy bit her lower lip. She hated being the cause of all this strife in this obviously close group of friends. She scraped her thumbnail on the granite countertop. "I'm sorry," she said quietly. "Maybe I should go."

"No!" Sarah replied, turning to face her. "No way. This is his problem. I don't know what's going on with him. This is pretty douchey even for him, but whatever this is, it's his problem. Not yours. You're more than welcome here, Daisy. Really."

"I didn't think it was such a big deal," Daisy admitted.

Sarah shook her head again. "Me, neither," she said. "I can't understand it. I mean, no offense Daisy, but Jimmy's been around the block *more* than a few times."

Abby snorted. "More like around the country. Very possibly *internationally*."

Daisy grimaced. Being one of a few was okay; being one of hundreds was a bit disheartening, even if she didn't like him that much.

"So, whatever this is," Sarah told Daisy, "it's not you." She grabbed a stack of bowls and handed them to Daisy. "We're going to have a nice dinner and take the boys' money afterwards. If Jimmy doesn't want to join us, well, that's not exactly anything new to me."

She nodded as much to herself as the other women in the room and ushered Daisy and Abby into the dining room to set the table. Daisy was surprised when the men wandered in and lent a hand. She deliberately chose a seat as far from Caleb as she could get. Even if this didn't work out long-term, she could get a hot meal and maybe make some money at the same time. Losing a little bit, as long as she still had a good time, would be fine as well. A few hours later, her stomach was pleasantly stuffed, and her wallet was hot on its heels.

"Read 'em and weep, gentlemen," Daisy she as she laid down her small straight.

"God damn it," Tex growled and threw down his own cards. "Okay. That's it. New rule. No women at the table. Period."

"Oh, hey now," Hawk argued, and gripped Tildy, who was sitting perched on his lap, a little tighter around the waist. "I need my good luck charm."

Daisy smiled. Apparently Tildy couldn't play for shit, but she was nice, if not a little sheltered, it seemed. She blushed at everyone's off-color jokes.

"Well, they can't play," Tex ordered. "They're all too damn good." He eyed Daisy across the table. "Your sleeves aren't long enough to stuff cards in them," he observed. "Where'd you learn to play like that?"

Daisy laughed. "Ricky Snell's basement. And you had to learn fast," she told him. "'Cause Ricky had a rule of his own: Only Strip Poker."

Tex snorted. "Typical Ricky."

Daisy laughed again. She had to admit that for guys who'd undoubtedly seen the worst of what humanity had to offer, they'd sure held on to their own. Even Easy, who may have lost a good bit of his sense of humor (assuming he'd ever had one to begin with), cuddled Sarah and Shooter's baby in a way told her that somewhere in there was a decent guy.

"So I had to stop losing fast," Daisy told them. "Because there was no way I was sitting around bare assed in a crowded room."

Abby sipped her martini and nodded. Thankfully, she'd sat out this round, because the girl had skills of her own. "I can relate," she said. "With Adam looking down at my ass for over an hour. Not comfortable."

"Who's Adam?" Tildy asked.

Tex leaned toward her. "Yes," he said. "I think I need to know who Adam is, too."

Abby blushed. "The tattoo artist."

Tex's jaw flinched. Apparently he hadn't given too much thought at this point about exactly how that tat ended up on his girlfriend's ass.

"Whew, yeah," Daisy agreed. "I don't know if it's better or worse for a semi-toothless guy named Old Joe with a ZZ Top beard to be looking or a guy as fine as that."

"I still want a tattoo," Tildy announced as she wrinkled her nose. "But I don't want a guy looking at my ass, toothless or hot."

Hawk looked at her, perplexed. "Why do you need a tattoo?"

Tildy shrugged and sipped her beer. "I just want one."

Hawk groaned and rolled his eyes. "You don't need a tattoo. And especially not one on your ass. And doubly especially if a hot guy is going to be giving it to you."

"I'm still trying to get over the idea of a hot guy looking at *my* woman's ass," Tex grumbled.

"It's okay, baby," Abby said, leaning into him. "I don't need any more tattoos. Plus, he's totally into Daisy."

Daisy rolled her eyes and looked away. "We were just talking shop. It wasn't a big deal."

"Wait a minute," Tex said, shifting in his chair. "Is this the scraggly guy at the bar the other day?"

"He's not scraggly!" Daisy and Abby protested at the same time.

Daisy held on to her indignation, but Abby backed down. "Not that I care," she said quietly.

"Damn right, you don't," Tex told her.

Even Daisy shivered at the tone in his voice.

"What are you going to do with all your dough, Daisy?" Sarah asked, rocking the baby in her arms.

Daisy tugged at the hem of her t-shirt. "Well, for starters I need more clothes. I don't have that many, and I don't want to spend any more time in that sorry excuse for a laundry room at the Rainbow than I have to."

Sarah wrinkled her nose. "Oh, God I know. The dryer-"

"Doesn't even work," Daisy told her.

"Really? It was on its last legs when I lived there. Can't say I'm surprised it finally gave out or that she didn't replace it."

"You lived there?"

Sarah nodded. "For a while, when I first came to town. It's awful, and so's the landlady. She tried to charge me for hooking in my room. As if I'd do that!"

Daisy plucked at her shirt again, recalling that the old lady tried to charge her, too. She felt a little better knowing it probably happened to everyone at that place.

"We can go shopping this weekend," Abby suggested. "Tildy and I are off."

"You work together?" Daisy asked, looking back and forth between the two. "I mean," she asked Tildy, "you work for her."

"Yeah," Tildy replied. "I quit my job last year. Just kind of walked away from it, no plan, nothing."

"What kind of job?" Daisy asked, curious.

"I worked at my parent's bank," she mumbled.

"Wow," Daisy replied. "That's like a *real* job. Like a career."

Tildy shrugged. "It wasn't for me. And my parents are, well, they're just..." She waved her hand dismissively.

Daisy nodded. "Yeah, I can probably relate to shitty parent stories. Never met my dad, but my mama's enough for the both of them."

"But Abby gave me a job," Tildy said with a smile.

"I didn't give you a job," Abby countered. "You *got* the job." To Daisy, she said, "Her Spanish is *outstanding*, so much better than mine. And the sales reports are a breeze for her. She's going to steal the place out from under me and run it better than I do."

Tildy blushed but grinned at the same time. "I would," she said. "But I don't have a gun."

"Huh?" Daisy asked, baffled.

Abby shook her head and waved her hand. "God," she grumbled. "You steal one hotel and they never let you live it down."

"You, wait," Daisy said. "You *stole* a hotel? With a gun?" She tried but failed to understand how that was possible.

Abby shrugged. "Sometimes you gotta go old school on people."

Daisy stole a look at Caleb, who merely shrugged right alongside the redhead. "I wasn't there," he told her.

"Huh," Daisy said. "Here I was looking to lay low, and I seem to have wandered into a den of thieves."

"Lay low?" Abby asked, grinning. "Are *you* a wanted woman?"

Daisy's cheeks flushed. "No," she protested a little too loudly. "I just- despite the tattoos, I'm not much of a lawbreaker," she told them, not making eye contact with Caleb.

Abby laughed. "Me, neither."

"Except for breaking and entering," Hawk chimed in.

Daisy gaped at her new friend.

"Doesn't count!" Abby protested and jabbed a finger at Tex. "It was *his* house!"

"We try," Tex drawled, "to stay on the right side of the law, as long as it's convenient."

"Good to know," Daisy replied.

She helped clear the table and set the dishes in the dishwasher as Sarah rearranged the fridge to accommodate the leftovers.

"So, you guys really are a family," Daisy observed. "You all work with each other. Or... for each other."

Sarah glanced over her shoulder and nodded. "Mostly 'with,' but yep."

"For me family's just me and mama, and most of the time it doesn't feel like family at all."

"You're not born into a family, Daisy," Sarah told her. "You choose one. And you fight like hell for them. Sometimes *with* them," she admitted. "But mostly *for* them."

"No one's ever fought for me," Daisy admitted.

Sarah considered this at length and then said, "Fight for *them*. If they're worth it, then eventually they'll come around."

CHAPTER TWELVE

Easy caught sight of Sarah's SUV pulling into the lot and frowned as she stalked across the lot. She had lunch with her but no Hope. Tex went out to meet her, but instead of letting him help her she shook her head, glaring past the older man's shoulder and right at Easy himself.

He grimaced. He knew he wouldn't get away with his tantrum last night. Slick never let him get away with anything. She was determined and unscrupulous to boot. So far, she'd nearly run over him and his mailbox, broke into his house and painted it, and once offered him a loaded .45 to put himself out of his misery.

The woman played fast and loose with the rules of polite society when it came to her family, and Easy had no doubt that for all the times that they'd locked horns Sarah Sullivan was as much his sister as Chris was his brother.

And now it was time to pay the piper- especially if he ever wanted to eat again. Tildy invited him over for dinner sometimes, but she'd been raised high-class with a family chef, and he only accepted her invitations out of politeness. Slick's cooking, on the other hand, was as close to God's Heaven as you could get on this green Earth. He sighed and put down the fan belt he was holding.

Without a word she slammed a few Tupperware containers into his arms. He took them and followed her into the break room. As he passed by he saw the corner of Shooter's mouth turn up into a lopsided grin. Easy glared at him, but kept a steady pace toward the chopping block.

"Where's the nugget?" he asked, lightly setting the containers on the table.

Sarah responded by slamming the door. "With Tildy," she told him. "I can't kick your ass with a baby in my arms."

Easy mashed his lips together. She was pissed, and it wouldn't do to laugh at her right now. A few months ago, at Shooter's request, Easy had given her some self-defense lessons, the idea being that she could actually get away from potential danger in the future without having to resort to killing. She wasn't bad, truthfully, for a female and a civilian, but she couldn't take down an ex-Army Ranger, no matter how many lessons she had.

She didn't seem to know it, though, because she marched right up to him and shoved his shoulder. Even with the leg, Easy didn't budge, but he had the good sense to look appropriately chastised.

"What the hell is going on with you?" she asked.

"I'm sorry," he told her, skirting the question. "I just didn't expect to see her there."

"Oh, no, Jimmy Turnbull," she snapped. "We're way past that. You screwed her in the *bathroom,* and I worked there so I know just how disgusting that it. Daisy is better than that, and so are you, if you somehow woke up with your head up your ass and didn't realize it. The bathroom? Jesus Christ! And cheating on Brenda- what the hell? She was-"

"She wasn't my girlfriend," Easy replied. He was a little irritated that Slick was up in his business, but he was trying hard to keep his cool. "It isn't cheating if you're not together."

Slick crossed her arms in front of her chest. "So, why aren't you together?"

Easy's eyes narrowed, and he scowled. "Just didn't work out."

"Bullshit! You'd better tell me what happened."

Easy shook his head, finally having had enough of this conversation and said, "I don't need lunch." He started to move past her, but she stepped in front of him.

"Don't ever," she warned him. "I know where you work, and I have the key to your place. I will dog you all day every day for the rest of forever until you talk to me."

Easy was determined not to get angry again. It would only piss off Shooter, who no doubt had one ear cocked, listening for any sounds of trouble.

"This is none of your business, Sarah," he said quietly. "This is *my* life."

He fully expected her to shout, throw something at him, or even throw a punch. Instead her face crumpled, her shoulders sagged. God damn it if that didn't eat through all his anger.

"You were okay," she said quietly. "You were getting better. That was the deal!" she said pushing at him again. He let her. "We were going to get better. *Both of us.* I'm happy. You're supposed to be happy." She stopped fighting him and wiped tears from her eyes.

When Easy had discharged from the VA assisted living and settled officially in Rapid City, he and Sarah, despite having survived very different traumas, were the only ones not on the road to... Easy didn't know if you could exactly *recover* from the shit they'd been through, but you could move beyond it to a better place. For the most part, Shooter, Hawk, Tex, and Doc had already found their way there. Only Slick and Easy were still stuck, unable to go back yet too damaged to move forward.

Sarah fell in love with Chris and decided there was nothing left to do but start healing, and she'd dragged Easy, kicking and screaming, along with her. She had been determined to save them both from themselves.

"We were better," she whispered and Easy could see how much it hurt her to think she was losing him.

He wrapped his arms around her and pulled her in close. She sagged against him, her tears wetting his shirt. "I'm better," he assured her.

She made a noise of protest, but he squeezed her tighter. "I am," he insisted. "Brenda wasn't the one."

Sarah sniffed. "You liked her," she argued.

Easy sighed and decided his pride wasn't worth her tears. She'd been through enough. "She made fun of my leg," he confessed.

Sarah gasped and backed up a step so she could look at him. "What?!"

"I called her for... a date," he said to spare her the details. "She made fun of my leg to her friends. She didn't know I heard it."

"That bitch!"

Despite the admission, he actually smiled. He, like Shooter, much preferred sassy Slick to sad Slick.

"I will kick her ass!" she shouted and Easy grabbed her arm as though she might try and go out to do just that. Hell, given what he knew about her, he wouldn't rule it out.

"Let it go," he told her.

"But-"

"I don't want her to know I heard. It's over. I'm over her. It's done."

Sarah considered this. "And Daisy?"

He scowled. "I was mad. She was there and into me. It was a shitty thing to do."

"So, you don't like her?"

He snorted but caught Sarah's glare and cleared his throat. "No," he replied truthfully. "I used her."

Sarah sniffed again and eyed him disapprovingly. "You should apologize."

Easy sighed.

Slick glared.

He looked longingly at the potato salad on the table. Then he imagined waking up to a purple bedroom. He shivered despite the late spring heat.

"I'll apologize," he promised.

Sarah continued to watch him.

"Scout's honor."

"I'll kick your ass if you don't," she warned.

He grinned at her. "It's so cute that you think you can."

"I can do other things to you."

He shivered again. "I know," he said solemnly. "I'll apologize. Tonight. I promise."

CHAPTER THIRTEEN

Easy stepped into Maria's and scanned the place for a five-foot blonde. The place was packed, which was typical on a Friday night. Bikers and cowboys were competing for buckle bunnies, leather ladies, and the occasional college co-eds who dared each other to visit the place. He didn't immediately see Daisy, but he didn't see Brenda, either, so that was something. Instead of going to the table where the others were sitting, he grabbed a stool beside Milo.

"How's it going?" Easy asked him.

The old man brought up his hand and ran it through his hair. "Got a haircut."

Easy checked it out and nodded.

"Supposed to help me pick up women."

The corner of Easy's mouth turned up. "How's that working out?"

Milo shook his head. "So far, nada. The hens won't pick up the phone when the cock is calling. So how are they gonna know about my new look?"

"Maybe if you stopped calling them hens..." Easy offered.

Milo grunted. "Says the guy getting his jollies in the head."

Easy turned away and sighed. The swinging door that led into the kitchen opened, and Daisy came through it, balancing two plates in her hands. She looked at Milo then spotted Easy, and the scowl on her face was unmistakable. She dropped off a plate to a guy at the end of the bar and then set the other down in front of Milo.

"Am I allowed to eat it?" he groused to her.

She shot him a look. "I don't know. I might just take it away. Guilt by association," she said, jerking her head to Easy.

Milo didn't waste time arguing. He tucked into his chili cheese fries with the fervor of a starving man.

"What do you want?" Daisy demanded.

Easy cleared his throat and shifted on his stool. If the girls were going to keep inviting her over, he couldn't very well keep pretending she didn't exist. "To talk to you," he told her.

She snorted. "We're not selling conversation tonight. If you're not ordering, I'm busy." She stomped away toward the tables on the floor.

"Smooth," Milo told him.

"Shut up."

"Just sayin'. Looks like I'm not the only one who lost his mojo."

"I haven't lost anything, Milo."

Milo chuckled and took a sip of his pilsner. "Not the story I heard."

Easy groaned and pinched the bridge of his nose. "Well, I don't know what you heard, but-"

"Heard Daisy was about as desperate as a woman could be, coming of a dry spell like she was, but you didn't ring her bell. Short ride, disappointing finish she said."

"Mind your own business, Milo."

Milo eyed him thoughtfully. "I'd tell you to try cutting your hair, but you don't have much anyway. Maybe you should grow it long, instead. You play the guitar?"

"What? Guitar? What? No, I don't play- just shut up. Jesus Christ."

"Just tryin' to help."

Daisy returned, tossing empties into the bin. Easy took the opportunity to try again.

"Listen," he said. "I-"

She stood up and squared her shoulders. She was definitely on the defensive, and that was his fault. If he hadn't been the cause of her ire, he might think she was cute, glaring at him like she was. He hadn't really noticed before how small her nose was or how blue her eyes were. Then again, he'd done her from behind, and he hadn't really an opportunity to see.

"You ready to order?" she demanded.

"No. I don't want to order."

"Then fuck off!" She started to leave again, but he reached across the bar and snagged her arm.

"God damn," he grumbled. "Just hang on. Jesus Christ, girl."

If he thought she was irritated before, she was flat out *pissed off* now. "Girl!" she cried. "*Girl!* Really? I told you before, *I have a fucking name!*"

Easy let go of her and drew back, chagrined. "I didn't mean it like that. You're just irritating the shit out of me."

"I'm irritating you. *I'm* irritating *you?*" She looked around dramatically. "Oh, I'm sorry," she told him. "I didn't realize that you *worked* here and were trying to wait tables, while someone came in to rub it in your face that they can't be bothered to call you by your name. My apologies!"

Easy let her go this time. There was no point in pursuing it, especially not here. She was likely to hit him with a tray or something.

"Lost your mojo," Milo said quietly.

Easy glared at him and got up off the stool. He'd fucked up, no question. He'd been pissed off and not thinking clearly, but he absolutely, positively had not lost his mojo. He headed over to the table where Tex, Hawk, and Tildy were sitting and slid silently into one of the empty chairs. Even Tildy was glaring at him. Easy held up his hands to stave off their anger. "That was not what it looked like."

"It looked like you were being mean to Daisy again," Tildy replied.

"I wasn't."

"You called her 'girl'. Like she's nobody."

"I didn't mean it like that," he insisted. "I was trying to apologize."

"Now you have to apologize for calling her 'girl'."

"I'm not apologizing to her at all," Easy told Tildy. "I'm done. It's over. She hates me. Fine. I don't care. It's best if we just leave each other alone."

Before Tildy could argue with him, Easy stood up again. "Want to play a round?" he asked Tex. The older man agreed, and they headed to an empty table.

"I don't want to talk about it," Easy said, pulling the rack off the hook. "Just heading you off at the pass. I don't want to talk, be analyzed, or any other damn thing."

Tex grinned at him. "Got it."

Easy slapped the rack onto the felt and started filling it up, grating on Milo's words earlier: Short ride, disappointing finish. He turned to grab a cue and nearly stepped on the toes of a brunette at the next table.

"Oh!" she gasped and tried to shuffle out of the way.

"Sorry," he told her, grabbing her at the waist. "Didn't you see there."

She giggled and looked up at him. Her hair was longer than Brenda's and curly instead of straight. Her face was a different shape, too. So was her-

"Ass." Daisy walked past, arranging drinks on her tray.

Easy shot her a look then grinned at the girl invading his space. "Haven't seen you before," he said, leaning in.

She giggled again and shook her head. "We've never been here before."

"How do you like it?"

"Nice. It's nice."

He grinned. "Not a word I'd use to describe this place. *You're* nice." He reached out and took a lock in his fingers. "Your hair's nice." His fingers reached the end of the length of hair, his hand hovering over her chest. He could tell he had her hooked when her breathing got a little heavier.

"We gonna play?" Tex prompted from the other side of the table.

Easy looked down at his fish. "Want to play?"

She looked at her girlfriend then back to him and grinned. "I'm not very good," she admitted, biting her lower lip.

"Oh, I can teach you," he assured her, in a tone that said he could teach her a lot of things.

"Okay."

In a matter of minutes, Easy had her bent over the table, ass pressed against his crotch, lining up a break. Tex didn't pick up women anymore, now that he had Abby, but he wasn't about to cockblock a brother, even if 'teaching' her was basically going to ruin the game.

The brunette, Holly (because he'd thought to ask), giggled and wiggled and was generally having a good time. Easy could ring her bell with very little effort. Across the bar, he winked at Milo and gave him a look that said "Mojo, my ass."

Holly took her shot, failed miserably to put enough on the ball to accomplish anything, and pretended to sulk.

"It's okay, baby," Easy assured her. "That part's hard." He took out his wallet and plucked out some bills. "Let's put some money on it," he told Tex. "To keep it interesting." Easy wasn't above losing twenty bucks to his brother to keep him placated.

Tex lifted his hand and tipped an imaginary cowboy hat at Easy and Holly. "Sure, I'll take your money."

Just then, Daisy, of all people, appeared and set down Holly's beer on the rail of the pool table. "Here you go, hon," she said, politely, with a smile even. *Who knew she could?* Easy thought.

"Can *I* get a beer?" he said, without thinking.

"Sure," she said, all politeness stripped from her voice. She plucked a half empty mug that she'd obviously just cleared from another table and slammed it down on the felt in front of him. Foam splashed everywhere, even onto his jeans.

"Damn it!" he hissed and wiped the denim furiously.

By the time he looked up, she was already gone.

Holly watched her leave then looked at Easy. "Do you know her?"

"No," Easy told her, moving the dirty mug off the table.

"She really doesn't like you."

Easy blew out a hard breath and raised his hands, plaintively. "Dunno," he lied. "Maybe she's just a shitty waitress."

Holly's eyes narrowed. "She's only mad at *you*," she pointed out.

Easy grimaced and shook his head. "I don't know," he repeated more firmly. He snuck a look at Tex, who had nothing to say on the subject, thankfully.

Holly took a sip of her drink and set it back down. "I'm going to go to the bathroom," she told him and whirled away.

When Easy turned to Tex, he caught the man's look. "You could go with her," Tex suggested. "Make it two for two."

Easy rolled his eyes. "Just play."

"You should probably tell Holly your side of the story," Tex suggested, lining up a shot.

"No," Easy insisted. "This'll blow over. We'll leave, Daisy will be out of the picture. No one needs to keep bringing it up."

"Need is a strong word," Tex replied. "Maybe she wants to."

Easy frowned. "Wants to what?"

"Keep bringing it up," Tex told him and nodded toward the bar.

Easy followed his gaze and saw Holly at the bar, talking to Daisy.

"Oh, god damn it!" he cried and tossed his cue on the table.

He headed across the room. The last thing he needed was Daisy telling Holly, or anyone else. "Hey!" he called out, getting their attention.

Holly looked at him inquisitively, Daisy, not surprisingly, just glared.

"What are you telling her?" Easy demanded.

"Nothing," Daisy snapped.

"Oh, so you just flagged her down to tell her about the specials?"

Daisy crossed her arms in front of her and cocked her hip. "I didn't flag anybody down. She came over here to talk to me."

"So, what'd you say?"

"Nothing!"

"You slept with her," Holly accused.

Easy glared daggers at Daisy. "Nothing, huh? So, you told her we had a quickie in the bathroom and you didn't come, which is probably your fault, not mine."

A slow smile spread over Daisy's face as she looked at him. "Actually, it was *Milo* who told her we had sex. *I* didn't tell her anything. And I sure as shit didn't mention that I didn't get off. Guess I don't need to now."

CHAPTER FOURTEEN

Daisy watched Jimmy retreat to his table and sighed heavily. Couldn't a girl just fucking work without people thinking they could bother her all the time?

"Hey, Daisy."

The hairs on the back of her neck stood at attention and she dragged her gaze from Jimmy to her left. Clad in another pair of black jeans and a matching black t-shirt stood Adam. His arms were crossed, too, like hers, and once more the sight of ink and muscles did strange things to her insides. *Scratch that*, she thought. *Here's a guy who's welcome to bother me.*

"Fun night?" he asked, watching Jimmy walk away.

"A riot," she told him.

"As in laugh a minute or Kevlar required?" he asked.

"Too soon to tell."

He grinned at her. "What time do you get off tonight?" Then he said, "That wasn't a reference to your personal problem, by the way."

Daisy laughed. "I don't have a problem. He does." She picked up a glass and began to wipe the counter underneath it. It seemed dangerous to look a man like this in the eye for too long. She was likely to end up bent over in the bathroom again. "I get off at Midnight."

He nodded. "Gonna let me see your stuff?"

For a moment her breath caught, and her face reddened. He grinned. "Your artwork, Daisy."

"Oh!" She let out a long breath and nodded, cautiously. "I... yeah... I guess you could take a look."

"Great. We'll head over to your place after work."

"I don't have a place," she told him. "Not yet. I'm staying at the Rainbow a few blocks over."

He grinned again, and Daisy thought she might need an entire pitcher of ice water to cool off. "I'll try not to read too much into that," he told her and walked away.

"Whew," Milo cried. "Now that guy's got mojo."

"There's not a lot he doesn't have," Daisy agreed. Then she glared at the old man. "I oughta take your fries away."

"You wouldn't!"

"Stop telling tales on me, Milo. Or the only thing I'm gonna serve you is a stewed boot and a salad."

Milo grumbled and dug back into his fries, mumbling about rabbit food.

Daisy pretended not to hear him. She also pretended not to see Easy glaring at her from his table across the room. *Oh well*, she thought, as she stacked glasses. She never could make friends without making enemies, too.

At Midnight, she clocked out and ran the palms of her hands nervously over her jeans. Adam was waiting for her when she came through the swinging door. He led her to a Harley and her stomach dipped again. She swung her leg on, wrapped her arms around his waist, and breathed deep. It had been a very long time since she'd caught that scent- male and musk. Adam started the engine and they roared off.

He parked two doors down from her room and let her off. She tried not to fumble the key as she stood at her own door. She opened it and flipped the light on. For the first time since arriving in Rapid City, she was actually happy she didn't have many clothes with her. Otherwise they'd be strewn all over the room, and she did not need Adam to see her underwear tossed haphazardly.

She did, however, have sketches on almost every available surface. Some were fully finished, hand drawn and colored in with pencil. Others were begun but quickly abandoned, barely more than dark smudges on crisp, white paper. Adam picked up one of each and studied them.

"Everybody has that one thing," Daisy said, a little nervously.

Adam grunted and nodded. He set down the pages and crossed to the bed. Daisy held her breath, but he picked up her sketchbook, and began to flip through it. He paused on something she'd finished a few weeks ago and held it up. It was Daisy, herself, but drawn in 50's pinup style. A short, polka dot dress flying up showing more of her panties than she'd ever have the guts to show in real life. Her lips were exaggerated, red and puckered for a kiss.

"This is good," he told her.

She could only nod due to embarrassment. She didn't really think of herself that way, as some kind of sex kitten, but it had been fun to draw.

"Very revealing," he teased. He tossed the sketchbook onto the bed and pinned her with a long gaze. "So, now I'm at the tough part," he told her.

Her hopes fizzled out. He didn't think she was good enough. In her heart she knew she was though, and if Adam couldn't see it then-

"...fuck you," Adam said, catching her off guard.

Daisy looked up at him, startled. "What?"

"I want to fuck you, Daisy. I think that's pretty obvious."

Daisy stood frozen in front of him.

"I didn't think you'd be this good," he said, indicating the sketchbook. "You could've been lying. Lots of people do. If you'd been blowing smoke up my ass, well, then we'd still be here, and I'd stick my dick up *your* ass, among some other places, and it wouldn't be a total loss."

Daisy gaped at him as he spoke.

"But you're good. Very good. And that's a problem."

"H-how?" she squeaked, still reeling from the ass part.

"I've worked hard to start my business. I had to hustle sharks for loans, built the space with my bare hands. I put everything I had into it, and I don't shit where I eat. Crude, I know," he said at her grimace, "but it's true. I can get pussy. Pussy's mine for the taking," he told her. "But good artists are harder to come by. As much as I'd like to taste you, Daisy, and keep tasting you 'til we're both tired of each other, you're worth more as an artist. If I take your work and show it around the same time you're showing me that sweet ass of yours, sooner or later it's not gonna work out between us. Then I've lost a woman *and* an artist. I'll take you either way," he said, and the deep baritone to his voice was almost hypnotic. It had Daisy imagining all the ways in which he could *take* her.

"It's up to you," said Adam. "You choose. If I take you to bed, I can't go into business with you. That's my rule. I'm not promising shit, in the bed or out of it. If we twist up your sheets a few times, and I've had my fill, I'm gone. If I show your work, and no one's interested, there's nothing I can do."

Daisy swallowed hard and tried to get her heart to stop pounding away in her chest.

"What's it gonna be, honey?"

CHAPTER FIFTEEN

Easy strode up to the dirty, orange door with the peeling paint and raised his fist. He pounded on it so loudly he even surprised himself. He steeled his nerves as the doorknob turned. He was God damn irritated, and there was a distinct possibility that everyone in this dump would hear about it soon.

The door opened just a few inches, and Daisy filled the empty space. Her face probably mirrored his, a mix of shock and annoyance. "What the hell are you doing here?" she asked.

"I want to talk to you."

"I don't have anything to say. Besides, I'm busy."

Easy scoffed. It wasn't like the Rainbow had cable. "Oh, really?" he sneered at her. "Doing what?"

A large hand curled around the edge of the door and pulled, revealing that asshole Adam, standing behind her. Easy felt another stab of irritation. So, she cockblocked him but was here trying to get some for herself? *Oh, that's some bullshit*, he thought to himself.

"Well, surprise, surprise," Easy bit out.

Daisy bristled and put her hand on her hip. "Shut up. You don't know me!" she snapped. "Who are you to judge me anyway? You and Ms. Snakeskin Boots should be very happy together. Why aren't you with her?" She cocked her head to the side and grinned at him. "Or are you done already?"

Easy felt a surge of anger and clenched his fists. "I didn't get the chance!" he argued. "You ran her off!"

"I didn't run her off! Milo did!"

"If you hadn't run your mouth at him, he wouldn't have known about it."

Daisy laughed and shook her head. "It was a public bathroom!" she reminded him. "About as private as doing it at the bus station! If you wanted to keep it a secret, you should've taken me someplace else. Guess you're as bad at keeping secrets as every other damn thing. Don't blame me!"

Behind her, Adam cleared his throat. "Daisy."

"What!" she shouted at him then bit her lip.

Instead of being angry, Adam looked vaguely amused at the whole situation. He flashed a piece of paper at her, but Easy didn't get a good look. "I'm taking this," he told her and brushed past the two of them as he exited the room. Over his shoulder he said, "I'll let you know how it goes."

He got on his Harley, which Easy noted darkly had a bigger engine than his own, and drove off. After he turned onto the road, Easy looked back at Daisy. Her clothes were still on, he finally realized. So were Adam's. "What was he doing here?"

She glared at him. "None of your business." She backed up and tried to close the door, but Easy placed a palm on it and pushed his way into her room.

"What are you doing? Get out!"

Easy looked around the shabby room that an army of housekeepers couldn't possibly make presentable. "Don't have anything *to* do, thanks to you." He plucked another piece of paper off the small table and studied it. It was a drawing of a skull with a snake coiled around it. Pretty standard MC fare. The room was covered in them, different images, some darker, some more feminine with flowers or hearts. They were all similar though, they had a certain *style* to them, he realized, for lack of a better term.

"Did you draw these?"

"Yes, Sherlock," she grumbled.

"So, this is what Adam wanted," Easy surmised.

Daisy blew out a frustrated breath and ran her hand through her hair. "I guess. Apparently, he decided for me."

Easy looked up from the paper. "What do you mean?"

"Nothing," she grumbled. "Why are you here? You can't care that much about Ms. Snakeskin Boots. Just go find another one."

Easy tossed the paper onto the table and avoided looking at her. What could he tell her, that she was the first girl he'd had in two years? That some small part of him was actually relieved Holly had ditched him? He, for damn sure, wasn't about to tell her he'd lost his mojo.

At that moment, he understood exactly why he'd shown up here, and it wasn't to give her hell over losing Holly. He might have been nervous about taking Holly home, but he'd already screwed Daisy, if not spectacularly badly. So what would it hurt to try again? And she didn't like him anyway. What could he possibly lose?

"You fuck Adam?"

"What business is it of yours?"

"I just want to know. Was he just here for the drawings, or are you fucking him?"

"Both!" she snapped, then sighed and waved her hand as if he was a gnat annoying her. "Or... either. One of those two."

Easy rolled his eyes at her. "Which is it?"

"He told me I had to pick. Screw him or have him take me on as an artist at his shop. He doesn't do both."

"And you picked working with him."

She glared at him. "I didn't get a chance to! You showed up, spewing your bullshit. Adam took a sketch and walked out. Like I said, I guess he chose for me."

Easy took a step toward her. Daisy continued to glare at him, but she didn't back away. "Would you have fucked him?" he asked her quietly.

She shrugged angrily. "I don't know. Probably. I sure as hell wanted to. God knows I'm about tired of getting *myself* off."

Easy grinned at her. "Yeah, I heard about your dry spell."

Daisy made an exasperated noise. "Fucking Milo!"

Easy moved forward and caught her face in his hands. He leaned down until he was just inches from her. He could hear her breath catch in her throat. "You need to get fucked, Daisy?"

It was pretty much a rhetorical question. He remembered her

clasping pussy and her cry of disappointment when he'd finished too early. He needed to prove he was still as skilled at fucking as putting together an engine as much as she needed to fall apart in his hands and around his cock, a perfect match. He didn't wait for her answer. He crushed his mouth over hers.

She tasted sweet, and her lips were soft, which made him wonder about the other pair. With one hand he yanked open the button of her shorts and pushed his hand inside. She was warm, but he needed her hot and wet. His fingertips grazed through her silky hair and found her clit. He worked it, rubbing it in slow circles until she groaned. Her arms slid around his waist, pulling him closer.

As before, it didn't take her long to go from surprised to supple. She spread her legs for him and pulled her head away from his as he dipped his fingers inside her. Her breath was hot and ragged on his neck. Her pussy was still tight, and he couldn't help but grin. Adam hadn't fucked her. She was still desperate and likely to be singing Easy's praises in just a few minutes, not that it would be over that quickly, not this time. The determination to fuck her as thoroughly as possible far outweighed his own excitement about the idea. His cock was as needy as her cunt, but it was his ego that took center stage.

He pushed two fingers into her and separated them, stretching her wide. She whimpered and made a half-hearted attempt to push away from him. Easy braced his other arm around her and held her in an iron grip. "You're fucking tight," he told her. "Need to open you up."

"Jimmy," she whispered and put her hands on his chest. He couldn't tell if she was resisting or urging him on.

"I'm going to *fuck* you," he whispered. "Balls deep and *hard*. You want me to hurt you, Daisy?" he asked, pushing in a third finger. "Or do you want to come harder than you ever have before? All over my cock."

If she wanted to argue, her pussy didn't. It clenched around his fingers sending a flood of juice into his palm. His lips found her ear, and he brushed over it. "Don't you want to come, Daisy?" he half-teased.

It turned out that was all it took for her to do just that. Her slick walls seized around his fingers and she dug her nails into his arms, panting hard. Before she was finished, Easy yanked his hand out of her shorts and pushed her back.

"Son of a bitch!" she snarled, her orgasm ruined. "You asshole!"

Easy didn't stop to consider how pissed she was. He didn't care. He had his belt undone done, his fly open, and his shaft out in record time. Daisy stopped mid-tirade to marvel at it. She seemed to realize several things at once. The first was that Easy had a giant cock. He didn't give a shit how many guys she'd been with, she hadn't seen one like this, or not often at any rate. She'd only felt it before but hadn't gotten a look at it. The second was that, true to his word, she was going to get pounded. His hard on was a rager and wasn't going down any time soon. And the last thing was if she wanted this pussy pounding to happen any time soon, she'd better get with the program.

He could tell when that last part kicked in, because she grabbed her shorts at the hips and shoved them down to her knees before he'd even got the condom out of the foil wrapper. She kicked the shorts, and with them her panties, across the room and Easy caught enough of a glimpse to notice that the carpet matched the drapes. He grinned again and grabbed her by the arm before she could get on the bed.

He jerked her around and pushed her forward. She caught herself with her hands on the mattress as he positioned himself behind her. Once again he got a good look at that round, creamy ass moments before he plunged in. He grabbed the head of his cock and forced his way into her. Daisy cried out, but she was already ripe from her half-orgasm and he knew he wasn't hurting her.

There was less of the frenzy of their first time. This time he pumped in and out of her steadily, a little further in each time until, as promised, his heavy sac slapped her swollen lips. She was bent over far enough that he might be hitting her clit, too, or near enough that she could feel it, anyway.

"You want this, Daisy," he growled and slammed into her. It wasn't that she needed convincing. Hell, she was pushing back against him as hard as she could. It was more 'You *like* this, Daisy,' but there was no need to be an asshole about it. She knew now what he could do for her, *to her*, as his fingers dug into the flesh of her hips and his cock filled her tight, little hole. She squeezed him then, and he knew another orgasm was building.

"Don't," he said firmly and slapped one round ass cheek with his palm to startle her. It worked, and she gasped in surprised. "I'm just going to keep going, even if you come. So, just wait."

"Hey!" she protested and craned her neck to glare at him over her shoulder.

He got the feeling she might call a time out or, worse yet, call their little game altogether. He reached forward, gripped her upper arms in his hands, and hauled her up until she was leaning against him. Her ass fit perfectly in the hollow of his pelvis, and his cock was nestled into her tight channel. "Just wait," he repeated and ran his hands under the hem of her shirt. He grazed her ribcage and found her breasts, barely a handful, but her nipples were hard and sensitive.

He couldn't pound her now as he had before, not in this position, but he rocked his hips into hers over and over, settling into a comfortable, lazy fuck. Her cunt juice ran down, coating his thighs, and she soon forgot her anger. She melted into him and rode each roll of his hips effortlessly.

He gently pinched and tugged her nipples as she groaned against him. He could finally feel his own orgasm building, and he made one last, hard thrust up into her, forcing her to her toes. Evidently he lied, though, because she didn't come hard. Seconds before he spilled into the condom, her walls tightened up, but Daisy was too far gone to care. Her head fell back into his shoulder, and he could see that her eyes were closed. Her cute little mouth was half open.

He pulsed inside her a few times for good measure then stepped back carefully. His cock slid out of her as she slid to the bed, limp and boneless. He slid the condom off, tied it, and tossed it into a nearby trash can. As he zipped up he watched her, naked from the waist down, curled up on the shabby comforter. Her eyes were still closed, but a slight smile played on her lips.

Having gotten what he came for and then some, he slipped quietly out the door and closed it behind him without a word.

CHAPTER SIXTEEN

Daisy tidied up the room for the third time and shuffled her drawings into a presentable stack. It was unlikely that anyone would actually come into the room- they were just picking Daisy up after all- but it couldn't hurt. Plus, Daisy had been ready for over forty-five minutes and had nothing else to do. She was too wired to sit and draw anymore.

She'd slept pretty well- the best she had in a while, actually- after Easy had shown himself out of her room. She was only mildly irritated by his sudden departure for a few minutes before she drifted off, head heavy on the too-thin pillow. She couldn't deny he'd given her exactly what she'd wanted, but he could have at least said good night on his way out. This morning, though, she was more concerned about going shopping with the girls than Easy's lack of basic manners.

Daisy only had one close friend, April, who'd taken off from Nebraska with her boyfriend just a few months before Daisy herself headed to South Dakota. April and Tiny had moved to Florida, hoping to make a go of it there. They'd invited Daisy and Matt to come with them, but Matt had said he had big plans of his own. Daisy hadn't known what they were, but she'd stuck around anyway to find out.

Friendship with April had consisted mainly of her borrowing Daisy's clothes and bitching about Tiny, but she'd been the only other girl Daisy's age who also lived in the trailer court, and that made for a pretty firm common ground. They both understood the nature of the other.

Daisy didn't think any of these women would want to borrow her clothes, and bitching about men was out. Well, they could bitch about *their* men, if they wanted. Daisy would listen, but bitching about Easy was a no-win situation. He'd been their friend longer and that made the situation awkward. As far as they knew, though, Daisy had only had sex with him the one time at Maria's. She was fairly certain he wouldn't go out of his way to mention last night to them. Neither would she.

Making new friends in her adopted home town was far more important than dishing about assholes. As far as Daisy was concerned, they were all pretty much assholes, and therefore it was pointless to complain about it.

Sarah pulled up in her SUV, which was big enough for everyone. Daisy waved and locked the door behind her. She slid into the backseat with Tildy, who beamed at her. "Did you bring them?" she asked, though it was obvious that Daisy had a small sketchbook in her hand.

"I did a few," she told Tildy and handed it over.

Tildy squealed with excitement and began looking them over.

Abby looked wistful and patted Sarah's arm. "Our little girl's all grown up and getting her first tattoo!"

Sarah laughed and caught Daisy's gaze in the rearview mirror as she backed out of the parking space. "Ugh," she said. "This place is such a shithole."

Daisy laughed and agreed.

"You really leave your stuff there?" she asked. "I was always afraid someone would steal it."

Daisy shrugged. "I don't have anything worth stealing," she replied. "Just some old underwear and colored pencils."

Abby laughed. "We can take care of the underwear today. There's a great shop downtown."

Sarah put the SUV in drive but paused with her foot on the

brake. She reached across Abby and extended her middle finger. Tildy gasped. Daisy followed Sarah's glare to the old woman who ran the motel. She was standing in the doorway, cig hanging from her lips, and looked like she wanted to return the bird but couldn't muster the energy.

Sarah didn't wait for a response and instead turned out of the lot and onto the road. "I never liked her," she declared, stomping on the gas. "She accused me of hooking. Right in front of Chris! Called him a john and said I owed her twenty bucks for taking him to my room."

"She did the same to me," Daisy confided. "Except it was ten."

Tildy patted her leg. "I'd pay twenty for you."

Sarah and Abby burst into laughter. Tildy turned red and scooted down into her seat. "That's not what I meant."

"So, we'll do lunch," Sarah announced, "and then we'll do some shopping downtown."

Daisy was a little concerned that she didn't have a lot of money to waste in a fancy restaurant, but Sarah surprised her by parking the SUV in a side lot and walking them to a Mexican place with tables on the sidewalk. Daisy breathed a silent sigh of relief when she quickly flipped the menu open and peeked inside. The prices were reasonable.

"This place is amazing!" Sarah told her. "They give you enough to feed a horse! And the drinks are insane."

Sarah ordered a margarita, apparently her first in quite a while. Abby got a martini. Tildy studied the drink menu until Abby ripped it from her hands and ordered her a sangria. Tildy didn't drink much, apparently, but when the waitress set the glass down, she gulped furiously.

"Slow down there, luscious," Daisy warned.

Tildy giggled and put the glass down. "I'm nervous." She looked at Daisy with wide brown eyes that reminded her of a puppy's. "Does it hurt a lot?"

Daisy wrinkled her nose, deciding what to say. "Well, it hurts some. But the spot you're getting it isn't bad. Don't drink too much though, if Adam's any kind of a decent artist, he won't do it if you're wasted."

"Drink a little bit more, though," Abby said, nudging the glass toward her. "Adam's going to be looking at your ass the whole time."

Tildy squeaked.

"No, he won't," Daisy assured her. "He'll have a towel. You'll be fine."

"Are you sure you want to do this?" Sarah asked.

Tildy took another sip and nodded. "Yep. I am resolved."

"The appointment's not for a few hours," Daisy reminded her. "You've got time to change your mind."

Tildy frowned and looked at the half empty sangria glass. "Can I get one of these to go?" she wondered out loud.

"The lingerie store isn't far from here," said Abby. "And Adam's shop is the opposite direction. We can walk to both places."

"I spend way too much money there," Sarah mused. "The lingerie shop, not the tattoo parlor. Abby loves it, too." She wrinkled her nose. "Though I don't know what she buys there. Nothing is made of leather."

Tildy giggled and Daisy raised her eyebrows. Abby waved her hand at Sarah.

"Leather?" Daisy repeated.

Abby rolled her eyes. "I do not wear leather underwear!"

"Just a leather collar," Tildy whispered looking around to make sure no one heard.

Abby's cheeks turned as red as her hair. "That's it! You're cut off," she said, grabbing Tildy's sangria.

"A collar?" Daisy asked, surprised.

Abby bit her lower lip and then dove for her martini glass. "Only in the bedroom," she mumbled.

"Not true!" Tildy said grinning and pointing to Abby's gold necklace. "That's the daytime one."

Daisy leaned forward and inspected it. It looked normal. Well, it looked like it was worth more than her mama's trailer but normal. "So, you're on the bottom?"

Abby blushed again and nodded. "I'm his... submissive. That's-"

Daisy nodded. "I have cable," she said. "Well, I didn't. Ricky Snell did, though. And one time we watched that movie 9 1/2 Weeks. It was hot... but creepy."

Abby laughed. "It's not exactly like that."

"Good. 'Cause he was an asshole."

"Tex isn't an asshole. He's... God... he's the most amazing man I've ever met."

Daisy leaned back into her chair. "Well, damn," she said looking at all three women. "I guess there are only three great guys in the world and they're spoken for. Figures that'd be my luck."

"Easy's not an asshole," Sarah told her.

Daisy made a face and sipped her drink.

"Really, he's not. He's just... had some problems lately."

Daisy snorted. "Yeah. His cock seems to have taken over for his brain."

"It's not like that," Sarah insisted. "I just... I don't want you to think that about him."

"Sarah," Tildy said quietly. "He did her in a public bathroom and didn't even ask her name."

"He was upset!"

Everyone stared at her and she put her glass on the table. "Okay," she sighed. "But you can't say anything. *At all.*"

Abby and Tildy put their glasses down as well and Daisy figured this was the part where they were going to dish.

"Brenda, that girl he was seeing?" she said for Daisy's benefit. "He caught her making fun of his leg."

Abby's mouth dropped open. "Oh, my God!"

"Witch!" Tildy cried, giving Daisy the impression that she didn't curse all that much, either.

Daisy could think of some other choice words for a girl like that. "What the hell is wrong with her?"

Sarah shook her head. "I don't know. But that's always been his biggest fear. He doesn't say it, but I know. He's afraid of what girls will think of his leg. It's why he's never gone with anyone until her."

Tildy looked puzzled. "He's with a different girl every weekend at Maria's."

"But he never goes home with them," Sarah pointed out. "And when we lived next door, he never had one over. Have you ever seen a girl at his place?"

Tildy considered it then shook her head. "Never."

"So, he never really dates them," Sarah concluded. "He just talks to them."

Daisy swirled her straw into her own sangria and watched the ice melt. "So, um, if he's never been with a girl that you know of, then how long...?" She let it trail off and finally looked up at Sarah, who seemed to have known Easy the longest.

"Almost three years," she told Daisy.

Daisy whistled and sat back in her chair. "Holy shit," she whispered. "*Three years?*"

"That explains a lot," Abby said quietly. "I didn't realize."

Daisy shifted uncomfortably in her seat. "I wasn't very nice about it," she said, feeling ashamed.

Sarah sighed. "Well, doing it in a *bathroom* was a bad choice," she pointed out. "If he'd have waited and had a... *connection* with someone, it would've been better."

Or maybe he just needed a little more privacy, Daisy thought, remembering the night before when Easy had played her like a six-string guitar, his fingers like magic, everywhere at once. And that cock...

She cleared her throat then snatched her sangria off the table to hide her discomfort. She liked these girls, but she wasn't about to tell them what had happened... or how he'd just walked out on her afterwards.

An hour later, Daisy had several pairs of new underwear that she probably really couldn't afford but hadn't been able to resist buying anyway. It was just a shame that she'd managed to have sex twice since coming to Rapid City, both times in her old granny panties. She grimaced at the memory of having worn them with the hottest guy she'd ever seen up close. Given how he'd walked out on her, it seemed unlikely she'd have another opportunity. Now, holding the door to the tattoo parlor open for a sober and nervous Tildy, she spotted Adam, the second hottest guy she'd ever laid eyes on, and further lamented that she wasn't going to get any of that, either.

She stepped inside, and he grinned at her from the doorway of a booth. His shop was nice, clean and well-thought out. There were semi-private rooms on both sides, one for each artist, she assumed. On the wall were large sheets of flash. She pictured having her own sheets up there someday, if her commission work started taking off. She'd never have the patience to learn to tattoo herself or to sit with annoying college girls or guys with roaming hands long enough to put on one on, but drawing was perfect. She could work alone in quiet, out of the way places and just watch the world go by.

Adam sauntered over, looking mouth-watering in leather pants. Daisy had never seen anyone but rockers actually be able to pull off that look. He greeted Tildy warmly and gestured to one of semi-private rooms. It had a large bathroom connected to it, and he told her there was a towel hanging on the rack. Tildy paled and looked like she might bolt, but, surprisingly, she rallied, and Adam went to make a photocopy of Daisy's hawk drawing while she changed.

"Daisy," Adam called out from the open doorway.

As she stepped out of the room and back into the larger lobby, he held out some cash to her. "The guy loved it," he told her. "I figured he would." He grinned at her. "Guess we settled on money instead of sex."

Daisy folded the bills and stuffed them into her pocket. "Better than money *for* sex, I suppose."

He laughed. "It's for the best," he told her. "I'm all for three-ways but not with another guy."

Daisy's face darkened and she shook her head. "There's nothing going on between me and Jimmy."

Adam laughed again. "Honey, a guy comes to your motel room looking to go to the mat with another guy, that's something. Trust me."

"He wasn't going to fight you!"

"He would have if I'd have stayed," he assured her. "He wanted you, Daisy. He wasn't there for coffee and conversation."

"Not true," Daisy grumbled and looked away.

"Did you have coffee and conversation? Or did the two of you twist up your sheets?"

Daisy felt her shoulders sag. "I didn't plan it," she mumbled.

Behind them, someone gasped, and Daisy whipped her head around. Abby, Sarah, and even Tildy, wrapped in her towel from the waist down, stood in a tight group in on the other side of the open doorway.

"Oh, my God!" Sarah cried. "*You did it again?!*"

Daisy groaned loudly. Adam's eyes twinkled. "Sorry, honey," he told her and walked away. Daisy turned to face the horde.

"I didn't plan it!" she repeated.

"Are you going to see him again?" Sarah asked.

"I'm not seeing him now!"

"You slept with him twice!"

"He just… keeps showing up!" Daisy cried.

Sarah stepped forward, suddenly concerned. "Daisy-"

Daisy put up her hands to ward her off. "I'm not going to hurt him, Sarah. I promise you. I get it now, all of it."

Sarah shook her head. "But-"

"I'm pretty sure it's over," Daisy told her. "He walked out on me, didn't even say goodbye. I think… well, I'm pretty sure he just wanted to prove that he could do better than the first time. Mission Accomplished. I… I wish he was interested in me," she admitted. "But he's not."

"He's just scared."

"I can't make him like me, Sarah."

Sarah bit her lip and looked at Daisy. "Could you *try?*" she asked.

CHAPTER SEVENTEEN

Tildy pulled up to a cute, white house with black shutters and parked her car in the driveway.

"This used to be Shooter's place," she explained as she got out of the car. "Before he met Sarah and bought the cabin for her." She nodded her head to the smaller, blue house next door. "That's his, too."

"Who lives there?" Daisy asked. When Tildy didn't answer, she tore her gaze from the house and to her new friend. "Oh, you're kidding."

Tildy shook her head and gathered up her shopping bags from the car's trunk. "Nope."

"I seem to have fucked myself into a black hole from which there's no escape," Daisy grumbled.

Tildy blushed but laughed. She unlocked the front door, ushered Daisy in, and closed it behind them. "I like it," Daisy declared.

"The bathroom's amazing!" Tildy told her and tossed the bags on the couch. "The kitchen's nice, too. All new appliances. If I can ever figure out how to actually use them. Sarah's trying to teach me to cook. It's going okay, I guess. But I'm not as good as she is."

"I've only eaten there once, and I think it's safe to say no one's as good as she is," Daisy agreed.

Tildy tugged at her waistband and grimaced.

"Itches?" Daisy asked.

Tildy nodded.

"Well, whatever you do, don't scratch it. The ink will bleed and it'll look terrible. Just take your pants off."

Tildy looked horrified and glanced around at the completely private living room. "Just... walk around in my underwear?!"

Daisy laughed. "Well, I certainly don't care. I doubt your man does."

The young woman frowned and skirted around the kitchen island. "I couldn't do that," she said and headed toward the hallway. "I'll be right back."

She appeared minutes later wearing an oversize jersey knit sleep shirt that hung just below her butt. It was pink, and not like anything Daisy would wear to bed, but it seemed to suit her. "That's what you wear to bed?"

Tildy blushed and nodded.

"Those panties are going be a big hit."

Tildy grinned and came back into the kitchen. She grabbed a bottle of wine off the counter and opened a drawer. "I know," she told Daisy. "He'll love them. He's not going to be thrilled about the tattoo, though."

Daisy shrugged. "He'll get over it."

Tildy filled two glasses and began pulling various items out of the fridge. "You want to stay for dinner?" she asked. "Such as it is?"

Daisy nodded. "Absolutely. Thanks." She wandered through the kitchen to the attached dining area, passing by the sliding glass door and did a double take. "Whoa," she said, stopping in her tracks. There was Easy, in total shirtless glory with a sheen of sweat covering his chest.

Tildy peeked over her shoulder. "Oh, yeah. He does that. Not that I watch," she amended.

"Damn," Daisy whispered. "Impressive."

"You've never seen him naked?"

Daisy shook her head. "Not even just his shirt."

Tildy nudged her. "I'll invite you over on Saturdays," she whispered, even though there was no one around to hear.

"Does he always wear pants?" Daisy figured he must be hot as hell mowing in the noonday sun in a pair of jeans.

"Always," Tildy replied.

"Have you ever seen his leg?" She turned to look at Tildy, who shook her head.

"No. Never. Not even Sarah has. When we go to the lake, he won't come."

"That sucks."

"He doesn't like to talk about it, either. At all. And he gets twitchy if you try to help him. When we first moved in, Hawk offered to mow both lawns."

Daisy snorted. "Bet that went over well."

"He ignored us for days. He hates being thought of as weak. It's hard to know, though, exactly what will set him off."

The sound of a bike engine rolling into the driveway had Tildy skittering away from the back door. "Don't tell him I was looking!" Tildy hissed.

Daisy laughed and saluted her with a glass of wine. "My lips are sealed, woman."

Tildy tugged nervously at her sleep shirt, and Daisy rolled her eyes. "Too late, now, Tildy. He's going to notice."

"He's going to be mad."

Daisy shrugged. "He'll get over it." "Or," she said thoughtfully, "he can get one for you. Then you're even."

Hawk's keys hit the lock and the door swung open. He stepped in and to his credit, only paused for a moment as he took in the two empty wine bottles and his half-naked wife. He glanced at the empty glass on the counter. "We're playing 'It's Five O'Clock Somewhere'?"

Tildy giggled nervously. "Yes."

"Are we having a sleepover, too?" he asked, looking at her shirt.

Tildy bit her lip. Hawk came further into the room and watched her carefully. Daisy was pretty certain that Hawk had eyes like his namesake and very little, if anything, ever got past him. "What'd you do?" he said casually.

"Um..."

Hawk looked at Daisy, but Daisy pressed her lips together, only re-opening them to take another huge gulp of wine.

"I'm making quesadillas!" Tildy chirped. "I have chips and salsa, too!" she told him. "Do you want some?" She turned and flitted toward the kitchen. "Wash up and I'll-"

"Freeze."

Tildy did as asked but turned back around to face him. Hawk's eyes narrowed and he strode toward her. Daisy saw Tildy gulp, and one of her feet lifted off the floor. "Don't even think about it," he warned.

The other woman gasped as her man grabbed her around the waist, swung her around so she was facing away from him, and yanked up her sleep shirt over her hips. He looked down at the gauze taped to Tildy's skin.

"Talk. Now."

"It's for you," Tildy chattered.

"I didn't ask you to do that."

"Well, I wanted to!" she argued.

"What is it?" he demanded. "I can buy you flowers. Whole bouquets of them, every Date Night. You don't-"

"It's you!" Tildy protested.

"It's what? You got my name tattooed above your ass like Abby? Babe, I know you belong to me. I don't need to see proof of-"

"Even better!" Tildy insisted. "It's a hawk." She looked at Daisy, her eyes begging for help. Daisy slid the folded piece of artwork out of her pocket and handed it over.

The large man plucked it gently from her fingers and opened it. He studied it for a good, long while. "I don't dislike it," he declared.

Tildy squealed. "He likes it!"

"I didn't say that," he corrected. "But I think we need to discuss it before making decisions, permanent decisions, in areas of-"

"It's my body!" Tildy countered.

Hawk looked down at her, crossing his arms in front of his broad chest. "Oh, so if I come home with a Prince Albert, you wouldn't have an opinion on it?"

Tildy's nose wrinkled. "What's that?"

Hawk grinned. "It's a stud that goes through the cock head and when we fuck-"

"Stop!" Tildy said, covering her ears, which were already turning purple.

Hawk obliged, but still smirked at her.

"I wanted it!" Tildy told him. "And it had to be now, because I won't be able to later. Maybe not for a long time. So I did it! And that's all there is to it!"

He cocked his head to the side. "Why now, exactly?" he asked her.

Tildy crossed her own arms and squared off against her old man. Daisy got the impression of a chihuahua going up against a mastiff. She suppressed a laugh and took another drink.

"I want a baby," Tildy declared loudly.

"A baby."

She nodded sharply. "Yes. Now. And you're not supposed to get a tattoo if you're pregnant. Which I want to be."

"So you keep saying."

Tildy gaped at him. "That's it? That's all you're going to say to me?" She slapped his arm harmlessly. "I just said-"

Hawk surged forward, seized her around the waist with both hands, and spun her until she was pinned against the wall. Daisy almost dropped her wine glass. Tildy wasn't hurt at all, but Lord above she was shocked as hell and nearly hyperventilating. Hawk pressed his crotch between Tildy's legs and Daisy got vicariously wet just from watching.

"I heard you," he said quietly. "You said you want my mark on your ass and my seed in your belly and since you've already got one, I guess that means we need to work on the other one."

Tildy made a kind of mewling noise and closed her eyes.

"Daisy," Hawk said, a bit more loudly.

"I'll show myself out," she replied, finishing off the glass and setting it down on the counter. "You two have fun!"

She slipped out the front door and closed it softly behind her.

CHAPTER EIGHTEEN

Easy finally finished the lawn and wrestled the mower back into the corner of the garage. He wiped his brow with the back of his hand and headed for the cool air-conditioning of his house. He wasn't particularly looking forward to an entire summer of this, but it wasn't like he had a choice, either. He grasped the handle of the large bay door and pulled. When it met the concrete of the driveway, he bent to twist the handle and lock it into position.

"Nice view."

He jerked his head around to see Daisy standing on the sidewalk, eyeing him appreciatively. He stood up and shielded his eyes with his hand. Ignoring her comment, he said, "What are you doing here?" It was a slight moment of panic or maybe just irritation. Surely she didn't think they had some kind of relationship, not just because they'd screwed a couple of times. He certainly hadn't meant to leave her that impression.

She grinned at him. "I was visiting Tildy."

He sighed inwardly and relaxed his guard a little. The last thing he needed was some chick breaking into his house or telling everyone they were getting married. Granted those things had worked out for Tex and Hawk, respectively, but Easy wasn't headed down that road.

"But if you're going to walk around shirtless," she told him, "bending over all the time, I might visit more often."

He frowned. There didn't seem to be anything to say to that

without putting ideas in her head. "Don't you have to work tonight?" he asked. Truthfully, he had thought to seek her out after her shift. Last night had been good, better than he'd been hoping for actually. The look on Daisy's face as she'd laid on the bed was all the evidence he'd needed to conclude she'd enjoyed it, too. She wouldn't be telling anyone else that story about the bathroom. He felt confident that he'd fucked the memory out of her pretty little head.

She was cute, he had to admit. Cover up the tats and take out the nose piercing and she'd be just his type. In the looks department. In the sex department she was pretty good, too, but that mouth of hers- yikes. He sure as hell didn't need a woman like Slick, picking fights and winning them, too. Even Abby, who no doubt used her mouth for something other than sassing Tex, at least in the bedroom, was too high maintenance with Dom/sub bullshit and constantly needed tending to. Tildy would've been perfect, if he'd met her in basic or on R&R and hadn't been blown to shit right after.

A beautiful, polite, nice girl who would move into a house on base and fill it up with kids while he earned his commission. But that possibility was long gone. In its place would be other women, a lot of them, for the rest of his life, which wasn't a bad way to live, he realized, now that he knew he could do it. At least he wouldn't have to settle for his hand anymore. As he looked at her now, he imagined her bent over again, her golden curls moistening as he used her in all kinds of filthy ways. It seemed dangerous to try that now, though. This was his place, and she'd caught him off guard. Everything about this moment had him off balance.

"My shift starts pretty soon. You could give me a ride," she suggested.

Easy frowned harder. One, he wasn't comfortable with trying it, and two, she might get ideas in her head. Before Hawk met Tildy he never let a woman share the saddle. "They get territorial," he'd explained.

Easy shook his head. "Can't. Got to shower."

She smiled at him again. "Me, too. Want to do your part to save the Earth and invite me in? I'll wash your back, if you wash mine, okay and your front, if you're nice. And maybe-"

Easy shivered at the thought of her seeing his stump and of

having to explain the white, plastic stool. Nothing about showering with him would even be remotely sexy. He turned and walked toward the front porch. "Later, Daisy," he said as he mounted the steps.

She sighed dramatically and turned away. "Later," she mumbled and started walking.

He wasn't willing to give her the upper hand here, but he had to admit he was grateful that she'd gotten him over the hump, so-to-speak. He could fuck her again tonight. One or two more practice sessions couldn't hurt. When he was safely inside, sitting under the hot shower spray, he ignored the fact that his cock had wanted desperately to take her up on her offer. He could stroke it now, he supposed, but he'd see her again in just a few hours, and a few hours after that he'd have her bent over again, screaming in pleasure. At that point his dick would forgive him for blowing her off.

He felt confident that, after last night, Daisy would forgive him, too.

CHAPTER NINETEEN

Daisy kept walking and didn't look back. She sighed to herself again. Jimmy Turnbull was a scorching hot mess. He wanted her- that tent in his pants made it more than obvious- but he'd turned her down anyway. Between the bomb and Brenda, he may never get right, she admitted to herself. She couldn't really think of a way to help him no matter how much Sarah wanted her to.

She dropped off her sketchbook at the Rainbow and trudged down the road to Maria's, vowing not to think about it anymore tonight. One look at Milo's face as he sat at the bar told her she wasn't the only one with problems.

"What's wrong, old man?" she asked, filling up his glass.

He sighed. "The interweb."

Daisy laughed and wiped down the counter in front of him. "Free porn isn't free, Milo. You ought to know better."

He shook his head. "Had three women," he told her. "Three hens in my hen house. I was cock of the walk," he said, squaring his shoulders. Then his face darkened. "But they all *friended* each other online. And now they know about each other. Turns out that's why they were ducking my calls."

Daisy tossed the towel onto the bar. "That's your problem? Seriously? That you were three-timing a bunch of women and got busted?" Daisy rolled her eyes at him. "Unbelievable."

"I'll one-time you," offered a scruffy looking guy Daisy had never seen before.

She rolled her eyes at him. "No thanks," she replied.

"What time do you get off... so you can get off?" he asked, waggling his eyebrows at her.

"I've never heard that one before," she said dryly. "Why don't you-"

As she spoke, the door opened and Hawk strode in. Daisy felt her cheeks flush as she remembered him pressing Tildy into the living room wall. The guy she wanted to go full-on cave man on *her* entered the bar right behind him. Maintaining his position as the King of Mixed Signals, he gave her a slight smile as he passed by the bar.

Daisy wasn't sure if she wanted to smack him or fuck him, probably both but one more than the other.

"Why don't I what?" the barfly asked, giving her a smile that wasn't nearly as sexy as the one she'd just gotten.

"Shut up and order another drink," she told him and stacked a tray with the shots and beers she knew Hawk and Jimmy would want.

She took off toward their table and rested her hip against the edge as she set down the drinks. Easy's hand brushed hers as he took the shot from her. It was obviously deliberate, and if she doubted it, the look he was giving her confirmed it.

"Thanks," he drawled.

Daisy looked away and set Hawk's beer down in front of him. "Where's Tildy?" she asked.

"Sleeping," he told her with a smirk.

Daisy ducked her head and laughed. "I bet."

"What time do you get off?" Easy asked her.

So I can get off? she thought, but didn't say.

"Early," she replied. "Which is good, 'cause I have plans." She picked up the tray and walked away. Truthfully, the only plans she had involved a shower and a semi-comfortable bed, but he didn't need to know that. Only one of them was nicknamed 'Easy'.

At the bar, the fly reached out and took hold of her arm. "You never gave me the drink I ordered," he told her. The way his eyes glittered told her he was one drink away from failing a sobriety test. She sighed and figured it was way too early to start arguing with drunks.

"Last one," she told him as she filled a glass from the tap. It was light beer, but he wouldn't notice.

"Much obliged," he replied and tipped the glass, a little too hard because the foam went everywhere.

Daisy cleaned up the mess and hit the other tables. There were some Badlands Buzzards, the local MC she guessed, getting rowdy at the pool tables, but she brushed away wandering hands and ducked intense gazes as she served them. When she got back to Easy and Hawk's table, she briefly considered swatting *his* wandering hand when it touched her leg above the knee.

It was under the table where no one could see unless they were looking. Daisy got distracted by the memory of those hands and forgot to tell him to stop. She hustled back to the bar, just wishing it was already time to leave. She had twenty minutes left to go, though.

She tossed the empties and grabbed a rag.

"One more," said the fly.

Daisy shook her head. "Nope. You're done."

He grinned at her. "Just one," he countered.

"You already have to call a cab," she told him. "Or walk. You had your last one."

He grabbed her wrist and held it tightly. "I'm paying; I'm drinking," he said.

Daisy tried to step back, but she had no leverage. She glanced across the bar at Easy's table. He was looking her way, his face growing darker by the second.

She pulled on her arm and tried to wiggle free.

"Hey now," said Milo, but he was twice as old as the fly. Milo also weighed more, but his pounds were in all the wrong places.

"Let go," Daisy demanded.

"Not 'til I get what I want," he said, and Daisy wasn't sure he meant another beer.

She looked back across the bar to see that Easy had risen from his chair and was headed their way. She sighed in relief. "Now listen," she said loudly. "You see that guy over there? The one who looks pissed as hell? Yeah, he's coming over here and if you don't let go and leave..."

Her words trailed off as Easy reached them... and walked right past. She watched in disbelief as he strode toward the opposite side of the bar. "Get your hands off her!" he shouted and Daisy's face felt flushed and prickly as she, and everyone else, turned to look.

Brenda had apparently shrunk a black mini skirt in the laundry that day until it was the size of the thong Daisy had on, the thong she'd just bought with the hope that someone might see it, the same someone who was now coming to another woman's rescue.

The fly let go, thankfully, but only because he was more interested in the argument at the jukebox than Daisy.

"What's your problem?" asked a long-haired biker as he had one arm wrapped around Brenda's waist.

Easy gave him a shove. The guy might've retaliated, but Hawk appeared directly behind Easy, and suddenly it wasn't such a good idea to continue arguing.

Easy grabbed Brenda's arm and pulled her to him. He bent his head and said something to her, but between the music and the crowd Daisy couldn't hear it. He turned and led her toward the door.

Daisy scoffed in disbelief and pushed off the bar. Turning, she stalked past Hawk, who'd convinced the biker to have a seat. She made her way to Maria while already untying her apron.

"Can I go now?" she asked.

Maria didn't look at her but nodded. She was too busy keeping an eye on the potential problem by the jukebox. Daisy hung her apron on the hook in the office and clocked out. She couldn't win for losing, it seemed, and slunk toward the door.

She was resolved to go home and cry in her non-existent beer, but when she stepped outside she spotted Easy and Brenda just a few feet from the door, and suddenly she didn't feel like crying anymore.

She turned away from the Rainbow and toward the arguing couple. Easy had let go of Brenda at this point, but instead of leaving, she was up in his face, tottering on four inch heels.

"You can't tell me what to do!" Brenda cried. "You can't do a god damn thing."

Daisy came up behind her and planted her feet on the loose gravel. "He can't, but I can."

Brenda turned, and Daisy waited until her nose was in full view before she swung. Her fist connected squarely with the other woman's face. Brenda stumbled back into Easy, who caught her.

"Jesus, Daisy!" he shouted over Brenda's howls.

Daisy ignored him and glared down at the woman. "You oughta stop running your mouth," she told Brenda. "It's caused enough problems. If you need me to duct tape it shut for you, I can do that."

"What the hell?" said Easy, trying and failing to put Brenda back on her feet.

Daisy was about to tell him that Brenda wasn't worth the effort when she heard a pair of boots behind her.

"Daisy Mae Cutter," came Adam's voice, as rough as the gravel he was standing on. He looked at Brenda, amusement playing on his lips, and back to Daisy. "You are a bundle of dynamite in one tight, little package."

Daisy grinned at him and shrugged. At least someone appreciated her efforts.

"You done for the night?" he asked her, noting her missing apron.

"Yeah. Just had a little business to take care of now that I'm off shift," she replied.

Adam smiled again. "Need a ride?"

She sighed and smiled back at him. "I sure do. Bye," she told the other two and then followed Adam to his bike a few spaces away.

Easy was still tending to the wounded Brenda. Daisy tried to pretend that it didn't irritate her. He shouldn't care so much about that bitch. She swung her leg over Adam's bike, settled her feet onto the pegs, and willed herself not to look back as he pulled onto the road. Easy had been flirting with her all night then Brenda waltzed in and it was like she didn't exist anymore. For a guy who said he was over her, he sure didn't act like it. Daisy refused to wonder what was so wrong with herself that he preferred a woman who'd insulted him so horribly over her.

CHAPTER TWENTY

Daisy stepped out of her clothes and into the shower, which was lukewarm on its best day. But it was hot out, so she didn't mind. She washed the stink of beer and fries out of her hair and was determined not to think about asshole Army Rangers or bitchy bar bunnies for the rest of the night. She'd dry her hair and crawl into bed and that would be the end of that. She hadn't even finished the hair drying part when someone pounded on her room door, startling her.

She slung the towel over her shoulder and checked the peephole. It seemed the rest of the night was shot as well, at least as far as forgetting about assholes was concerned.

She unlocked the door and opened it. Easy swept into the room like he was the one paying for the place.

"What the hell was that?" he demanded.

She shrugged, not feeling conversational.

"Running her mouth? What did you mean by that?"

Daisy sensed she was on dangerous ground here. Easy had a lot of pride and it wasn't smart to stomp all over it by admitting that she knew the real reason he'd broken up with Brenda. She threw the damp towel onto the bed and crossed her arms in front of her. "Well in case you forgot, she called me a slut in front of the whole damn bar. And she took a swing at me first! I don't know who she thought she was coming back to Maria's after all that, but I'm not about to let that shit stand."

He seemed to consider this at length, and if he doubted her, he didn't say anything. Instead he moved toward her and took hold of her hand. He turned it over in his, inspecting her knuckles. Angry that he only cared about her now, as an afterthought, she jerked it back. "I know how to throw a punch, Turnbull. Been doing it all my life."

"You're right," he told her. "She shouldn't have come to the bar."

Daisy glared at him. "And maybe if you weren't gawking all over her, exactly like she wanted, she would've just left."

His gaze darkened. "That guy she was messing with is bad news, a one-percenter. She was in for a whole lot of trouble with someone like him."

Daisy let out an exasperated breath. "Oh, so you just had to be the one to save her. Good thinking. Maybe she'll give you a Thank You blowjob once she can breathe through her nose again!"

"It wasn't like that! She was going to get hurt. I couldn't let that happen."

Daisy turned away and, for lack of anything better to do, pushed a sketch around on the table next to her. "No, but you'll let *me* get hurt," she said quietly.

There was a long silence between them before he said, "You don't need my help. You can take care of yourself just fine."

Daisy scratched the surface of the table with her thumbnail. Of course she could take care of herself. That wasn't the point. The point was to have someone who cared enough about you to fight for you. She'd taken Brenda down a few pegs for insulting Easy, that's what you were supposed to do. She sighed to herself. He didn't know that's why she'd done it and she could never tell him.

"You're right," she told him and turned to face him. "What happened between me and your girlfriend is our business, not yours. Long as she stays the fuck away from me, I'm over it now. But I work there, that's my *job,* so keep her out."

"She's not my girlfriend."

"Bullshit. You showed up here to bitch at me about it, about *her.* She's yours and that also means she's your problem."

"That's not why I'm here and you know it."

For one crazy moment, Daisy thought he was going to confess to her the truth about Brenda. She imagined him telling her everything, about why he hadn't been with a woman in so long and how badly it must have hurt him to hear her say those things about him.

"So, why are you here?" she asked, challenging him.

But instead of talking, he caught her in his grasp again, taking her wrist in his hand and pulling her forward. His mouth slanted over hers. She briefly considered making him stop, forcing him to confide in her instead, but instinctively she knew he wouldn't. If she pushed him, he'd just walk away from her, maybe to Brenda, who had clearly realized her mistake in letting him get away.

She opened her mouth and pushed her tongue inside his. He tasted like that shot of whiskey that he always had with his beer, warm and dark. She felt his hand press at the small of her back, keeping him close. His other hand grazed the front of her shirt, his calloused hands moving roughly over the fabric. He moved it lower, catching the waistband of her panties with a finger and diving inside.

As he pushed between her thighs, he pulled away from her and dragged his mouth to her ear. "Did Adam give you one ride or two?" he asked. Not waiting for a response, he dipped a finger inside her. "Just the one then," he determined as he explored her not-yet-wet pussy.

Her body felt heavy, like she was drunk or high. He was good at this, that couldn't be denied, but he already had too much power over her. Every time he snapped his fingers -or did something else with them- she obeyed his every command. And then he just walked away. She grabbed his wrist and pulled his hand out of her underwear. He was surprised but didn't argue.

"You're going to give me one," she informed him.

He cocked his head and looked down at her. "I am?"

She hooked the leg of the chair nearest to him with her foot and pulled it forward. She grabbed a handful of his shirt and shoved him backwards. "Sit," she demanded and felt a thrill of victory when he complied. Daisy stood in front of him and nudged his knees apart. She grasped the hem of her t-shirt and pulled it over her head. Her damp hair fell across her shoulders and her nipples puckered and tightened when exposed to the cool air of the room.

Easy reached for her and ran his thumbs over her hardened nubs. His hands were rough but they'd never bothered her. That was what a real man should feel like, she thought, rough and hard but not use any of that to hurt their woman. "Nice panties," he told her, gazing at them appreciatively.

"They're new," she said with a smirk and hooked her thumbs into them.

Easy watched her wiggle her ass and tug them down slowly. Daisy enjoyed the idea that she was making him desperate for once, instead of the other way around. She pushed the black thong aside with a toe and stood in front of him without a stitch on.

"Ready for a pole dance?" she asked, eyeing the tent in his pants.

He unbuckled his belt and unzipped his fly, releasing his thick erection. It sat heavy in his lap as he pulled a condom out of his front pocket. Daisy watched him roll it on and was slightly dismayed to discover that she was just as eager for this as she wanted *him* to be. The heaviness in her breasts and lower belly told her that in just a few seconds, she was going to be beyond caring that she'd lost yet another round.

She spread her legs and slowly lowered herself over him. The tip of his cock hit her clit, making her gasp, then found its way toward her center. The condom was lubricated enough to get him inside, the familiar stretch and burn was heightened by the fact that she wasn't quite ready for him yet. She slid down anyway, enjoying the sensation of being filled up. His hands were on his thighs and he cupped her ass as she seated herself in his lap.

"Oh, God, girl," he half-groaned.

She squeezed her pussy in response. "Daisy," she told him.

"Daisy," he whispered and closed his eyes.

She planted the bare soles of her feet on the carpet and pushed herself up. The hard length of him dragging against the walls of her pussy. When she got to the head, she sat back down, just as slowly. With her hands on his shoulders, she arched her back and he took the hint immediately. He drew a nipple into his mouth and slid his tongue over it. Daisy ran her hands over his short hair, her fingernails grazing his scalp lightly. She silently lamented he didn't have more to hold on to as she pushed his head closer. His hot mouth sealed over her breast and he bit her gently.

Daisy rocked her hips into him, fucking him harder, driving her nipple further into his mouth and his cock all the way into her pussy. It felt like he was all over her, covering her. His fingers dug into her ass as he pulled her closer. It was a delicious kind of pain, and she moaned encouragingly.

She felt that wave of euphoria starting to rise, her orgasm just out of reach. Easy must have sensed it too, because he dragged his mouth away from her breast. "Fucking come, Daisy," he rasped. "Tighten up that hot, little pussy for me."

Daisy's wetness had puddled around them, mixing with their sweat and slicking their thighs. Effortlessly she rose up, feeling that empty ache as he left her channel, and plunged back down again, giving them both what they needed. The wave finally overtook her and she lifted her feet to feel all of him inside her at that moment. The ache in her pussy subsided as came, around him and on him, flooding them both with more of her juices. She squeezed over and over, milking him thoroughly after she felt the first jerk of his cock inside her.

She rested her head on his shoulder, gasping for breath. Easy wrapped his arms around her and pulled her close, cock still inside her, throbbing occasionally. When she felt her legs would hold her, she stood up and moved away from him. Her clothes were strewn about the room and she set about getting herself dressed again as he disposed of the condom.

As she pulled her shirt back down over her head, there was a sharp knock at the door. Easy was buckling his belt as he strode toward the door. "Jesus Christ," he muttered and glanced at Daisy who was stepping back into her panties. "How many people go through here every day?" he asked, grasping the knob.

"That's exactly what I want to know."

Daisy looked up to see the old hag who ran the place standing in the doorway. She scowled right back at the woman and snatched a pair of shorts off the bed.

"What do you want?" Daisy snapped, though she knew very well why the woman was here.

"Got a lot of men traipsing through here," the old woman

replied.

Easy shot Daisy a look and Daisy glared at him. "Just you and Adam," she assured him. "Adam didn't even come in tonight," she told the old woman, "and you damn well know it."

The old lady jerked her head at Easy. "Where's my cut for this one?"

Before Daisy could respond, Easy laughed sharply. "Woman, do I look like I pay for pussy?"

She smirked at him. "Maybe you're a freak."

"Maybe *you're* a freak!" Daisy shot back. "How long were you standing outside that door?! Ew."

"I'm not giving you shit," Easy told the woman. "She's my girlfriend."

It was hard to tell who was more shocked by this declaration, the hag or Daisy, but Daisy felt certain they both looked a bit stunned.

"Keep giving her shit," he said, "and my friend Caleb can come over. You might remember Caleb. About this high," he said, raising his hand. "Dark hair, *shiny badge*."

The woman turned and huffed off down the sidewalk. Easy jerked the door the rest of the way open.

"Bitch," Daisy mumbled.

"She tried that shit with Sarah, too." He adjusted his clothes and ran and hand through his hair. "Anyway, she won't bother you now. Long as you don't have anyone else in your room."

Daisy's breath caught a little. Was he telling her they were exclusive? Did he really mean it when he said-?

"If Adam keeps showing up, she's not gonna buy that girlfriend line."

Daisy felt her hopes deflate but was determined not to let it show. "Yeah. Thanks," she said.

He nodded to her and left the room, shutting the door behind him. Daisy kicked the chair they'd just fucked in and it toppled over onto the floor. "Idiot," she muttered.

CHAPTER TWENTY-ONE

Daisy's phone rang again and she sighed as she checked the caller ID. Settling down in Rapid City was all well and good, but she couldn't go on pretending that Delay and the people in it didn't exist anymore. She tapped the screen and brought the phone to her ear.

"What do you want?" she asked, deciding that it was best to just cut through the bullshit.

"Hey, Daisy," came Matt's voice through the phone. "How are you doing?"

"Fine," she said while stuffing one foot into a cowboy boot.

"So, are you really staying there? In South Dakota?"

"Yeah. I like it here."

"You're not... you're not hooked up with one of them bikers or anything, are you?"

It was hard to tell if he was really concerned about her. It was possible, though, considering the fact that the first -and last- group of one percenters Matt had run into had beaten the shit out of him. It wasn't hard to imagine what guys like that would do to a girl like Daisy.

Daisy had to admit she'd also had an unrealistic idea of outlaw MC's before they'd arrived in Sturgis. To Daisy, they'd just been cowboys on steel horses and though it was obvious they weren't exactly law abiding citizens, she hadn't taken the time to consider what that really meant.

When Matt had stumbled back to their motel room with a swollen eye, a busted lip, and a broken nose, she'd had to reconsider what it would mean to be someone's old lady. She would've been Matt's old lady, if as he'd planned, he'd been accepted into whichever gang at the rally had impressed them the most. Daisy hadn't known a damn thing about how someone actually got *into* an MC. Matt had apparently had his own ideas about it. Once they'd checked into their motel room, he'd unzipped a bag of freshly cooked meth. Daisy had gone apeshit. Drug dealing was far beyond anything she was comfortable with.

Matt assured her he'd trade the crystal for a place in a gang and Daisy, though not happy about it, believed him. He'd come back quite a bit worse for the wear and relieved of all his 'product'. When she said "I told you so," Matt had slugged her and left her in Sturgis.

"No," she told him. "I didn't hook up with anyone in an MC."

"Well, when are you coming home?"

She scoffed. "Never, Matt. This *is* home."

"Oh, bullshit," he replied. "Who do you even know there? I'm not there. April's not there."

"April's in Florida."

"They're coming back," he told her. "Tiny couldn't find work. Your mom's here, too. So, come home."

"I'm not coming back, Matt. I'm done with Delay. And I'm done with *you*."

"None of that was my fault! And anyway, you're the one who kept on about joining an MC. Life on the road and all that shit! That was all you!"

"Well, I didn't tell you to cook up some meth!" she argued. "I told you to stay away from that shit!"

"I wasn't using it! I was going to sell it!"

"That's not any better! And you're going to end up in jail, Matt. You can't-"

"I don't sell it, either," he said quietly. "Believe me. I learned my lesson. So just come home. I've got some things going and-"

"What things?" she demanded. "If you're not selling drugs, then what?"

"I took a job at the plant."

A heavy silence hung between them and despite everything, Daisy still felt sorry for him. Matt had been determined not to end up like his old man, wasting away at the plant until his bad knees and messed up shoulder had put him on disability. Since she'd known Matt, the topic of most conversations was how to get the hell out of Delay. That he'd taken a job at the plant meant he'd given up on ever leaving.

"I can't, Matt. There's just no way."

"Why not?" he argued. "What the hell do you have going on there that's so great?"

"I have to go," she told him.

"Go where?"

"Out. With friends."

"What friends? You hooked up with some asshole?"

Daisy sighed. Honestly, that was the long and the short of it. She was hooked up with someone. And usually he was an asshole. "Bye, Matt," she said and disconnected the call.

Hawk's truck pulled into the parking space just outside her room and she went out to greet them. Tildy moved closer to Hawk so Daisy could fit.

"How's your ink?" Daisy asked.

"The scab's nearly gone."

"Don't pick at it," Daisy advised.

Tildy shook her head. "I won't," she said and leaned back in the seat. "This week has been so crazy. My dress came in. Along with Sarah's. It's been murder trying to find a tux that would fit Hawk."

Daisy grinned. "I believe it," she said glancing at the large man. "He doesn't seem like the tux type."

Hawk grunted, but kept his eyes on the road. "Only for her."

"He looks so good in it, though," Tildy insisted.

"I believe that, too."

"Abby's got the ballroom ready and the menu is all sorted out."

"You're having it at her hotel? Fancy."

"Well, she's giving us a break," Tildy explained. "Otherwise we could never afford it."

Daisy frowned. "So, your folks aren't helping out?"

It was obvious to anyone with eyes that Tildy came from money.

Everything from the way she spoke to the way she accessorized her outfits, said she was high class. She never wore a lot of expensive jewelry, but there was always a scarf or a matching handbag.

Tildy was quiet for a moment, then shook her head. "No. They don't even know. We haven't talked in a long time."

"What's a long time?"

"About six months."

Daisy whistled. That was almost as long as she'd gone without speaking to her own mother.

"I don't know how it'll all work out," Tildy said. "I decided not to invite them to the wedding." She looked impossibly sad and Daisy couldn't feel anything but sorry for her. "I don't know what would hurt more, them not coming, or coming and putting me down. Or Hawk. I *won't* let them insult him."

The large man said nothing but patted her knee gently. He pulled into Shooter and Sarah's driveway and killed the engine.

"Where are you going on your honeymoon?" Daisy asked as she climbed out.

"New Mexico," Tildy replied, shutting the door behind her.

Daisy raised an eyebrow. "New Mexico? Not even *Mexico* Mexico?"

Tildy grinned. "The woman who raised me lives there. I haven't seen her in a while. And Hawk doesn't mind."

"Wasn't planning on letting her leave the hotel room much anyway," he told both of them. "Desert seems as good a place as any with a view."

Tildy giggled and slapped his arm. When they entered the house, Daisy saw a blur of white streaking down the stairs. The Sullivan's cat clawed her way up Hawk's leg. Daisy winced in empathy, but the man didn't even flinch. The cat nestled into the crook of his arm and purred loudly.

"I don't know how a deaf cat always seems to know we're here," Tildy told Daisy. "But she always does."

"She smells him," Caleb replied from across the room.

Hawk flipped him off as he sat down.

Daisy noticed Easy sitting in an armchair, but only spared him a furtive glance. She didn't really know where she stood with him.

"So?" Abby prompted. "Did you get the dress?"

Tildy beamed and nodded. "It's amazing!"

"Totally agree. You'll look great in it."

"I feel like I need more time," Tildy said, then caught her breath as everyone looked at her. "To plan!" she clarified. "I mean everything's ready, the food, the flowers, the invitations... Oh!" She whirled on Daisy and grabbed her arm. "I sent out the invitations before you came to town. You're coming, right?"

"Um..." Daisy blinked at her. "To your wedding? I don't... I mean, I don't even know when it is or-"

"It's in two weeks. And you don't need a date or anything."

Without meaning to, Daisy glanced at Easy, who immediately looked away. Well, there was an answer of sorts about where they stood.

Tildy seemed to realize her mistake and hurriedly tried to fix it. "I-"

"I don't have a dress," said Daisy, interrupting her before things got any worse. "And I can't really afford one," she added.

Daisy had never been to a wedding, but it stood to reason that if it was being held at a fancy hotel, a fancy dress was required, and that would cost about as much as she'd earned so far.

"We're about the same size," Tildy pointed out. "You can borrow one of mine."

That only left the matter of a gift. Daisy sighed inwardly and vowed to figure out something. "Okay."

Tildy hugged her tightly, then pulled her into the next room. "Teach me how to win at poker," she said. "Abby and Sarah have tried."

"No luck?" Daisy asked.

Tildy made a face and shook her head.

"Here, sit next to me," Daisy said, and pulled out two chairs.

Shooter grimaced as he sat down. "I thought we said no more women."

"We always say that," Tex reminded him. "But they're so damn cute..."

Shooter grunted and shuffled the cards.

Tildy reached out and ran her fingers over Daisy's arm. Daisy grinned at her and leaned closer and whispered loudly, "I don't swing that way."

Tildy blushed and took her hand away. "I was just looking!" she insisted. "You have so many. Why?"

"Tildy," Hawk warned.

Daisy waved her hand at him. "It's fine." She held out her right arm so Tildy could get a better look. "My daddy left before I was born and it was always just me and mama. She works nights at the processing plant, always has, and sleeps during the day. She could never afford a babysitter, so I had to be real quiet. She'd put me in front of the TV with some paper and some crayons. I knew I'd get a belt if I made any noise, so I just drew. All day long."

Tildy's face fell and she withdrew a little bit. "My mom... my mom was like that," she half-whispered.

Daisy nodded patted the girl's arm. "Take away the money and we're all the same," she said. "Everyone's got problems, not all the *same ones*, but everybody's got them. Anyway, when I got older, I started staying after school to work in the art room where they had more than just crayons. I had a teacher who thought I had talent, which was better than my mama who never thought I was good for much of anything at all. And when I turned sixteen, I got my first one." She pointed to a small skull on her forearm.

"I loved it," she told Tildy. "It hurt like hell, but it was worth it. I could see, right there, plain as day, that I was worth something, that I had something no one else in Delay had- talent. And they could see it, too. Now, anyone who looks at it knows I've got something special about me."

Tildy wrinkled her nose. "But they don't know," she pointed out. "I mean, you could've just had someone else draw them and put them on."

Daisy shrugged. "Why would I care what strangers think? If they take the time to get to know *me*, then they know I drew them."

"I love mine," said Tildy. "I look at it in the mirror all the time." Then she leaned a little closer. "Do you know what a reverse cowgirl is?"

Abby laughed from across the table. Hawk shook his head and groaned.

Daisy grinned at her. "Honey, I've ridden more cowboys than horses."

"Hawk likes to look at it while we're... you know."

"That's why tattoos are sexy, honey. They're a tiny little piece of your soul that you wear on the outside so everyone can see what you love the most."

Tildy sighed wistfully and looked at him across the table. "He's my soul mate."

Daisy squeezed her arm and smiled warmly. "Well, hold on to him, honey. Not everybody gets one."

CHAPTER TWENTY-TWO

Two days later, Daisy walked to Tildy and Hawk's place from the Rainbow. She glanced at Easy's living room window, but the blinds were pulled and she couldn't see in. Sighing, she mounted the steps of the other house and rang the doorbell. Tildy answered, in real clothes instead of a sleep shirt, and let her in. Daisy glanced around but didn't see Hawk.

"He's still at work," said Tildy. "Easy, too. But they knock off early on Saturdays."

Daisy shrugged. "Wasn't all that interested. I'm here to try on dresses."

Tildy gave her a knowing smile and Daisy scowled. "Okay, I'm a *little* interested," she admitted. "For whatever that's worth. He doesn't seem to care."

"We'll put you in something *fabulous*," Tildy replied. "Then you'll see."

She led Daisy down the hall to the last door. In the Master bedroom, the closet doors were open and Tildy's wedding dress was hanging from one of them. It was off-white and short, as far as wedding dresses went. Daisy guessed it would hit Tildy just below the knee. It was strapless and had a bit of satin trim at the top and a matching strip at the waist. Daisy ran her hand over the creamy fabric and sighed. "This is beautiful, Tildy."

Her new friend beamed. "I love it. Of course, my mother would hate it. It's not traditional enough for her." She shrugged. "Then again, neither is Hawk. He's about as far from Tate as you could get."

Daisy looked up from the dress. "Who's Tate?"

Tildy blushed and bit her lip. "My ex-fiancée."

Daisy grinned. "Tildy! Getting around all over town! Did you dump him for Hawk?"

Tildy shook her head. "Not really. I dumped him and Hawk happened to be there. It was... complicated. But I made the right choice. Hawk is... " She sighed. "He's everything Tate isn't and everything I need."

"Better in the sack, too, I'm guessing."

Tildy flushed scarlet but laughed. "Way better," she whispered. "I only slept with Tate once, but I can tell I'm not missing anything." As she gazed down at her wedding dress, her hand fluttered to her lower belly.

"How long 'til you know?" Daisy asked.

"Another week," Tildy sighed. "It's torture! I'd give anything to know. Hawk is so excited. It's all he can talk about."

"So, he likes kids?"

Tildy nodded. "He loves them. He's got two little nephews that he adores."

Daisy considered this. "Good in bed, loves kids, and the cat likes him. I don't know this Tate, but I'd say you traded up."

Tildy turned and pulled open the closet door. As she sorted through some dresses, she said, "Definitely." She hesitated, then said, "Hawk's so much... bigger, too."

Daisy laughed. "The more I get to know you, Tildy, the more I like you. A size queen trying out all the men in town until she found the right fit. I'm starting to think maybe we should've gotten you a tramp stamp, instead," she teased.

"Oh, hush!" Tildy scolded and pulled out a blue dress. "This one matches your eyes. Give it a try."

Daisy took it from her and looked it over. It was sleeveless and short, as far as reception dresses went, she supposed. Tildy was the same height but a bit more on the scrawny side. "Tildy?" she asked. "How sure are you that my boobs are gonna fit in this thing?"

Tildy frowned and looked down at her own chest, then at

Daisy's. "Hmm. Wear a thin bra," she suggested.

Daisy went to the bathroom and shut the door from behind her. There was a huge tub nestled in a corner under the window and Daisy knew she'd give anything for a soak. "Holy crap!" she said loudly.

"I know, right?" came Tildy's voice through the door.

"How many people can you fit in there?" Daisy asked, stepping out of her shorts.

"Um... at least two."

"Tramp!" Daisy called out. Tildy laughed in response.

Daisy squeezed into the thing and managed to zip it halfway up on her own. She frowned at herself in the mirror, not sure what to think. She'd never owned anything this nice. It felt, and looked, so strange that she couldn't judge it for herself. Her tats stood out against the bright fabric and she had to admit her tits looked nice, too. She had more going on than Tildy by comparison, but it still wasn't a lot. The dress made her look like she had more cleavage.

She opened the door and stepped back into the bedroom. Tildy gasped.

"You look so pretty, Daisy!" She moved forward and swept Daisy's hair off her shoulder. "Easy's going to love it."

Daisy frowned and shrugged. "He won't even be my date."

"Well, he'll be there anyway," Tildy reminded her. "He won't be able to resist." She put one of the castoffs back on the hanger. "How's it going with him?" she asked quietly.

Daisy sighed and shimmied out of the winning frock. "He's a tough nut to crack," she admitted. "And by nut I mean I think he might be slightly certifiable."

"Daisy!"

"Oh, come on. The guy lives in perpetual fear of being judged because of how he looks, but he keeps on doing it to me. For a guy who's so self-conscious, he's about the least self-*aware* person I've ever met."

"He just needs time," Tildy insisted.

"Time I've got, but I can't change who I am, even if I had forever." She hung the dress back on the hanger and slipped the plastic over it. "Maybe I'm just the bridge girl," she told Tildy. "The one who helps him get over it, on his way to something else."

"You're not! I mean, you'll help him get over it. And then he'll see he's been an idiot and you'll stay together."

Daisy shook her head. "Yeah, the thing about bridges, Tildy, is they usually end up getting burned."

CHAPTER TWENTY-THREE

Easy raised the door to the garage and pulled out the lawn mower. As he came around the corner of the house, on his way to the back lawn he stopped short. Tildy and Daisy had apparently camped out on Tildy's lawn. They had towels spread out and were wearing bathing suits like they were at the fucking beach.

Daisy spotted him and grinned. "Mow that lawn, baby. Give it hell!" she shouted.

He stalked over toward them, stopping at the edge of the towel Daisy was laying on. She propped herself up on her elbows and looked at him over her sunglasses.

"What are you doing?" he asked.

"Objectifying you."

"Jesus Christ," he muttered.

"It's cheaper than a strip club," she said, lifting a glass of sangria. "But I've got some ones in my wallet. If you come a little closer, I'll stuff some in."

"Give me a break," he scoffed.

"Well, if you want fives and tens you're going to have to shake that ass a little more. And lose the shirt."

Tildy giggled. Easy frowned. "Well, stay out of my way," he told them.

"We're all the way over here. Doing important things," Daisy pointed out. Tildy held up a wedding magazine for good measure.

"Well," he said, flustered, "keep it that way."

He stalked back to the mower and jerked on the handle a bit. He couldn't very well tell Tildy not to be in her own damn backyard, but he didn't much like the idea that they'd be watching. Eventually he'd slip in the grass and then what? They'd laugh. Or worse, get all concerned. Either way he didn't want to deal with it.

He glanced around the lawn, sizing it up. The grass was too long. It had to be mowed immediately. He could perhaps put it off, but the wedding was tomorrow. If Hawk saw that it wasn't mowed, he might offer to do it for him, and that made him almost as pissed off as the idea that the girls would laugh at him. He decided it had to be done and that there was just nothing for it. He leaned down to grab the pulley.

"There you go!" Daisy shouted from across the yard. "Very nice!"

He growled and shook his head, wishing he could angle himself differently so that she wasn't looking right at his ass. But it would take longer to adjust his position than it would to just pull the goddamn starter.

He fired the thing up and set his mind to the task in front of him. It made no difference at all that there was a cute little blonde in a string bikini eyeing his every move. He set the mower on the first pass across the yard and got started. Midway through, though, his ankle twisted and his heel slipped a few inches on the loose cuttings. He quietly glanced over his shoulder at the girls. Daisy was smiling, but not at him. Tildy was showing her something in her magazine. He sighed in relief and vowed to be more careful.

After several more passes, being careful was starting to wear on him. He should have been at least halfway done by now. It was getting hot as hell out here, too. But hurrying through it would only result in falling on his ass. He grit his teeth and re-aligned the mower. He'd just have to suffer through the heat.

He was in the middle of doing just that, suffering and wiping the sweat off his brow with his forearm, when he noticed Daisy waving at him. She was up off her towel, standing at the edge of Tildy's lawn. He debated simply ignoring her and returning to work, but Daisy didn't strike him as the type to take being ignored all that well.

He let go of the safety bar and the mower's engine died. He

headed over to her, careful to keep the glare affixed to his face so she'd know just how much she was annoying him right now. She remained pleasant, though, a bright smile played on her lips and he had a moment of weakness as he remembered kissing them. Then he glanced down and caught sight of her tits and remembered kissing those, as well. He came to a stop just in front of her and prayed she wouldn't notice the bulge in his khakis.

"What?" he practically barked at her.

"It's hot."

"Jesus fucking Christ, seriously? I didn't notice."

She held up a bottle of water. "I thought you might want a drink. I would've brought it to you, but you said to stay over here."

Easy was now officially torn. He didn't know which he wanted more, the water or the girl offering it. He hesitated in taking the bottle, though. Daisy had angles. All he could see, though, was a pretty girl smiling up at him so he reached out and grasped the bottle from her.

As he took his first sip, she asked, "Are you going to take your shirt off?"

"Maybe," he replied replacing the cap.

"You definitely should. It's downright oppressive out here."

"Then why don't you take *yours* off?" he teased.

Instead of being cowed into silence, she said, "Good idea,'" and left with his water.

He watched as she tossed the bottle down onto the towel and picked up another one, sunblock this time. Ignoring Easy, Daisy leaned forward and whispered something to Tildy. Tildy put down her magazine and took the sunblock, squirting a copious amount into her hand. Daisy turned to face Easy, a slight smile on her face, and reached around behind her back. She untied the strings at her neck and they fell. Then she untied the other set.

"Daisy!" Tildy gasped, but Daisy just shrugged. Easy got an eyeful, just before Daisy laid down on the towel. Tildy moved next to her and began rubbing on the lotion. Easy was glad Daisy had moved further away because the bulge in his pants wasn't quite finished growing.

"You'd better be looking at the blonde."

Easy turned to see Hawk standing next to him. He must've come up the side yard between their houses.

"You better *not* be," Easy warned.

Hawk raised his eyebrow. "You staking a claim on that?"

Easy's jaw twitched as he realized he might have been. "No," he replied. "Your woman is right there. And Tildy might put up with a lot, but something tells me she won't take too kindly to you dogging other chicks."

Hawk grunted in amusement. "She knows she's the only one for me." Now that Tildy was done with Daisy, she put some more sunblock in her hand and began applying it to her arm. As she got to her shoulders, she paused thoughtfully.

Hawk grunted again, though this time he was not amused. "You take your top off in public," he said loudly, "and you'd best be considering what else you'll be doing. *In public.*"

Tildy squeaked and dropped the bottle. Then she laid down next to Daisy, blushing furiously.

"Daisy's a bad influence," Easy observed.

"Nah," Hawk replied. "If you weren't here, I'd let her do it."

Easy scoffed. "You would not."

Hawk leveled his gaze at him and Easy saw not only amusement, but also desire glittering in his friend's eyes. "The hell I wouldn't. We'd have to burn that towel, too, when we were done."

He left and Easy headed back to the mower, trying not to think about Daisy, topless and just a few feet away.

CHAPTER TWENTY-FOUR

Daisy watched as Easy turned off the lawn mower and began pushing it back to the front of the house. She briefly considered letting him go and waiting to see if he'd come back over, now that he was done. Something told her, though, that he wouldn't. She got up off her towel and headed across the yard.

"Bye!" Tildy called out, teasing. "Don't come back!"

Daisy trotted across Tildy's lawn and onto Easy's. She mounted the wooden steps of his deck and tried the back door. She discovered it was unlocked and slid it open quietly. She shut it behind her and stood in his kitchen. The place was immaculate, and that impressed her. The only men she'd been with lived like pigs, among old pizza boxes and dirty socks.

She crossed into the living room, noting the homey touches. The place was painted a soothing green color and it made the small house seem cooler on such a hot day. Sarah had done a nice job on the place. The couch was nice, soft and comfortable looking. Daisy briefly imagined cuddling up to Easy on it, watching a movie, not that he was the cuddling type.

She was reminded of this when the front door swung open, and he stepped inside. The dark look on his face told her he wasn't happy to see her.

"What are you doing in here?" he demanded, slamming the door shut behind him.

"Waiting for you," she replied as he moved toward her.

"Daisy-"

She reached out and ran her hand along his forehead, tousling his short hair. "You need another shower," she told him.

"You need to go."

"I don't want to." She tugged at the hem of his t-shirt and slipped her hands inside. His abs were hard and slick with sweat.

"Daisy," he said again, but it was less stern this time, and she knew she was winning.

She stood up on her tiptoes and touched her lips to his. He smelled warm and musky and she pressed her hands to his back to get closer to him. For a brief moment he let her do all the work, teasing his lower lip and running her tongue along it. Then he gripped her around the waist and pushed her back.

He came with her, though, his body dangerously close to hers, and soon they were against the wall of the hallway- the hallway that must lead to his bedroom. Daisy desperately wanted him to take her there.

Instead he placed one large hand on each of her hips and kissed her hard. His cock ground against her through the thin fabric of the bathing suit. His fingers found the ties at each side and tugged. The bottom half of the suit came loose, and he yanked it roughly away. Daisy's heart thundered as she realized that was exactly what she'd envisioned him doing when she borrowed this bathing suit of Tildy's in the first place.

Easy's fingers pressed against her mound until she spread her legs for him. He grazed over her clit as he reached down and dipped into her. He pulled back a little and smirked at her as he realized she was a little wet already. Daisy wasn't embarrassed, though. She'd been watching him for the better part of an hour, waiting as patiently as she could until this moment.

She grabbed his hand and guided him, pressing his fingers farther into her. With her other hand, she found his massive erection through his khakis. She gripped it tightly, rubbing it between her fingers. He groaned and felt as though she'd scored another victory. He pulled down the top of her bikini, revealing her breasts. He ran his thumb over her nipple, and she shivered.

He moved closer to her and kissed her again. He pressed her hard against the wall, and Daisy realized he was going to win this round. His fingers were in her pussy, and his tongue was in her mouth. Though she still had a hold of his cock, that was nothing compared to being opened and penetrated. His fingers moved rhythmically inside her, and she clenched every time he pulled them out.

With his free hand, he fumbled with his zipper, and before she could react Easy had both his hands wrapped around her thighs. He was lifting her and pulling her legs apart. His eyes held her for the briefest of seconds, waiting for some sign that she wanted this. Daisy couldn't catch her breath enough to say anything so she simply swallowed and nodded.

He impaled her in one quick stroke, his bare cock sliding through her wetness and into her core. Daisy cried out and grabbed at his shoulders. His hands cupped her ass and held her firmly as he thrust up into her. He buried his head first into her neck, before she felt his lips on her shoulder. His mouth found its way further down as she rode him. He bit her gently at first then harder.

"Oh, God!" she gasped as his fingers dug into her ass and his teeth sank into her breast.

He slammed into her hard, over and over. The pain of the wall behind her warred with the amazing feeling of him moving inside her. She felt her belly tighten and knew she was about to come. She did, loudly, clawing at him to keep him inside her as she clenched around his shaft.

"Wait, wait, no!" she demanded as she felt him trying to pull out.

"Daisy," he rasped into her ear. "I'm going to come."

"Not yet!" she cried as the last of her orgasm rippled through her. Only the last few moments were foiled as he pulled himself out of her at the last second. Jets of thick, hot cum coated her inner thighs and belly as he climaxed.

He set her down, more like he'd simply let go of her. She leaned against the wall, panting, trying to regain the ability to stand on her own. His eyes were closed as he also took a moment to recover. When he opened them, he tugged his khakis up over his hips but didn't bother to fasten them. He pushed off the wall, moving away from her, and headed down the hall.

Daisy only watched as he stepped into the bathroom. He closed the door behind him, and in the ensuing silence she heard the sharp snap of the lock.

CHAPTER TWENTY-FIVE

Daisy stepped into the cool confines of Adam's tattoo shop and let her eyes adjust to the light. It was blazing hot outside, but the shop was nicely air conditioned.

"Can I help you?" a girl said from behind the counter.

"I'm-"

"She's my muse," Adam announced dramatically.

Daisy laughed.

"And an artist in her own right," he added. "Are you almost done with that flash book?"

She nodded. "Nearly, but I need new pencils. And some other things for a project I'm working on. Point me in the direction of the nearest art supply store."

Adam took a business card off the counter and picked up a pen. "There's one downtown," he said, scrawling the address on the back of the card. He started to hand it to her, but then caught hold of her wrist and extended her arm. "You need a touch up," he remarked.

"No, I don't."

"Yes, you do. Come on," he said pulling her toward the door. "No charge."

"It must be a slow day," she said, following him.

"Afternoons are always slow. Not that it matters. If I can't have you in my bed, I'll have you in my chair."

He gestured and Daisy sat down in a brown leather recliner near the wall. "When did you get this one?" he asked, examining a tiny skull.

"That was my first time."

Adam's eyes twinkled. "Ah, memories."

"It's terrible."

"All first times are," he replied. He lifted his shirt and revealed a tribal tattoo around one of his nipples.

Daisy bit her lip and tried not to laugh. "You didn't cover it up?"

"Nah. Some fuck ups stay with you forever."

She nodded. "That's why I never got mine covered. Life lesson: don't rush into things."

Adam smirked at her. "You ever take your own advice?"

She sighed. "Rarely. Not sleeping with you was the best decision I've made so far."

Adam paused. "You know, no woman has ever said that to me before."

He snapped on some gloves and wiped her arm down. The sharp smell of alcohol stung her nose. He unholstered the gun. Daisy didn't flinch when he touched the needle to her skin. "We could go crazy," he told her. "Give you a whole new one."

"Not today."

"You sure? What about a tramp stamp that says Easy?"

Daisy rolled her eyes at him. "I'm pretty sure that's the wrong message to send. To anyone."

Adam shrugged. "If you break up, it still works," he teased.

"We're not going to break up."

"That good, huh? Can't say I'm not jealous."

Daisy shook her head. "We can't break up, because we're not together."

"We men are complicated creatures."

"If by complicated you mean dumb, then yeah."

Daisy caught a glimmer of gold as Adam leaned over her. She reached out and tucked her finger into the neck of his shirt. He paused and looked down at her. "Thought we settled this, Daisy," he said quietly.

She laughed. "We did." She fingered the gold cross around his neck. "I'm just looking. This is nice. Did you get it around here?"

He nodded. "There's a store downtown. It's not too far from the art supply place."

"Pricey?"

"A bit, yeah. If you need God in your life, Daisy, you should go to church. It's free."

"Not looking to get struck by lightning, thanks."

"God forgives," Adam replied.

Daisy grinned. "Only if you stop sinning."

CHAPTER TWENTY-SIX

Daisy dabbed concealer on her skin, just above the bust line of her borrowed dress. Easy had managed to give her one hell of a hickey, right where everyone could see. She slapped the cap back on and tossed the tiny bottle onto the table Tildy had been using to get ready. She caught sight of Sarah looking at her in the mirror and shook her head.

"Don't."

Sarah held up her hands. "I didn't say anything," she insisted, but she was grinning from ear to ear.

"Good," Daisy replied. The sex had been good, phenomenal really, but she didn't want to talk about how he'd just left her standing naked in the hallway. As she looked at the small, black box that housed Hawk's wedding band, Daisy couldn't help but be reminded of the silver one she'd discovered when she'd snooped in Easy's room afterward, looking for a shirt.

She was startled out of her reverie by Abby pounding on the bathroom door. "Have you gone yet?" she demanded.

"Yes!" Tildy called back through the door.

"What does it say?!" Sarah practically shrieked.

Tildy flung open the door. Her face was red, and she was close to hyperventilating. "It takes three minutes!" she reminded them.

"You've been in there for fifteen!" Abby cried.

"I can't go when I'm nervous!" Tildy looked like a strange

combination of innocent and guilty. She was clad in a white bra and panties with a slip over them. Her long, beautiful hair hung in curls around her shoulders. Sarah had done her makeup, light and fresh, and altogether Tildy looked like one of the models in her wedding magazine. She was also glancing furtively at the plastic stick in her hand.

"You're not the first person to take a pregnancy test on their wedding day," Daisy assured her.

Tildy wrinkled her nose. "Do you think he'll know?"

"Well, he's pacing outside the door," Abby pointed out. "So, yeah, I think the cat's out of the bag, hon."

"Not Hawk! The minister!" Tildy whispered fiercely.

"He's seen Hawk," Daisy said helpfully. "He's probably wondering why you don't already have two or three."

"Oh, God!"

"Don't say *that* around him," Daisy replied.

"Don't worry about it," Abby said. "He's making an honest woman out of you. It's fine."

"Is he, though?" Sarah asked and reached for the stick. All four women leaned in and peered down at it.

"What's that mean?" Daisy asked, never having taken one herself.

Sarah screamed, and Tildy fumbled the stick. Suddenly Daisy was drawn into a screaming, giggling mass of arms, perfume, and hairspray. The door burst open, and Hawk's huge frame filled the doorway. Tildy broke free from the girls and flung herself at him.

Hawk swept her into his arms and held her tightly. "Yeah?" he asked quietly.

Tildy nodded into his broad chest.

Hawk beamed as Tildy stepped back and swiped a hand over her cheek. "You have to go," she told him firmly.

He grinned at her. "Babe, I've already seen you. It's too late."

"I'm naked!" she hissed.

"This isn't naked. You're *going* to be naked, though. When I get you alone I'm going to-"

"Go!" she cried and pushed him out the door.

He laughed but complied. Tildy slammed the door and sagged

against it. She was smiling, too.

"Dress!" Abby declared, snatching it off the bed. "Then we'll fix your makeup again."

Daisy tugged at her own dress as Tildy finished getting ready. Now that she was used to it, she kind of liked it. The heels were a little more than she was used to, but she'd manage. She smoothed her hair and tried to pretend there was nobody in particular she wanted to look nice for.

When Tildy was finally ready for her walk down the aisle, Abby and Daisy headed to the ballroom to snag some seats. Abby took the chair next to Tex in the front row, and Daisy sat beside her. She caught sight of Easy seated at the end of the row and cradling baby Hope in his arms. Well, if that wasn't enough to make a girl's panties melt, Daisy didn't know what was. She tore her attention away from the two of them when music started.

Hawk and Shooter, looking damn fine in their tuxes, made their way up front and stood with the minister and waited for Sarah, who looked just as beautiful as Tildy in a very light pink dress. She grinned at her husband as she headed down the aisle. Daisy thought that must have been the look she'd had on her face when she'd gotten married herself. Shooter couldn't take his eyes off his wife, and Daisy was glad to see it. They seemed like great people.

The march started, and Tildy appeared at the large, double doors. She looked a bit nervous, even though the room was hardly packed. It seemed Tildy and Hawk had only invited their closest friends and family. Maria sat next to Milo, probably to keep him in line during the ceremony, and there were a few other faces Daisy didn't recognize.

Tildy began her slow walk down the aisle. Her nerves seemed to fade away, though, as she watched the man she was about to marry. In truth they looked as though they were the only two people in the entire world. Tildy reached the front and stood next to Sarah. Hawk reached out and took her hand to hold it during the ceremony. They exchanged rings and kissed to the applause of the small group watching them. Ushers cleared the folding chairs, so that Hawk and Tildy could dance under the twinkling white lights of the decorated hotel ballroom.

Daisy sipped some champagne and watched them, then she caught sight of Easy handing Hope back to Sarah. Sarah disappeared out of the ballroom, probably to feed her, and Daisy slipped up next to Easy. "You look nice," she told him, gesturing to his suit.

He tugged at it uncomfortably. "I guess. Haven't worn anything close to it since the Army," he grumbled.

Daisy waited for him to say something about her dress, but he didn't. Undeterred, she set her empty glass down on a nearby table. "Dance with me," she said.

Easy looked stricken. "What?"

She sighed, irritated. "You heard me."

"I don't want to dance."

"It's a wedding. Everyone's dancing. Even Milo." Daisy pointed to the old man who was doing something alright, though even Daisy had to admit it was a stretch to call it dancing.

"Not interested."

"No one's going to notice. It'll be fun. It'll-"

"No," he snapped and tried to walk away.

Daisy snagged his elbow and tugged him back. "How about a honeymoon, then?" she asked, batting her eyelashes at him for effect.

"What?"

"Apparently the honeymoon suite comes with the ballroom," she told him. "But Hawk and Tildy are catching a plane tonight." She grinned at him. "Abby gave me the key. There's a mini bar and a Jacuzzi tub."

"Jesus."

"I didn't borrow Tildy's bikini, though," she told him. "I forgot."

"Still not interested."

"Why not?" she asked, though she knew goddamn well why not.

His eyes narrowed, and he leaned toward her. "We just fucked yesterday," he said quietly. "Can't you get enough?" He pried himself loose of her hand and turned.

"Apparently not," she told him harshly. "Guess I'll scout the place out for a real man. A *whole* man."

Easy turned on her, anger blazing in his eyes. "What did you just say to me?"

"You heard me," she said quietly, not wanting to attract attention. "You're sure as shit aren't a whole man. And it's got nothing to do with your leg." She raised her hand and jabbed a finger at him. "I know exactly what's underneath that pant leg of yours," she whispered fiercely, "even though you won't show it to me. I know, and *I... don't... care.*" She continued her one-woman invasion into his personal space. "But you sure as shit aren't a whole man, Jimmy Turnbull! I'm also telling you that you better locate the missing pieces of that heart of yours. And you better do it right quick, 'cause I am not waiting forever for you!"

She crossed her arms in front of her chest. "Now, I'm willing to forgive a lot, because I happen to know a thing or two about needing someone to look beyond what's right in front of them and into the soul of a person. And no matter how much you treat me like a piece of shit, white trash, *bathroom lay*, don't think for a second that I don't see how you hold Hope, like she's the most precious thing in the world.

"So, there's something inside you, Jimmy Turnbull. Something that kinda looks like a heart. Something that maybe used to *be* a heart. Like the *ghost* of a heart. It's just missing so many pieces that there's not room for a whole hell of a lot of people in there."

She stomped away before he could respond, careful not to totter on her high heels. She would have preferred to just leave, but Tildy blocked her path. She was holding a large, cardboard cylinder in her hand. "You didn't have to get a gift!" she gushed.

Daisy felt heat creeping up her face and blamed Easy for it. Her stomach turned as she felt another kind of embarrassment. "I... " she said weakly. She'd buried the 'gift' behind all the other wrapped presents on the corner table, hoping neither Tildy nor Hawk would notice it. "I didn't really," she mumbled.

To Daisy's horror, Tildy pulled the top off and began pulling the rolled paper out of the tube. She bit her lip and looked at her feet. It wasn't a toaster, or a clock, or whatever else people gave as gifts for a wedding like this.

Tildy rolled it flat onto a table and gasped. "Oh, Daisy."

A fair number of people gathered around to look. Daisy was used to colored pencils more than anything else, but she'd opted for charcoal this time, and it had taken several tries to get it just right. The drawing was large; it took up half the table. Most of the details she'd drawn from memory, which hadn't been hard because she saw the place almost every day.

It was Maria's bar, minus Maria- or anyone else. The jukebox was against the wall; the glasses and bottles were lined up on the shelves. The only two people were Hawk and Tildy, dancing alone in the center of the room, just like they had moments earlier for their first dance as a married couple.

In the drawing, Tildy's head rested against his chest. Her eyes were closed, her face serene. Hawk had his chin against the side of her head. His eyes were closed, too. Hawk Red Cloud, with his huge muscles and large frame, looked even larger when compared to Tildy's wispy figure. They looked like a couple that shouldn't work, a hulking bad ass and a rich princess, but they fit together perfectly. And they only had eyes for each other. Daisy didn't actually know what that felt like, to be with someone in a crowd of people but still be alone together.

CHAPTER TWENTY-SEVEN

Daisy sat alone in the hotel room, keeping one eye on the door. As much as she'd meant it when she said she wouldn't wait forever, she had to admit she was doing just that. She sighed and grasped the neck of a bottle of champagne that Abby had thoughtfully left in a bucket of ice.

As she tugged on the cork, she made another cursory inspection of the suite. It was beautiful with thick, plush carpet and a huge, four-poster bed. The comforter was a deep, royal blue that matched the walls. The only thing Daisy regretted, other than being alone here, was the fact that she'd have to give it up in the morning.

The cork burst, and champagne bubbled out. Surprised, Daisy quickly held the bottle over the bucket. She didn't want to know what the cleaning bill was for a place like this. Her mama's carpet was permanently stained and bore more than a few cigarette burns. It was vacuumed regularly (because Daisy was the one who did it), but it had never been cleaned.

In fact, nothing had quite made her acknowledge the dinginess of her life the way this room did. She poured some champagne into a glass and sat on the edge of the bed- the large, unused bed. Jimmy had problems, of that there was no doubt. His insecurities were a large part of the reason they hadn't moved forward. Daisy hated having to consider the fact that the other reason might be because he thought he was too good for her. Just because he'd let Sarah, Hope, and to some extent Tildy into his life didn't necessarily mean he was interested in Daisy joining their ranks.

There was a knock at the door, and she jumped up, spilling a bit more champagne.

"Damn," she whispered, and for a moment she couldn't decide whether to reach for a towel or the door. The door won out as her heart pounded. She twisted the knob and flung it open.

Instead of Easy, Sarah stood outside the door. Daisy could tell by the look on the other woman's face that she wasn't the bearer of good news.

"He left," Sarah told her, and Daisy nodded like she already knew it. And she had, hadn't she? She'd been sitting here long enough to have figured that out. "Can I come in?"

Daisy stepped back from the door and gestured with the half-empty glass still in her hand. "Sure," she replied. "Misery loves company."

"I'm sorry, Daisy."

Daisy shrugged and took a seat at the table next to the bucket. "Want some?" she offered.

Sarah nodded and slid into the remaining chair.

"Whatever," said Daisy, though Sarah hadn't said anything else. "I had a nice time. Got to wear a dress I could never afford to own and sleep in a bed I couldn't afford to rent. I came out ahead on the deal."

"He just needs time."

"I think he's had plenty of that."

"Don't give up," Sarah pleaded.

Daisy played with the glass stem of her flute. "Maybe I'm not the one giving up," she replied quietly. "What happened?"

"It was an IED. It killed-"

"Yeah, I got that. Bomb, half the team died, and then discharge. But what *happened*?"

Sarah was silent so long Daisy thought she wasn't going to answer. Then she said, "He wanted to die."

Daisy took another sip and considered this. "So, he comes home and everything's fucked up and-"

"No," Sarah told her. "Right then. He wanted to die *right then*, right when it happened. He knew his leg was gone, and there'd be nothing anyone could do. So he asked Caleb to kill him."

"Like shoot him in the head?"

"Chris said they'd do it with morphine."

"*Chris* said?"

Sarah nodded. "He didn't mean it, though. He just wanted Jimmy to believe it, because he was so scared and in so much pain. They didn't do it. They only gave him enough to make him sleep."

"Why didn't he do it himself when he came home?"

Sarah shifted uncomfortably in her chair. "He's Catholic."

Daisy nodded to herself. "He's afraid the real Hell might be worse than the one he's living in now."

"It's not Hell!" Sarah insisted. "He has family, people who love him. People who-"

"It's not about you," Daisy interrupted. "It's about him and how it's got to be ten times harder for a man like him to accept that this is the way it's going to be."

Sarah stopped and looked at her. "What do you mean, a man like him?"

"He's an engineer. He builds things, gets them working again. From what I hear about Burnout, they're all pretty damn good at it. It's got to be a special kind of punishment that the one thing he can't put back together is himself."

"So... are you done?" Sarah asked, tears brimming in her eyes. Daisy felt like crying, too, not that it would help anything.

"I like him, but I don't love him, Sarah. How can I? He won't even let me try. I know he's important to you. I know you want him to find peace, but I'm afraid I'm just *a* piece."

CHAPTER TWENTY-EIGHT

Easy sighed as his boots crunched the gravel under his feet on the way into the bar. Apparently Sarah was out with Hope today, so there would be no lunch delivery. Shooter and Tex had opted to eat at Maria's, which they always did when Sarah didn't feed them. So, it was either go hungry or possibly face Daisy, and he wasn't certain he was interested in either one.

She was always pushing him, sometimes too far. He found himself wishing she was more like Sarah, or the guys, and would just leave him be. Why couldn't she ever back off? He had fully expected to fuck her that day after he'd finished mowing the lawn, had showered, and was presentable. He just hadn't expected her to barge into his place uninvited. She was too much in his face all the time, expecting too much.

As he followed Tex inside, he felt an odd mix of comfort and disappointment that she was working today. With Daisy, he never knew if they were going to fuck, or fight, or both. Today, though, she didn't seem interested in any of the above. She gave them all a cursory glance as they chose a table on their own. Her eyes passed over him with the same general regard she had for the others.

The heated gaze she used to pin him with was gone, and he was surprised at how deeply its absence affected him. Daisy, it seemed, *could* actually get enough. And she reached her limit with him. She didn't bother to walk over. Instead, she filled her tray with ice water for Shooter, the sweet tea Sarah had taught Maria to make for Tex, and she popped the top on a can of Coke for him. She didn't spit in it, though, and he supposed that was something, at least.

She dropped the drinks off at their table. "You want the usual?" she asked. "Wings?" she said to Tex, who nodded. "Two cheeseburgers and a basket?" she asked Shooter, combining Easy's order with his. After Shooter confirmed it, she left to put in the order with Thomas in the kitchen.

"Chilly in here," said Tex, and he didn't mean the air conditioning.

Daisy brought their food and set down a bottle of steak sauce in front of Easy without saying a word. He figured she was just doing her job rather than really caring that he preferred it on his burger. Before he could thank her, Milo came through the door and drew her attention away.

The older man flopped dramatically into a chair at the table next to them. "Daisy," he called out. "I need a beer. And some chili cheese fries." After thinking better of it, he said, "Two chili cheese fries."

"Old man, what do you need two orders of cheese fries for?" Daisy asked.

Milo looked up at her plaintively. "Well, who am I looking good for?" he whined.

"Oh, here we go," Daisy muttered. "What happened now?"

Milo shrugged. "Nothing really. Made up with Cora and Jan, sort of. Though mostly because Jan got lonely and Cora dropped a fork in her garbage disposal. They want me to choose, though."

"Seems reasonable," Daisy replied, offering him no sympathy. "Pick one."

Milo frowned. "I don't want to," he groused. "Don't know how I could, anyway. They're too different." Milo considered this for a moment. "Maybe I could flip for them."

"What?" Daisy asked.

"Flip a coin. Heads Cora, tails Jan."

"You can't be serious," Daisy argued.

Milo fished a quarter out of his pocket and held it in his hand. He shrugged at her. "Makes sense."

Daisy was quiet a moment then said, "Okay. Fine. Flip a coin."

Milo flicked his thumb and watched the silver piece spin through the air. That was how he missed Daisy's open palm streaking toward his face. She connected with a sharp smack.

"Ow!" Milo cried.

From across the bar, Maria laughed hysterically.

"Are you crazy?!" Daisy yelled as the old man rubbed his face. "You can't flip a coin, Milo. They're people! You just pick one!"

"How do I do that?!" he shot back.

"You pick the one you like the most!"

"Well, Cora's not so bad in the sack," he told Daisy. "But she ain't much of a looker. Plus, I think she's a little sweeter on Ben Carver than me."

Tex grunted appreciatively. "Who knew the elderly got around so much?" he mused out loud.

Shooter lifted his burger and prepared to take a bite. "I can believe it. I'll still chase Slick around the retirement home."

"And Jan's a good cook," Milo said, "but she's still in love with her husband. Talks to the urn on her fireplace and everything. It's a little weird."

Daisy crossed her arms in front of her chest and glared down at him. "And there's not a woman in Rapid City who's the total package?"

Milo shifted in his chair. "Well, Alma," he replied quietly. "Probably."

Daisy lifted an eyebrow. "Now, we're getting somewhere. What's wrong with Alma?"

"Nothing that I know of. She's the prettiest woman in town, and I know she's a great cook 'cause she fed me once. Best chicken Kiev I ever had," he said wistfully.

"So, what's the problem?" Daisy demanded.

"Me and Alma, it just ain't in the cards," Milo told her.

"Did you try stacking the deck?"

"I knew she was cheating!" Tex whispered loudly. Daisy rolled her eyes and shook her head but otherwise ignored him.

"She's too good for me."

"Did she tell you that?"

Milo frowned at her. "No, but it's obvious. She's a classy lady, and I'm just the guy who mows her lawn."

"Is that what we're calling it?" Tex asked.

Without looking at him, Daisy snapped her fingers to shut him up. To Easy's amazement, the most dominant man he'd ever met sat quietly with only a tiny gleam in his eye. If that had been Abby, she'd probably be bent over the table by now getting a spanking. Shooter laughed softly after seeing the tiny blonde put him in his place.

"Well, the next time you're out with her," Daisy declared, "you just sit her down and tell her how you feel. If she-"

"Out?" Milo asked, shaking his head. "We don't go out."

"What do you mean you don't go out?"

Milo shrugged. "I just mow her lawn. One time I fixed her fence. And once a shingle came off her roof, and she needed me to fix it before the next storm." A twinkle lit up his eyes as he spoke. "She called me at night for that one. Saw her in her nightgown."

Daisy stared at him and then blew out a harsh breath. "Are you telling me you play Mr. Fix It for this woman, and you've never even had a date?"

"Didn't think she'd agree," Milo admitted. "I'm hoping maybe someday she will. I can just keep mowing her lawn, and maybe someday-"

Daisy threw up her hands in exasperation. "Jesus, Milo! You've got to stop that."

Milo's face darkened. "But she needs me."

"Does she? Or does she keep calling because you keep picking up the phone? You know, it's okay to sacrifice for other people if they're worth it. But if you keep doing it without getting anything back, then eventually they have everything, and you ain't got jack shit."

CHAPTER TWENTY-NINE

As Daisy fixed her hair in the bathroom mirror of her room at the Rainbow, her phone rang again. She sighed. As soon as she found herself a place, she was going to get herself a new number. She glanced down, though, and saw that it wasn't Matt -again- but Sarah calling.

"Hey," came Sarah's voice over the phone. "I just wanted to make sure you're coming tonight."

"Yeah," she replied. "I just need a ride."

"Abby will come get you. If you start early and have a good night, you'll be able to afford your own car soon."

Daisy laughed. "I don't know if they'll let me play. Tex thinks I'm cheating."

"He just wishes he could. He's a man of questionable morals."

"Don't we all want one of those?"

There was a bit of a silence after that. Sarah was still disappointed things hadn't worked out with Easy, but probably not as much as Daisy. There was no point in re-hashing it.

Changing the subject for both their benefits, Daisy said, "I have enough saved up for first and last on a new place."

"Awesome! I'll help you look this weekend, if you want. We'll take my car."

"Preferably something close to Tildy's place," Daisy told her. "I like hanging out with her."

"Absolutely," Sarah replied. It was hard to tell whether she was enthusiastic about the idea in general or the fact that being close to Tildy meant being close to Jimmy. It was hard to believe the woman would give up so easily. She cared about the stubborn ass too much.

They hung up, and Daisy headed outside to wait for Abby. She made it to the sidewalk before her phone rang again. She pressed the button and held it to her ear.

"Forget something?" she asked.

"Daisy?"

Daisy frowned and silently cursed. What was the point of Caller ID if you were too dumb to remember to check it?

"Matt, I'm busy."

"No, you're not."

"I am actually. I have plans."

"It's Thursday night."

Daisy shielded her eyes from the setting sun and searched the street for Abby's car. "It's poker night," she told him.

He laughed. "Remember when we used to play at Ricky's?"

Daisy rolled her eyes. "I'm trying to forget."

"Best tits I ever saw," he drawled.

She made a face. Matt hadn't been so bad himself, not as hot as anyone she'd seen in Rapid City so far, but a well-hung bad boy on a bike had always gotten her motor revving. Too bad they were never good for the long haul.

Matt's tone turned sharp, and Daisy had already gotten over the call. "You ain't stripping for your new friends, are you?" he asked.

Daisy groaned. "No, Matt. I've grown up a little since then. You should try it."

"I am!" he shot back. "I told you! I got a job and-"

Daisy spotted Abby's car, and she sighed in relief. "I gotta go. My ride's here."

She disconnected the call and pocketed the phone. The next thing on the list was definitely a new number.

When Daisy entered the Sullivan house, she saw Sarah with the phone pressed to her ear. She waved Abby and Daisy over. "Tildy," she told them.

"Happy honeymoon, Tildy!" Abby called into the receiver as Sarah held it out.

"Hey!" said Daisy. "So, Hawk gave you a break long enough to call us?"

"Daisy!" Tildy chided over the speaker phone.

Abby laughed. "It's amazing," she said. "You can almost hear her blushing over the phone."

"How's New Mexico?" Daisy asked.

"It's beautiful!"

"Did you go to that cafe I told you about?" Sarah asked.

"Yeah," said Tildy. "I think I ate enough for *three*."

"Well, enjoy it until the morning sickness kicks in," Sarah replied.

"Ugh. I'm not looking forward to that."

Sarah smiled at Hope as Shooter held her across the room. "It's totally worth it," she told Tildy.

"Enjoy the rest of your trip!" Daisy told her and headed to the kitchen to get herself something to drink. She pulled a bottle out of the fridge and pried off the cap. She turned and stepped right into Easy, who had come up behind her. She jerked back and sloshed beer all over herself. "Damn it," she said and reached for a paper towel.

"Sorry," he replied and picked up the mostly empty bottle.

"It's not your fault. I didn't hear you." She sopped up the mess, dabbing at her shirt and avoiding looking at him.

"Daisy-"

She sighed. "Do you have anything to say that I actually want to hear?"

Before he could respond, her phone rang again. She threw down the sodden paper towel and yanked her phone out of her pocket. "The assholes are coming out of the woodwork tonight," she muttered and stabbed the answer button.

She brushed past Easy and headed toward the back door. "What?" she snapped into the phone. She didn't really want to talk to Matt, but she definitely didn't want to talk to Jimmy, either. *The devil you know*, she thought as she opened the screen door and stepped outside.

"Stop hanging up on me!" Matt demanded.

"I was kind of hoping you'd take the hint," she replied. "What do you want, Matt?"

"I miss you."

Daisy rolled her eyes and plucked a leaf off a nearby tree, twirling the stem in her fingers.

"Come home."

"I told you. I am home."

"You don't sound like it," he pointed out. "In fact, you sound damn miserable."

"No one's smacking me around," Daisy replied, "so there's that."

He sighed. "I said I was sorry for that. It won't happen again."

"Matt-"

"It never happened before."

That part was true. Matt had done his share of yelling and pushing, but he'd never hit her before that day.

"So, just come home. I miss you," he repeated. "I miss how we used to be."

Daisy pressed her lips together. She didn't miss Nebraska or Matt for that matter, but she had to admit it was nice to be wanted. It just sucked that it was the wrong guy saying it.

"I got a place of my own," he told her. "And I can put in a good word for you at the plant."

"They're never going to hire me," Daisy told him, because it seemed easier to say than arguing about being over him.

"They might."

"Matt, they're not going hire a girl with a prostitution conviction. It won't happen. I've got a good job here and-"

"So, *they* hired you. The plant'll hire you, too."

Daisy bit her lip and felt guilty about lying on the application. She'd probably have to lie for the rest of her life. She didn't relish the thought.

"Forget it, Matt. We're done."

"Daisy-"

Daisy hung up on him, hopefully for the last time, and shoved her phone back into her pocket. She turned around and came face to face with Easy, lurking in the shadow of the house.

"Jesus!" she cried. "You scared me."

It was getting dark outside, but she could still make out his face. She froze.

"You're a whore," he said quietly.

Daisy's heart pounded, and she felt like she was going to be sick. "Jimmy-"

"You're a fucking whore."

Daisy shook her head. "It's not really like that. I-"

"I let you into my life!" he shouted. "Into my *house*! And you're a god damn *whore*!"

Daisy's eyes flitted to the house. The back door opened and Sarah came through it. Daisy felt on the edge of panic and took a step toward him. "I'm not," she told him quietly. "Please don't-"

"Do not fucking touch me!" Easy shouted.

"Jimmy!" Sarah yelled and Shooter followed the sound of their voices out into the backyard.

"She's a hooker!" he told Sarah loudly, then he turned back to Daisy. "I guess that's where you've been for the last eight months!"

Sarah looked from Easy to Daisy. "Daisy?"

Daisy pressed her lips together as Tex, Abby, and Caleb came out. They weren't exactly surrounding her, but she felt trapped just the same. She shook her head and refused to answer. The sting of tears pricked the back of her eyes, and she blinked rapidly, willing them not to fall. Crying would solve nothing, and the last thing she wanted to do was explain.

"She just got out of jail," Easy informed them. "For prostitution."

Daisy laughed, sharp and bitter, and glared at him. "You forgot resisting arrest and assaulting a police officer."

"Maria doesn't hire felons," Caleb pointed out.

Daisy shrugged. "She's also too busy to do background checks."

"You bitch," Easy snapped.

"Easy," Shooter said quietly.

"You *bitch*!" he yelled louder. "You come here and lie- to *all* of us. You're nothing but a skank ass *whore*!"

"That's enough," Caleb said, trying to defuse the situation. He crossed toward her, reaching out his hand. "Daisy-"

She jerked back from him, nearly stumbling. Tears welled up in her eyes and blurred her vision. "Don't touch me!" she shouted at him. "Not you! *Never you!*"

She looked around, searching desperately, for what she had no idea. Sarah looked horrified, Shooter pretty much the same. Abby and Tex were quiet. Daisy could see there was nothing for it. Whatever she had thought she'd found here was lost- or possibly had never really existed at all. She could lie and say it was all mistake, but they probably wouldn't believe her. So she told a bigger lie instead.

"I want to go home," she whispered.

CHAPTER THIRTY

Things had settled down in the last week, or at least Sarah, Tildy, and Abby had gone from yelling at him to not really speaking to him at all. Daisy hadn't answered her phone when they'd tried to reach her, and they blamed it on him. Apparently, she'd cleared out of her room at the Rainbow and hadn't even told Maria she was leaving town. Easy tried to point out that it was more proof Daisy was unreliable and dishonest, but the girls were having none of it.

Work was the same as it always was, with the guys pretty much leaving him alone. Only Caleb had tried to talk to him about. Easy simply asked if Caleb had ever accidentally fucked a whore. Caleb had nothing to say to that and had since given up, or so Easy thought.

He barely looked up as an RCPD squad car pulled into the lot at the garage. Caleb got out and crunched the gravel with his heavy boots as he walked toward the open bay doors.

"What's up?" Shooter asked him, since Caleb rarely stopped by the garage, especially when he was on duty.

"Been up to Lead," he replied, glancing at Easy, but Easy wasn't about to take the bait. He picked up a socket wrench and walked away, back to the engine he was working on.

Ignoring Easy's attempt at indifference, Caleb said, "Thought I'd talk to the cop that arrested Daisy. See what his impression was of her."

Since Easy didn't respond, Shooter did. "Oh, yeah? What'd he have to say?"

Caleb shook his head. "Didn't. I couldn't reach him." He hooked his thumbs into his utility belt and sighed. "Apparently, he's doing his own bid right now. Year and half for sex abuse."

Easy kept his eyes on the engine, but paused.

"Sex abuse?" Shooter asked.

"Seems a concerned citizen saw him in plainclothes heading into a no-tell motel with a young girl and called it in. Turned out she was fourteen, a runaway. He told her if she didn't play nice, he'd take her right back to her step daddy who was already crawling into her bed at night."

"Jesus Christ."

"Any asshole can be a cop," Caleb replied darkly. "Least this one got caught."

Easy fought back the black spots before his eyes as he gripped the wrench tightly. He stood up and turned on Caleb. "Did he hurt Daisy?" he demanded, gripping the wrench so hard his knuckles turned white.

"I don't know," Caleb replied quietly. "She pled guilty to all the charges right out of the gate. Never tried to make a deal. She did her whole bid with no behavioral issues, and they released her."

"And no one's looking into his prior arrests?" Hawk asked.

"They are, but they're doing it quietly. They reached out to some girls, including Daisy while she was in jail, but she wouldn't talk about it. The DA didn't pursue it. Mostly, they just want it to go away. I had to go through five people before I could find someone who'd even tell me *that* much. For what it's worth, Daisy's got no other priors. Not even a juvie record that I could find. She's lived her whole life in Nebraska and never got into trouble until she came up to Sturgis."

Easy tossed the wrench toward the nearby workbench but missed, and it clattered to the floor. He turned and walked toward the parking lot.

"Easy," Shooter called after him, but he ignored the man. "Jimmy!"

"I just need... a break," he said. "I'm going home. I'm done for the day."

They watched him go without trying to stop him. The last thing he needed was to be around people right now or have to look at their accusing glares. Nothing they could do or say could make him feel worse right now. He nosed the bike into traffic and drove home, but it turned out that being alone had its own pitfalls.

Easy sat at his kitchen table with a bottle of Jack Daniels, a belated Christmas Gift, and one hell of a guilty conscience. The truth was he didn't need the box or the bottle, so he'd finish off one and toss the other in the garbage.

He was reaching for the bottle when the back door slid open. A shadow fell across the floor. He was reminded of the time Daisy had come into his house, uninvited but not exactly unwanted. He could say a lot of things about Daisy, about himself and how he'd treated her, but he'd always wanted her. It wasn't that he didn't want *all* of *her*, he just didn't want to give all of himself.

Hawk pulled out a chair and sat down. "So, you're going to sit here and get drunk and wonder why you didn't just ask her for the truth?"

"I didn't want the truth," Easy admitted. "The *truth* is I was looking for a way out. And I found one. She could have told me it was all bullshit. I wouldn't have believed her, because I didn't *want* to believe her. I didn't want to believe *in* her."

Easy leaned back in his chair and studied the ceiling. "This... foul mouthed, sassy little girl blows into town and everything's on *her* terms, always. She doesn't give a shit what anyone else thinks. Like she wouldn't even let anyone take *that much* from her. If he hurt her... "

"You don't know that."

"I didn't *ask*! Too busy feeling sorry for myself." He reached for the bottle again.

Hawk eyed him as Easy poured himself another drink. "You could stop," he suggested. Easy wasn't sure if he meant feeling sorry for himself, or the drinking, or both.

"I am," Easy assured him.

Hawk frowned. "Doesn't look like it."

Easy shook his head. "It's not a bender."

"Then what is it?"

"The end of the road. Or the beginning of it. Fuck, I'm not sure."

"Deep," Hawk said with a smirk.

"Fuck you. I'm drunk. And this shit's all going away," said Easy, gesturing to the table.

Hawk reached out to pluck the silver box from the table. On instinct, Easy reached for it to stop him. Then he blew out a boozy breath. "Fuck it," he proclaimed. "I don't need it." He pushed it away, and Hawk picked it up. He took off the lid and peered inside. Easy felt a flood of warmth coursing through his body. He wasn't sure if it was the booze, or embarrassment, or what.

"You're getting rid of this?"

He nodded sharply. "It's time," he told Hawk. "I don't need it anymore. I'm done with that."

Hawk frowned. "Are you sure?"

"Fuck yeah, I'm sure!"

"Well, it's not my thing," Hawk told him. "Or my business. But are you sure you don't need it?"

Easy gaped at the man. "What the fuck?!" he demanded. "So... you're writing me off? Just like that?"

Hawk looked just as surprised. "No. Of course not. But I'm not sure you should give up on the idea of-"

"*Fuck. You!*" Easy shouted and snatched back the box. He slammed it down on the table with a resounding thud. A glimmer of gold caught his eye and he looked down. He stared at it for a moment before reaching inside. His fingers trembled as he tried but failed to grasp the small chain. At last his fingers pinched the clasp and he held up the small gold crucifix. It dangled above the silver box and twinkled in the afternoon sunlight coming in through the window.

"Son of a bitch," he whispered.

Hawk was silent a moment before he asked, "What was in it?"

Easy blew out a harsh breath and looked at him. "A hollow point," he said finally.

"Jesus, Jimmy!"

"I'm over it!" he insisted. "Like I said, I don't need it anymore. I haven't thought about needing it for a long fucking time. I was gonna put it back in the ammo box with the others."

Hawk spun the box around on the table. "Fucking Christmas box, too," he muttered. "Drama queen. But you were getting rid of it?"

"Yeah."

"What changed your mind?"

Easy looked at him.

Hawk smiled. "It figures."

"Why does it figure?"

"I'll let you in on a little secret," Hawk told him. "We never save the girl. The girl always saves us."

CHAPTER THIRTY-ONE

Easy was acutely aware of Shooter's gaze on him as he stepped out of Slick's SUV. The slightly larger man watched calmly but curiously as his wife followed Easy to the garage.

"It's your day off," Shooter said to Easy.

Easy nodded. "Got business."

Shooter cocked his head. "Tempted to ask what kind of business involves my woman." He looked at Sarah, who had her lips pressed together. Since Easy had called her the day before, she'd barely been able to contain her excitement. It was a wonder that she hadn't already told her husband everything already. But Easy wasn't flat on his back, choking on dust, so he figured she'd managed to keep things to herself.

Shooter tucked a rag into his back pocket and cast Easy a look. "What-?"

Before he could finish, a rumble of engines caught his attention. Down the street, two Harleys and a jacked up truck were coming their way. The riders were sporting club colors. Shooter moved forward and took hold of Sarah, pulling her toward him. Tex appeared on Shooter's other side, keeping a watchful eye on the caravan.

"Easy," Shooter growled, and there was an entire interrogation packed into that one word.

"They're just a club," Easy assured him. "I checked them out."

"So, I don't need to get my gun?" Tex asked.

Easy shrugged. "You could. They might come down on the price." He left the group and headed across the lot, waving at a large, burly man with a salt and pepper beard and aviator sunglasses. After a cursory meet and greet, the man stepped back and gave Easy some space.

The Softail was a gleaming mass of black and chrome, but Easy ignored the shiny bits and went right to business. He checked the twin cam engine and the caliper brakes. Satisfied with what he saw, Easy stood up and reached for his wallet. "It's in good shape," he confirmed as he handed over a cashier's check.

The beard grinned. "She's my baby," he said. "Take care of her."

"I will."

The beard jumped into the truck, one Harley lighter and a few thousand dollars richer. Easy gave him a final wave and turned as everyone came up behind him.

"Nice," Hawk declared, eyeing the bike appreciatively.

Shooter's mouth quirked up, and he could barely contain his grin. "So, this is why you needed a ride."

Easy smirked at him as the door to Slick's SUV banged shut. The sound caused everyone to look. She'd gone to retrieve two bucket helmets from the cab. Shooter raised an eyebrow at her.

"Actually," said Easy. "I'm taking your wife for a ride."

Shooter watched Sarah hand Easy the second helmet then put on her own. "Last time you tried that," he told Easy, "I kicked your ass."

"No, I kicked *your* ass, not that you deserved it. I'm going to drop my pants in front of her, too. You're going to have to work overtime to win back her love once she sees my package."

"Jimmy!" Sarah cried and slapped his arm.

Shooter's jaw twitched. "You can show her anything you want. You touch her, and I'll rip your leg off and beat you with it."

Easy grinned at him. "Do it with the cheap one."

Shooter ignored the cryptic comment and turned to Sarah. "How long have you known about this?"

"Um... since yesterday."

"And yet you didn't think to mention it." Sarah didn't answer. "Fucking Slick," Shooter muttered.

Sarah slid on the back of Easy's new ride and put her arms around him.

Easy grinned at Shooter and patted her hands.

"Higher," Shooter growled.

"Chris," Sarah groaned but moved up her hands.

"When are you coming back?"

"Not 'til after dark. Tildy's at the house with the baby. Bye!"

Easy rolled out of the lot before Shooter could live up to his nickname. He turned onto the street and settled into the leather seat. The shifting was fluid, and his leg felt okay for now. By the time they hit the highway, he was comfortable. He hit the gas and shifted through the gears seamlessly as he and Sarah headed northwest.

In the sterile room, he felt less comfortable than he had on the bike. The cool breeze of the open road had been replaced by the chill of the air conditioning and his one bare foot on the floor. He took a deep breath and reached for the privacy curtain.

"You don't have to do this if you don't want to," Sarah told him from the other side of the room. "I can wait outside."

"No," he said, and pulled the curtain back.

Sarah made a small noise, and Easy's stomach twisted. "That bad?" he asked quietly.

She shook her head, face flushing. "It's not... " She cleared her throat. "You're in your underwear."

He glanced down. "Well, yeah. How's he going to look at it?"

"I don't know!"

He smirked at her as he slid into the chair next to hers. "You just can't keep from looking."

"Oh, I can," she countered. She reached down to the floor and grabbed a helmet. She plunked it into his lap.

Easy looked down at it and sighed. "Perfect fit. If only they made condoms in my size."

Sarah slapped his arm. He laughed again. She was quiet for a moment then reached out and tousled his hair. "You look good."

"If only you weren't married. And your old man didn't have a . 45," he teased.

"I mean it, Jimmy. You look good."

He was the one who cleared his throat this time. "You don't think I should grow out my hair? Go for a rocker look like Milo?"

"I don't know. I've always known you like this. I don't think so. You're perfect."

She threaded her fingers through his and rested her head on his shoulder. "Remember when you used to do this for me?"

"Get you naked and compliment you? Somehow I would've remembered."

She squeezed his hand. "You used to hold my hand when I was pregnant. When Chris... "

Easy rested his head against hers. Shooter hadn't taken Sarah's pregnancy complications well. He'd whittled himself down to survival mode, like they'd done in the field. It was understandable, after all; he'd had twice as much to lose. Along the way he'd lost sight of the fact that although his wife was one hell of a fighter, she wasn't a soldier. She'd needed comfort when Shooter had none to give. Instead he'd immersed himself in blood pressure readings and daily medication.

There had been no formal discussion about it, just a tacit understanding that Tex would watch over the lieutenant while Easy cared for Sarah. It had seemed the obvious choice. Easy had been showing her how to protect herself physically. It only made sense that he'd help her emotionally, too.

The door opened, and a doctor in a white lab coat came in. Easy recognized him from his previous extended stay. He shook the man's hand. "Is this your girlfriend?" he asked, taking Sarah's hand as well.

"No. She's my sister-in-law."

Sarah grinned at him.

The doctor pulled up a chair and examined Easy's prosthetic. "Is your socket hurting you?" he asked. "We've been through several already, but if this one's not working we could try-"

"No, this one's good," Easy told him. "A little numb for the long rides but not too bad. It's the most comfortable so far."

The doctor nodded, checking the fit of the neoprene sleeve. "So, what are doing today?"

Easy took a deep breath. Sarah squeezed his hand. "I think... I think I'm ready for a custom prosthetic."

CHAPTER THIRTY-TWO

Daisy woke just before the alarm clock kicked on. Three weeks of early mornings had turned her into an early bird, an irritated early bird who might peck out your eyes. She stumbled to the shower, hoping for hot water. Her mama got off work just as Daisy was going on, and Daisy was faced with either getting up *even earlier* to shower comfortably or dealing with cold water. Neither option was all that appealing.

Joe was working her like a dog at the Silver Spoon, open to close five days a week. She was grateful, though, that he'd hired her back under the circumstances. And in case she wasn't, Joe was quick to remind her that she should be. The pay was terrible, and the tips were at least as bad as she remembered. Worse, actually, since now they had the occasional 'What does five bucks get me?' written on the side, or similar.

She waffled between taking it or telling them to shove it up their asses. But in the end, practicality won out. The sooner she had some money saved, the sooner she could leave again. At this rate, though, she'd need a second job to be able to afford it. Opportunities were scarce in Delay already and there weren't enough hours in the day as it was.

Matt had tried, without asking her, to get her a job at the processing plant. She was actually glad it hadn't worked out, because the last thing she wanted was to feel beholden to the jerk. Her plan was to avoid Matt altogether until she blew town. With all her hours at the Spoon, and his hours at the plant, that actually seemed possible.

She'd ditched her phone when she'd come to town. There was no one left that she wanted to speak to, and mama had been grateful for the upgrade. So grateful, in fact, that she let Daisy stay in her old room basically rent free, although Daisy had to do all the cooking and cleaning to compensate. That wasn't too bad a deal, until Daisy realized that her mama had apparently done no cleaning at all, possibly in the entire time Daisy had been gone. By the time Daisy got through the mess, she'd likely be ready to move again.

She washed her hair, toweled it dry, and threw on a pair of jean shorts that looked reasonably clean. Mama only let her borrow the car to take clothes to the laundromat just off Main Street, but Daisy couldn't muster enough energy to go more than once a week. She pulled on her boots and headed out the door. Summer was scorching, but winter would be nice- at least it would be in Colorado. It would be as cold as Nebraska, she figured, but at least there would be more to do.

She trudged out of Vista Valley and down Main Street toward town. It was a decent walk over the train tracks, a little shorter than her daily trek to Maria's had been. She frowned, not wanting to think about it. She could have made a good life for herself in Rapid City, but she could do that in Denver, too. She crossed the street and opened the door to the Silver. Grease hung thick in the air, and though Joe had banned smoking in the place almost ten years ago, it seemed that the smell of smoke would never truly go away.

She pulled her apron out from the shelf behind the counter and tied it on. Before she even finished, Cole Barton barked out, "Coffee!" as he came through the door.

Daisy refrained from rolling her eyes as she poured him a cup. The good Christian people of Delay, Nebraska had never treated her very well, even before she left. Things had only gotten worse since she'd returned. Tips were bad, even dismal. Last week someone left her a sermon instead of cash.

The farmers and plant workers filtered in, and Joe was too busy to yell at her, so that was something at least. Being busy helped fill the hours, if not her wallet, though the lulls between meals were brutal in their boringness. Daisy wiped down the tables and the counter, while Joe grudgingly fired her up a burger.

She slid onto the last stool at the counter, in the corner and out of the way then set down her plate and her travel guide in front of her. She was only allowed to read on breaks, but she was grateful for the distraction. She didn't make it to the end of the chapter before the bell above the door jingled again. She sighed and pushed her half-eaten cheeseburger away with one hand and closed the book with the other.

She got off the stool, took a step forward, and almost collided with the man who'd come up behind her. He had black motorcycle boots, dark blue jeans, a gray t-shirt, and a face she recognized. She nearly stumbled back and used the stool behind her to keep herself from falling. She ran a hand over her still damp hair and cursed herself or maybe him. It was hard to be sure.

"What do you want?" she snapped.

The air seemed to vibrate around them, or maybe it was just her, shaking from anger. Easy moved forward, skirting her, and sat down on a stool as she watched in disbelief.

"I said what-"

"The usual," he said. "Cheeseburger, fries, and a Coke."

Daisy didn't move, she only blinked at him.

"Delilah!" Joe shouted and she jumped.

She moved behind the counter to get him his Coke. Joe was trying to figure out how a man he'd never laid eyes on before today had a *usual,* but he slapped a patty on the grill anyway. Daisy took her cue from the ice she was scooping into his glass and let her sudden burst of anger melt away. She turned and slammed the soda down on the counter. She stood in front of him, silently watching as he wiped up a splash off the counter with a napkin.

If he'd said anything, she was ready to pounce on him, to kick his ass out of *her* town, run him out on a rail just the way he'd done to her. But he said nothing at all. Pretty soon Daisy was soundly reminded just how much Delay was *not* her town, such as it ever was, when the door opened and the lunchtime crowd started to trickle in.

They filled up the tables and the counter, barely grunting their orders to her. Soon she was too busy to wonder why Easy had come all this way just to yell at her. Except he wasn't yelling at her. He was just... sitting there.

Tom Parson sent his egg salad back just to fuck with her, and she stepped around behind the counter to dump the nearly finished sandwich into the trash. Out of the corner of her eye, she saw Easy reach out and snag her book. He slid it over the counter toward himself and inspected the cover.

Well, let him look, Daisy thought, bristling with anger. He could rest assured she'd never go back to Rapid City, corrupting his town and his friends with her wicked, wanton ways. Parson finished the second egg salad and tossed a quarter on the counter as he left. Daisy felt her face flush with humiliation as she was forced to pick it up and pocket it, if only to clear the space.

When she came back up front, Easy slid off his stool and slowly stood up. She held her breath, for what she didn't know. He turned and walked toward the door. As he stepped outside, Daisy sighed and sagged against the counter. Her chest felt tight. She didn't know if she was disappointed or furious, if she was going to scream or cry. Someone snapped his fingers at her as though she was a dog, and Daisy, caught up in a roil of emotions she couldn't exactly identify, yelled, "I have a *name*!" Though it wasn't clear who she was talking to.

She glanced down and saw that Easy had left enough for his lunch plus a five dollar tip, which was too much for the bill. It felt like a slight, a joke he was playing at her expense. She stood staring at it, not touching it. She was afraid to pick it up.

What will five bucks get me?

She grabbed it and shoved it into her pocket without looking at it in case anything was written on it. She'd never felt more like a whore.

CHAPTER THIRTY-THREE

Easy had to leave before someone died or was beaten to a pulp at the very least. He'd spent the better part of an hour watching a slew of people treat Daisy like shit, talking down to her if they bothered to talk to her at all. One guy had tossed her some spare change after running her ragged. It wasn't hard to see why she'd want to move to Denver and get away from that.

He started the Harley and headed toward the edge of town, back the way he'd come. He parked outside the tiny gas station and headed inside.

"Did you find the Spoon?" the clerk asked.

Easy nodded. "I did," he told the older man.

"Decent lunch."

Easy nodded again, although his definition of decent was obviously very different. He missed Thomas' burgers and chili cheese fries. And the tattooed blonde who served them. She'd forgotten his steak sauce this time, but that was okay. She'd been flustered to say the least.

He set a newspaper and a hot rod magazine onto the counter. "I need a place to stay," he told the clerk.

The man looked surprised. "You want to stay in Delay?"

Hell no, he didn't want to stay. But he hadn't gotten into this mess in a single day and it was clear to him that it would take more than a day to untangle it.

"Keep heading down Main Street," the clerk said as he rung him up. "There's a motel on the other side of town."

"Thanks."

He stuffed the reading material into the saddlebags and turned back toward Main Street. He parked in front of the Spoon again and held the door for a guy in overalls before heading back inside himself. He took the same stool he'd sat at before, still available because the lunch crowd had thinned out.

He took his newspaper out from underneath his arm and spread it on the counter. It didn't take long before a pair of cowboy boots came stomping up behind him. It seemed Daisy was over her initial shock at seeing him, and she'd settled on being pissed instead.

"What is going on?" she demanded.

Easy didn't look up from the paper. "They're widening the road out by the bridge," he told her, reading from the article.

She hesitated. "Is this a joke?"

"Gary Burns thinks so. Though I'm pretty sure it's because he lives out there and doesn't want his yard torn up."

Daisy lunged forward. Easy didn't flinch. If she was going to hit him, well, he deserved worse. This really wasn't the time or place for a serious discussion, though. Her hand came down on his paper and not his head, so he supposed maybe she thought the same.

"What are you doing here?!"

"Delilah!"

Easy looked up at the guy who was apparently Daisy's boss. "What's going on?" the older man asked. "I don't want trouble." He turned to Daisy and jabbed a finger at her. "I told you when I hired you back that I don't want-"

"I came to eat," Easy declared. It was none of the old man's business if he'd come to eat crow or cheeseburgers.

"You already ate."

Easy shrugged. "Sign says 'Breakfast, Lunch, and Dinner'. So, I want dinner." To Daisy he said, "I want meatloaf, mashed potatoes, and a slice of apple pie. In five hours."

"Five hours!" the man barked.

Easy kept his eyes on Daisy. "You'll still be here?"

She hesitated, then nodded slightly.

Easy picked up his paper and shook out the wrinkled pages. "Meatloaf, mashed potatoes, apple pie," he repeated. "In five hours."

CHAPTER THIRTY-FOUR

Daisy was too stunned to do anything but nod. He was really going to just sit there for five hours until dinner time? The only thing she could think at that moment was *Why?* But she couldn't bring herself to ask.

Doug Geer came in for his dinner before his swing shift started, and she was relieved for the distraction. She poured Doug his usual black coffee, and he ignored her in his usual way. She put in his order for chili and waited for Joe to plate it. As much as she'd rather avoid Easy, she couldn't. Silently, she picked up his glass and refilled it with soda and placed it back down in front of him.

"Thank you, Daisy," he said loudly then looked at Doug.

Doug shifted uncomfortably on his stool under the weight of Easy's gaze. Easy finally had mercy on him and went back to reading his paper. When Doug finished his chili, he grunted something that sounded remarkably like thank you to Daisy, left her a dollar, and shuffled toward the door.

During the lull, he broke the lingering silence between them. "What's in Denver?"

Daisy grabbed some napkins to fill up the dispenser on the counter and began stuffing them in. "Restaurants, movie theaters, mountains, snow," she replied. "No assholes," she added, watching Doug walk out the door.

"There are assholes in Denver," Easy told her.

"Well, I'll avoid them. I've learned my lesson." He remained silent, which infuriated her for some reason. "Well, you're not in Denver!" she snapped, just in case she hadn't made her point.

Easy looked at her from across the counter. "No, I'm not."

Daisy didn't know what to say to that, either, so she grabbed a rag and started wiping down tables instead. She did her best to ignore him for the rest of the afternoon and into the evening, inventing new things to take care of, like organizing drinking straws by color and rearranging ketchup bottles.

He hadn't *said* anything or *done* anything. He was just *here*. And for some reason, to her that was worse than saying or doing anything, even calling her a whore again or telling her she'd better never set foot in Rapid City. That would be something at least, something to argue about or agree with, since she had no plans to ever go back to South Dakota. Easy was just sitting there doing *nothing at all*.

So why did it feel like something?

Easy ate his meatloaf and mashed potatoes silently and thanked her loudly for the pie. Then he tipped her more than he should have-again. He waited for her to push in the chairs and sweep the floor. Then, after she folded her apron and stuffed it on the shelf behind the counter, he held the door open for her. She still managed to ignore him, while ducking her head and stepping outside. Once her boots hit the sidewalk, she turned to head home.

"Do you want a ride?" he asked her, gesturing to a bike she'd never seen before. It was beautiful, larger than the one he'd had before. She was half-tempted to say yes.

She blinked at him and then glanced around her, as if this was some kind of joke or a dream where she could manage to wake up. "No! I don't want a *ride home*." She passed by him, refusing to give him another glance. She nearly made it to the end of the block when she heard him coming up beside her. Before she could react, he grabbed her hand. His fingers threaded through hers and held her firmly. Daisy was too surprised to struggle.

"That's okay," he told her casually. "It's a nice night. We'll walk."

She broke her stride for a moment, unsure what to do. She didn't know what was going on, but she did know that she wanted desperately to get away from him. She gave a futile tug with her captured hand before giving up. In a daze, she put one foot in front of the other and crossed the street.

"I got a new prosthetic," he told her casually. "Custom made. I've been walking a lot, breaking it in. This will be good for me."

Once they arrived on the other side, Daisy faltered again as she looked up and saw the Reverend Wilcox and his wife headed their way. She gripped Easy's hand tightly, though she wasn't certain whether she was trying to hurt him or convince herself he was actually real. Daisy felt shame, or embarrassment, or panic rise up in her throat as the older couple stared at them. For the first time since she was a little girl, she ducked her head.

When they passed, furious whispers ensued behind them, and Daisy hung her head again. She was used to people in town talking about her. She didn't know why it mattered to her this time. This was nothing new. As she turned the corner, she stopped in her tracks. Before them was the faded sign for the trailer court. The paint was peeling, and a large crack spidered up from one corner across the bottom half.

Over the years she'd gotten used to the people of Delay calling her trash. But suddenly she wasn't comfortable with Easy saying it. She couldn't stand him seeing it and confirming every bad thing he'd ever thought about her. She took a step back and tried to wrestle her hand from his, but he wouldn't let her go.

"Come on," he said, and half-pulled her forward. Daisy could do nothing but continue to move. "Have you ever been to New Orleans?" he asked her. Confused, Daisy shook her head. Her pace had slowed so much that it rivaled a snail's, but he didn't seem to mind. "I grew up in a row house," he told her. "That's New Orleans' version of a trailer park. At least *my* neighborhood was."

Daisy looked up at him and blinked.

"My mom works in the same cannery where she's always worked since I was born. I guess you could say my old man's retired now, or he gave up job hopping and *called* it retirement. He could never seem to hold onto a job for more than a year or two. When he was in between gigs, we didn't have much, not that we had a lot when they both worked. But when he was on unemployment, sometimes the only meal I got was lunch at school."

"Catholics are supposed to have a bunch of kids," he told her. "That whole thing. But I think my mom realized more kids would just make things harder. Plus, she never really wanted *me*, so she wasn't about to keep making the same mistake."

They had reached her place and Daisy's gaze skittered away from it and from him. She scraped the crushed gravel of the driveway with the heel of her boot. "This is me," she said quietly, indicating the trailer.

Easy let go of her hand and lifted her chin. "It's not you," he told her. "It's just where you live." He leaned forward, and she held her breath. His lips touched her forehead gently. "Keep your head up, Daisy. I'll see you tomorrow."

CHAPTER THIRTY-FIVE

Daisy walked into the trailer and shut the door behind her, putting a barrier between herself and whatever had just happened. She looked around at the lumpy couch and the stained carpet and tried to imagine Easy growing up in a similar place. She couldn't picture it, but then he and his friends had homes with yards instead of weeds. She'd just assumed it had always been that way for him. Maybe she was just as guilty of judging appearances.

In the morning, she grabbed a quick shower (only because it was cold) and slowly got dressed. She headed out the door but couldn't force herself to do more than take slow, deliberate steps. He'd said he'd see her today, but maybe he'd changed his mind. Maybe after he left he'd taken a walk around Vista Valley and Delay proper and decided to go back home- without her.

She paused just before the railroad tracks. *Without her.* Did she want him to take her back to Rapid City?

It didn't matter if she did; he hadn't offered. Nor was he likely to, not now that he knew the truth. So why was he here? Just to apologize? Maybe he was making amends, she mused. He'd bought a bike, gotten a new prosthetic, and now that he was starting his new life, he was making up for the old one.

In the time she'd known him, Easy hadn't been a heavy drinker.

She doubted he was addicted to alcohol, but maybe depression was its own kind of addiction. You just got so used to being in the gutter that it was easier to stay there. She knew a thing or two about that.

Her mama, it seemed, had long ago given up on having anything better. Even stocking her fridge for her on-again, off-again man seemed a little more like habit than hope. Daisy had never gone down that road. She knew that once you started- and if you kept on it long enough- the way back was longer than the way through, and you just kept on going- right up until you died. She wasn't going to own a fancy hotel or run a restaurant; she'd barely finished high school. But she'd be damned if she'd die in a dirty trailer in Delay, Nebraska.

She couldn't blame Easy for pulling himself up, and now it seemed he was finally recovering from his own bump in the road. It was just hard to feel happy for him when she wasn't sure why he was here. If he wanted to rub it in, then why had he admitted he'd grown up basically just like her? If he was here to apologize, why didn't he just do that and leave?

As she approached the diner, her heart knocked in her chest as she saw him outside leaning up against his new bike. He remained silent as he held the door for her. She shuffled inside and grabbed her apron as he chose a stool at the counter again. She ducked her head guiltily, as Joe glared at them both.

As if to legitimize his presence, Easy said, "I'll have steak and eggs, scrambled. With coffee."

Daisy filled his cup, along with everyone else's, and started her shift. When Easy finished his breakfast, he pushed the plate away and unfolded a newspaper. Daisy knew there was nothing newsworthy going on in Delay, certainly nothing of interest to a man like Jimmy, but he continued to read for the better part of the morning.

Daisy was about to take his lunch order when the bell above the door jingled. She looked over Easy's shoulder and scowled. Matt stomped up to the counter, looking surly.

"What do you want?" Daisy asked him.

Easy looked up from his paper, first at Daisy then at Matt. Matt eyeballed him with disdain.

"Heard some asshole was in town sniffing around."

"He's not," Daisy replied. "And it's no business of yours,

anyway."

Matt ignored her and glared at Easy. "Daisy's mine," he declared loudly. "So you can just fuck right off, because you don't belong here, and you sure as shit don't belong with her!"

Daisy watched as Easy put down the paper and got up off the stool.

"Hey!" yelled Joe. "I don't want no trouble in here! You take it outside."

Daisy was certain she heard the old man mutter that she wasn't even worth it, but she was too busy staring at Matt and Easy to care.

Easy drew himself up to his full height, which was a head taller than Matt. Matt's jaw twitched, but he didn't back down.

"Well, you're right about one thing," Easy replied. "I don't belong here. But you're wrong about something else. Daisy isn't yours."

"The hell she's not."

"If she was," Easy told him calmly, "you wouldn't have left her in Sturgis. And don't think for one second that I've forgotten that you hit her before you took off." Easy's eyes narrowed as Matt's widened. "So, how about it, *Matt*?" he said, managing to make 'Matt' sound like 'shit'. "Want to talk about this outside? I'm ready."

It was probably a combination of Easy's deadly calm voice and the Army Ranger tattoo prominently visible on his forearm that caused Matt to rethink his strategy. He mumbled something about needing to get back to work before he turned to leave.

Easy slid back onto his stool, once Matt had left. Several other people were staring at him and Daisy. She didn't know what to tell them or what to make of what had just happened. Deciding it wasn't worth agonizing over, she cleared the counter and wiped it down. What had really happened? Not much, she decided. Matt had come in spoiling for a fight, not knowing who he'd be up against.

Easy had changed his mind with just a few words. Daisy reminded herself that none of those words had included claiming her for himself. He didn't want her. He wasn't apologizing and he still hadn't left. Angrily, she threw down the rag. It was busy, too busy to just confront him. Hell, if she thought Joe would let her, she'd tell Easy to meet *her* outside. As it was, she'd just have to wait until they were alone, and she could tell his ass to leave.

Easy didn't belong here. She did, at least for now. And it was time to end whatever this was.

By the time dinner service was over, she was spoiling for a fight herself. She stalked to the door Easy was holding open for her and passed through it. The only difference was that she wasn't about to back down. It turned out, though, that she was forced to do exactly that. When she opened her mouth to give him what for, he asked, "So, your dad took off?"

Thrown off balance, she could only stare at him. Ignoring her confusion, Easy slid his hand into hers and started walking.

"My old man took off, too. I mean my *real* old man. My mom got knocked up in high school, but he took off once he found out. Not sure why the guy I call my dad agreed to marry her, except they were young, and her old man, my grandfather, wasn't the nicest guy in the world. Maybe he felt like saving her. I don't know."

"I don't think she wanted to be saved, though. Or she was angry that she needed it or something. Because she drank a lot, and she'd go off on a tear, yelling about the shithole we lived in and the crappy job she had to work to pay the bills. And she'd remind him that I wasn't his."

"I wanted to be, though. I was always trying to make him proud of me. But nothing I did was ever good enough. Not my grades or football, even though I was damn good at both. And you would think that I would have wised up, that I would have just stopped fucking trying, but I never did. Although, after a while, I didn't want to impress him anymore."

As they walked, Easy squinted into the setting sun that was orange against the purplish sky. "After a while, I just wanted to piss him off," he admitted. "So, I'd be better than him, I decided. We were flat broke, no money for college. I figured I'd join the Army, and they'd pay for my education. And then I joined the Rangers, because they were elite. I had it all planned out. A few tours, a fat commission, then I'd come home and get married. To a nice, pretty girl who'd take care of my house and raise my kids and never, ever mouth off to me."

Daisy jerked her hand again, a bit more forcefully this time. "Well, that's not me. So, I don't know what you thought you were doing hooking up with me in the first damn place. Because I'm not like that!"

Easy let go of her hand, but before she could get away he grabbed her shoulders. "No one is like that, Daisy. That girl, she was never real. She was never even a *person* to me! She was just like the football trophies and the medals, just another *thing* I could parade in front of my old man. I never once thought about how much I'd love her, only how much *she* would love *me*."

"Well, you're in luck!" Daisy shot back, pushing against his chest. "Because I don't love you! I'm ugly, and tattooed, and mouthy. And I'm a whore, too. Just ask around! No one's surprised. They all knew what I'd turn out to be. And you did, too. So, go back home, Turnbull. Because *this* is where I live, and you don't want any part of it."

His grip on her shoulders tightened, and he pulled her in closer. Daisy fought, though, and tried to get away. "Just leave me alone!" she cried. "I don't love you. *I don't love you!*" she cried even as fresh, hot tears spilled down her cheeks. This fucking hypocritical bastard tracked her down just to stomp on what was left, and it wasn't fair. It wasn't fair at all.

He held her so close she could smell his cologne and the musk underneath that she'd always loved about him.

"*What do you want?*" she sobbed.

Instead of answering her, Easy swept her hair out of her eyes and kissed her forehead. "See you tomorrow, Daisy," he told her, and then he walked away.

CHAPTER THIRTY-SIX

Easy checked his watch as he waited outside the Silver Spoon for the third day in a row. She was either late this time or not coming. He could go to her trailer, he supposed, but that seemed a little too invasive. He'd almost given up when he caught a glimpse of her coming down the street.

"You're not working today?" he asked her.

She shook her head, then peered at him. "I wasn't sure how long you'd wait."

"A long time," he assured her. "Will you take another walk with me?" he asked her, nodding across the street. "We could go over there."

She hesitated, then nodded, and they crossed the road toward a small park in the middle of town. Easy took her hand again and noted with some satisfaction that she didn't fight him this time. They sat down on a park bench at the edge of the sand playground.

"Why are you here?" she asked quietly.

"I've got a lot to make up for."

She nodded. "I figured."

"You figured what?"

"New leg, new bike, new life. Time to burn the bridge," she added quietly.

"Time to what?"

"Nothing."

Easy reached out and tucked a strand of hair behind her ear. "Did he hurt you Daisy?"

"Who? Matt? No, not really. I've been hit harder."

"Not Matt," Easy replied. "The cop."

Daisy glanced at him for a moment and looked away. "That's got nothing to do with you."

"I'm asking anyway."

"What do you want me to tell you?" she snapped. "That it was all a mistake? That I'm innocent. Think whatever you want about me. I don't care."

Easy leaned in and kissed her softly. His little warrior girl put on a strong front, but he realized she wore her heart- and her soul- on her sleeve, if you gave enough of a shit to look for it. He wasn't surprised she'd never shown him much in the way of emotion. He'd sure as shit never given *her* anything.

When he pulled away, he rested his forehead against hers. "*I care, Daisy.*"

He could get down on the only knee he had left and say it louder, if he thought that was what she needed, but it wasn't. Daisy didn't need some big gesture that was as much about the people watching as it was about her, not that there was anyone watching. They were alone, and it was his chance to be intimate with her in a way that was about more than just putting his dick inside her.

"I care, Daisy," he repeated, because he was certain she'd never heard it before. She might have heard *I love you*, but who had said *I care?*

She broke away from him and wiped tears from her eyes. "He didn't hurt me."

They sat in silence while he waited for more.

"I was in a bar," she said finally. "Pissed off because I was broke and had no way to get home. Some guy bought me a drink, and I told him I was stuck. He asked me what I'd be willing to do for some cash." She kicked at the dirt underneath her boot. "Here's the part where I cement your shitty opinion of me and tell you I considered stripping. But I didn't think I could do it, even just once. Not with a bunch of people watching."

She laughed bitterly. "You'd think I wouldn't care after Ricky

Snell's basement, but I did. And I didn't know how many times I'd have to take my clothes off before I had enough money. I thought with sex it'd just be one time. It'd be over fast and I'd have the money I needed. I could just go home and put it behind me. So, I told him to buy me another drink."

"We went out to the parking lot. I let him fuck me. But he stopped and took off the condom. He wanted me to suck him off, but I wouldn't do it. We argued. He grabbed me, and I punched him. Then he dragged me out of the car and told me he was a cop. He called someone else to cuff me. He told them I was turning tricks in the parking lot and offered to blow him."

"But you didn't tell anyone what really happened?"

"I did. The first guy who showed up, I told him. But all he saw was a drunk slut with too many tattoos. Trailer trash versus a cop. He didn't believe me. Later, a lawyer came to see me and tried to talk to me, but it didn't matter. It *doesn't* matter."

She turned to look at him. "I did it, Jimmy. I let some sleazy asshole stick his dick in me for a bus ticket. Nothing else matters. I'll always know that I did it."

Easy pulled her in close and held her against him while she cried. After a few minutes, he said, "Sometimes bad choices seem like the *only* choices. I know how that is. You looked in my box."

She pulled away to look at him. "You have so much."

"I do," he agreed. "I have family that loves me, a little niece to watch grow up. But for a long time I didn't realize it. I treated them like shit. Worst of all, I had a girl who loved me, and I treated her like shit, too." He smoothed back her hair so he could see her face. "Can I have you again, Daisy?"

She looked up at him with clear blue eyes, and he held his breath. Her lips parted, and he waited on a knife edge to get a glimpse into his own future.

"I'm sorry. Are we interrupting a Hallmark moment?"

Daisy gasped in surprise, and Easy let go of her. Matt had enlisted two mouth breathers to back him up. They stood behind him and tried to look menacing. Easy would have laughed if he wasn't so damn irritated.

"I told you, Daisy's mine."

Easy shook his head. Matt didn't give a shit about Daisy. It was more likely that his ego was bruised, and in a small town like this everyone had heard about it. Easy weighed the merits of explaining that if he needed two other guys to finish the job it still wouldn't be a victory, not that they stood a chance. Two pissants and a loudmouth were hardly intimidating.

"These are shitty odds," Easy told Matt. "You should've brought more guys." He stepped forward, putting himself in front of Daisy, just in case one of them had brought a gun. "Obviously, you were too stupid to get it the first time, so let me be perfectly clear. Daisy... *is mine*. So suck it up, boy band, because she's leaving with me."

"Like hell," Matt shouted and lunged.

Easy side stepped him and swept his legs out from underneath him. He went down in the dirt, just as the other two charged. Easy pivoted and rammed his elbow into the large one's gut. He doubled over with a grunt. The third one was still advancing. So, Easy threw a punch, catching him squarely in the face. He went down harder than Matt, blood misting from his nose.

The one he'd winded was back for more, so Easy grabbed his shoulder with one hand and made several quick jabs with the other. Somewhere around the third or fourth strike, he felt a rib crack under his knuckles.

Matt was up by now and swinging hard. He caught Easy in the back with a kidney punch. Easy stumbled a bit. Matt kept up his pursuit, but the younger man was all enthusiasm and no strategy. When his next swing missed, he over-extended himself. Easy brought his fist down hard, cracking Matt's jaw and sending him to his knees.

"Want to go another round?"

Matt didn't respond, and Easy turned away. A body slammed into his, but this one was small and female. She was sobbing and he wrapped his arms around her.

"Everything's fine," he murmured in her ear.

"I know."

"Then why are you crying?"

"Because you fought for me."

Easy pushed her away a little and wiped her cheeks with his thumbs. He grinned at her. "Is one of these guys Ricky, by any chance? If not we could go looking for him. I'm on a roll."

She laughed through her tears and leaned in to kiss him. He lifted her to her toes and pressed his lips to hers.

"Yes," she told him when he let go.

He knew which question she was answering.

CHAPTER THIRTY-SEVEN

Daisy barely got off the bike before Tildy tackled her. Easy watched in amusement as the two women hugged each other fiercely.

"You didn't answer your phone!" Tildy accused in between sobs.

"I got rid of my phone," Daisy told her.

"Well, get another one!" Tildy cried. She took a step back and wiped her eyes with the back of her hand.

"You really missed me," Daisy said grinning. "Either that or pregnancy hormones."

"Both," Tildy replied.

Hawk snorted. "Yep. Let's blame the hormones," he said wryly. Before Tildy could yell at him, he said, "Slick's taken over our kitchen. Family dinner."

Easy followed Daisy into Shooter's old house. There were more hugs between the women, while the men set the table. Easy had met Sarah over Family dinner, one she made especially for him. She squeezed his arm as she passed by, and he wondered if she was remembering the same thing. He'd been a dick to her that night and on many other subsequent nights.

"Give me that," he said, taking a serving bowl from her. He set it down on the table and picked a chair next to Daisy.

"Run into trouble?" Shooter asked, noting Easy's bruised knuckles.

"None whatsoever," he replied.

"There were three of them!" Daisy protested.

Hawk laughed. "Need more than that to take down a Ranger."

After dinner, Easy helped clear the dishes into the dishwasher. As he stood up he heard Caleb say, "Daisy, can I talk to you?"

She bit her lower lip but nodded. Easy watched as he took her out the back door and onto the deck. His first instinct was to follow them, if only to comfort her, but he decided if she wanted him there, she'd ask.

"He wants her to make a statement," Shooter said quietly from beside him.

"She probably won't."

"She told you what happened?"

He grimaced and nodded.

"Bad?" Shooter asked.

"Bad enough," he replied. "Broke, desperate girl and cop who took advantage of her, got rough with her."

He fought the urge to go to her again. Shooter must have sensed it, because he said, "He won't push her."

Easy sighed. "I know."

"He just wants her to know he'll go with her, back her up. If she ever wants to do anything about it."

Caleb and Daisy talked for a while. She finally seemed to relax around him and even smiled a bit once in a while. When they were done, he opened the door for her, and they came back inside.

Easy swept her into his arms and hugged her. "Okay?" he whispered.

She nodded into his chest. "I just want to forget about it," she said quietly.

He squeezed her tightly in response then took her by the hand and led her to the door. "We're going home," he told the group and did not miss the smiles of everyone watching them.

In the house, she didn't waste any time. She walked straight to the bedroom, and he followed her. He turned on the light for them, and she kissed him, tasting like sunshine and warmth. He would have pulled her closer, but she moved away, out of his reach. Her blue eyes sparkled, even in the dim light. "Are you ready?" she asked him.

He took a deep breath and nodded.

Daisy grasped the hem of her shirt and lifted it over her head, revealing smooth white skin and the silver glint of her belly button ring. She reached behind herself and unclasped her bra, letting it fall to his bedroom floor. Slowly, she unbuttoned her jeans and pushed them down, along with her panties.

She stood before him, naked and gorgeous, and for a second he felt a sting of self-doubt, before he pulled his own shirt off over his head. This was the awkward part, and he hated doing it, but Daisy looked nothing but ready for him. He sat down on the edge of the bed and unlaced his boots. He pulled them off and tossed them aside. Hesitating only for a moment, he unbuttoned his jeans and slid them down over his hips.

His cock was already hard from watching her undress for him; it lay heavily against his lower abdomen. He ignored it and pushed his jeans down over the black neoprene sleeve. Daisy watched silently as he disconnected the prosthetic and laid it carefully on the floor at the foot of the bed. He debated whether or not to stop there, but he was all in, he had to be. Stopping now would only insult her. She was here, and she wasn't running away.

He gripped the tight material and rolled it down, revealing the cotton comfort sock, which he also tugged away. Those he dropped on the floor. He knew he shouldn't, but he still felt a little scared sitting there naked, his stump revealed, ragged and ugly.

Daisy moved forward and knelt down on the floor in front of him. She placed her hands on his thighs. He watched as she leaned forward and kissed his leg, just above the amputation line. Her warm breath tickled his skin. She dragged her lips higher until they reached the base of his cock. He sucked in a sharp breath as she licked him. His hands twisted in the sheets on either side of him as he got the first blowjob he'd had in over three years.

She was slow and methodical, alternating between licking and kissing his shaft as she worked her way to the head. A drop of pre-cum had already beaded and she glanced up at him holding him with her gaze as she extended the tip of her tongue to catch it. She licked her lips as though he was the best thing she'd ever tasted, before she opened her mouth and drew him in.

He would have closed his eyes, but he was fascinated watching her. Her ripe, full bottom lip ran along the underside of his cock, and he groaned. She slid him in, nearly to the back of her throat, and then back out, making love to him with her mouth. As much as he loved it, if she didn't stop soon, that would be the only part he made love to.

His hands threaded through her hair and he moved her away. "Daisy," he rasped.

She rose to her feet and placed one knee on either side of him. With one hand on his chest, she pushed him down onto the bed. As she straddled him, she grasped his shaft and placed the head at her entrance. She took him into her by inches, so warm and wet.

Daisy rode him gently, placing his hands on her breasts and gazing down at him. He couldn't help but feel it was deliberate, the way she looked at him, watching him. She'd seen everything, and she still wanted him.

He felt his breath catch in his throat and he swallowed hard. "Daisy," was all he could manage to get out.

"Come here." She took hold of his arms and pulled him up until he was sitting. "Put your heart next to mine."

She held him tightly, her chest pressed to his. "You're mine," she whispered in his ear.

He held her tightly, as close as he could. "Always," he whispered in her ear.

CHAPTER THIRTY-EIGHT

Daisy woke in the morning light, naked and tangled up in Easy's sheets- their sheets, she supposed and smiled to herself. Her back was to him, and she felt his fingers tracing over her bare shoulder. She rolled over to face him. "Are you trying to decide where you want your mark on me?"

His gaze darkened, a look that always made her catch her breath. "Yes," he admitted.

She grinned at him. "You first."

"Done. Anything you want, anywhere you want it."

"Oh you better be careful saying something like that. I might take advantage."

He laughed. "Just don't put any daisies on my ass."

It was supposed to be funny, but she cupped his face with her hand. "Do you think I'd do anything to make you feel like less of a man?"

He hesitated then shook his head. "No."

She pulled him to her and kissed him. "I could though," she mused. "What about one that says Property of Daisy Cutter?"

He kissed her shoulder. "Daisy Turnbull."

She froze and looked at him. "Was that a proposal?"

"No," he told her. "Not yet. But I'm a forward thinking guy, and let's not do anything that'll have to be fixed later."

"Jimmy Turnbull! Is this... *optimism* I'm hearing from you?"

"Glass is half full," he murmured, while moving over her. "Speaking of being full..."

He thrust into her hard, burying himself inside her.

It wasn't really a fucking quite yet, she decided, just a claiming. He didn't move inside her, just held her and filled her up, as he'd said.

Daisy gasped and wrapped her legs around him. "Nice way to wake up."

"Hmmm."

"I know what I want," she told him.

"Tell me slowly." He swiveled his hips, grinding into her.

"I mean the tattoo," she said before she lost her train of thought.

"Less exciting," he replied, and the fucking began.

She dried her hair as he was putting on a shirt. He caught her gaze in the mirror and turned to her. "Really?" she asked, slightly irritated.

"What?"

"A stool? That's what you're so goddamn worried about? That's the reason we can't shower together?"

He blushed a little and looked away. "It's not sexy," he mumbled.

Daisy threw down the towel and put her hand on her hip. "What?! You're actually standing there and telling me that you don't remember the chair?"

Easy paused while reaching for his wallet on the top of the dresser. "Oh, God. The chair." He could actually feel his dick twitching in his pants.

"You forgot about the chair."

"Baby, I didn't forget. I was just... I..."

She shook her head and held up one hand. "Don't. Don't even."

"I'll make it up to you."

She paused and eyed him. "How?"

"I'll think of something."

She sighed and pulled a pair of shorts out of her backpack. "Fine. I'm going to Maria's to apologize and see if she'll hire me back."

"She will," Easy assured her.

"How do you know?"

"I already talked to her."

Daisy bit her lip and looked at him. "What... what did you say?"

"No one told her the truth. When I decided to get you back, I just said that you'd had some personal problems come up and asked her to give you another chance. She doesn't know."

Daisy sat down on the edge of the bed and picked at the sheets. "I should tell her."

"That's up to you."

"Is it always going to be like this?" she asked. "What if people find out? Do you want to be with-"

"I want to be with you. And I don't give a fuck what anyone else thinks. If things don't work out at Maria's for some reason, Abby will hire you. Or Shooter. We're getting enough business to get a receptionist."

"Really?"

He crossed the room and pulled her to her feet. "We're family, Daisy," he reminded her. "And we take care of each other."

She nodded. "Okay."

CHAPTER THIRTY-NINE

She pulled the door to the bar open and stepped inside. Milo spotted her first. "Thank God!" he cried. As Daisy crossed the nearly empty bar, he turned on his stool. "I need help," he told her. "I've got a date with Alma, and my hair's not right. And I don't know where to take her. And *she's* no help," he said, jerking his thumb at Maria.

"I'm not comfortable with the idea of him dating," Maria replied. "He's a horny teenager in an old man's body. The visuals are killing my appetite."

Daisy smiled. "We'll get your haircut," she told Milo. "And take her to a restaurant."

"Not this place," Maria warned. "I want nothing to do with this."

Daisy looked at Maria while Milo grumbled. "Can we talk?" she asked, shoving her hands into her pockets.

Maria nodded and headed into the office.

Daisy sat in the empty chair facing the desk and took a deep breath to steady herself. "I'm sorry I bailed on you."

"You're not the first."

"I guess Easy told you I had some... stuff going on."

"Guess he did."

"I didn't," Daisy said. "Have stuff. I *had* stuff. A while ago. And I thought it was behind me, but... " She shrugged. "Maybe it never will be."

Maria leaned against the desk. "Stuff like prostitution and resisting arrest."

Daisy tensed.

"I finally caught up on my paperwork," Maria told her. "Background checks and the like."

"I'm sorry," said Daisy. "I know what you think, and I don't blame you. I shouldn't have lied, but I needed a job, and I knew you wouldn't hire me if you knew."

"Well, nice to know that you know so much about me. Guess I don't need to do my own thinking then, since you're nice enough to do it for me."

Daisy blushed from embarrassment. "I-"

"Can I tell you what I think?" Maria asked. "Or are you just going to keep telling me what I think?"

Daisy, wisely, shut her mouth.

Maria got up from the desk and moved to the chair. She pulled open the bottom drawer of her desk and brought out a bottle of scotch and two glasses. She poured one for Daisy and one for herself. Daisy thought it was a little early in the day, but said nothing.

"When I was eighteen, I ran out of my mama's place like my hair was fire," she told Daisy. "No plan, no money, no God damn common sense, either. Thought I'd find me a motorcycle man. A fine ass man with a fine ass bike, and I'd be his old lady." She paused and took a sip of her drink. Daisy did the same and grimaced as it burned her throat on the way down.

"Well, I settled for two of the three. I ended up a house mouse for a one-percenter. On the good days, he smacked me around. On the bad days, he *passed* me around."

"God," Daisy whispered.

"But it was a place to stay," Maria explained. "So... I stayed. I don't know your story. You can tell me if you want to. But whatever you were before, you're a smart girl now. Got a plan, got a good man to stand up for you. I got a second chance; I'll give you one, too."

Daisy stayed to help Maria do inventory, until Easy and

everyone else showed up after work.

"Told you she'd hire you back," he told her.

She grinned at him. "I start tomorrow officially." She spotted the group taking over the largest table in the place and took a step toward them.

"Hang on," Easy told her, snagging her arm.

"What?" she asked.

He grinned at her. "Figured out a way to make it up to you." He took hold of her hand and pulled her in the opposite direction.

"Jimmy," she said quietly. "We're not going to the bathroom. I-"

"Nope. I would," he told her, eyes glittering. "But it's against Maria's rules."

"So what are-?"

He tugged her to the middle of the dance floor and stopped. "We can dance, though," he said. "She won't mind."

He pulled her close and put his arms around her waist. She leaned into him and sighed contentedly.

"I meant it, you know," she told him.

"What?"

"You're mine."

THE END

VEGAS

BURNOUT SERIES

DAHLIA WEST

A NOTE FROM THE AUTHOR

I want to thank all the people who contacted me to say they loved Tex. Don't worry, I won't name all of you. Your secret's safe with me, but I'm so glad you loved it! I wrote it for you. Well okay, I wrote it for *me*, technically, but I wrote it because I knew I wasn't alone. I knew if I existed, then you existed and we all needed more than we were getting.

Rest assured that I will be writing many, many more dark/BDSM erotica titles in the future. I know my upcoming projects are a little mainstream, but I haven't forgotten you. Just don't forget about me when I finally get around to releasing them!

CHAPTER ONE

"Alright, pet?"

Abby flexed her fingers. Her wrists were chained, arms over her head, naked, with her bare feet on the concrete floor. Alright was a relative term. Her heart was beating a staccato tattoo in her chest, she was nervous, but she was unharmed. Which was really what he was asking. She looked up at her boyfriend Mark and nodded. The ball gag in her mouth prevented her from giving more of an answer than that.

Mark was shirtless, his hard muscles rippling over his large frame. Abby was certain no man had ever looked this good, especially when he was being so bad. He stalked around behind her, the air between them practically crackled with electricity. When she was no longer able to see him, a crack of another kind tore through the air. The riding crop came down hard on her ass. Abby jumped and sucked in a sharp breath. The sting of the blow soon gave way to a spreading warmth and she closed her eyes. When she'd lived in Las Vegas, she'd been surrounded by hedonism, but never once been a part of it. If someone had told her before she moved to Rapid City, South Dakota, that she'd be the part-time pet of an ex-Army Ranger with a penchant for heavy spankings, she wouldn't have believed it. But here she stood, in the garage where Mark worked during the day building custom bikes, trucks, and cars.

Except now Burnout was more of a dungeon of pleasure and

pain, heavy on the pleasure part. Doing anything kinky outside the safe walls of the house they shared was always as nerve-wracking as it was exciting. Of course, Mark knew that. He'd lured her here by telling her that he'd left something in the office. The bastard. She'd give him a sassy look, if she could see him from where he was standing. It would earn her another stripe, a punishing one at that, but it might be worth it.

Right now was just the warm up, the steady swats of the crop stinging her ass and thighs as she struggled in the bindings. It was good, though. With Mark it always was. He seemed to want to remind her of that just then, and she felt the triangle shaped end of the implement slide slowly down her back and then slip between her legs. She moaned as he rubbed her pussy with it. Mark always knew to how give as much pleasure as pain and somehow always left her wanting more of both.

His lips were at her ear; his breath hot against her skin. "Little wet pet," he teased. He replaced the crop with his fingers, caressing her folds and dipping into her. Lost in her need to come, she pushed back against his hand. Mark chuckled, amused, and let her masturbate herself with his fingers for a moment. His fingertips grazed her clit, just enough to drive her crazy. Just as she was feeling satisfied with her own efforts, he pulled his hand away. She groaned again, this time in frustration. Mark knew, too, how to keep her on that knife edge of almost-orgasm. In fact, he called it 'edging' and he did it a lot. Mostly it irritated her, but that was the point, she supposed.

"I control your pleasure, pet," he reminded her softly.

Abby was disappointed, but not furious. Her orgasm would come... eventually. Mark never left her unsatisfied unless he was punishing her. She had to admit, her orgasms after an edging session were harder and longer than regular ones.

Mark brought the crop down again before moving in front of her, trailing it along behind him. It slid over her hip and across her taut belly, making her shiver. He looked down at her with a dark gaze that she'd learned to covet with every fiber of her being. That look that said he was about to play with her, and Mark's 'playtimes' were nearly transcendent. He skimmed the crop over her breasts and she took in a deep breath. She knew what was coming, but that didn't make it easier. He swiftly brought it down over one nipple. Abby yanked on the chains, trying to move away. She couldn't though. Mark hit her other breast, leaving two small red welts competing with her flushed areolas.

She was breathing heavily now and juice ran freely from her pussy, trickling down her thighs. Mark skillfully worked her breasts over until she almost come from that alone. She knew, with no small amount of satisfaction, that even though Mark could let her come that way, he wouldn't. He could never resist being inside her when she peaked. He could tell she was close now. After more than a year together he could play her body like an instrument he'd built himself, with careful patience and expert hands. He never seemed to lose control until he was fucking her; his desire for her overwhelming him just as it did her.

He tossed the crop onto the work bench beside them and unzipped his jeans. He freed the large bulge and Abby admired it now just as she had a thousand times previously. His thick cock jutted up and she knew it was only a seconds before he impaled her on it. He moved forward, his large hands spanning her hips on either side. Abby deftly wrapped her legs around him, locking her ankles together at his back.

Mark slid his hands behind her, holding her ass, which was buzzing from the earlier whipping. The sensation only added to the experience. He slid in slowly, letting her adjust to him. The anal plug she was wearing made her pussy tighter and it ached when he filled her. She whimpered and he gripped her tighter.

"I know, pet," he whispered hoarsely as he fucked her. "I know what you need."

Mark needed it too and he was taking her maddeningly slowly. She felt every inch of him spreading her wide. She squeezed him tightly, like a good little pet should, and he groaned. "Come with me, pet," he ordered. "Come for me." He withdrew almost completely before slamming back in. Abby's pussy grasped and clenched, trying to keep him inside. She was so desperate to follow his order that she bounced hard against him, trying frantically to get pressure on her clit. Mark slid out again, pressed the head of his cock against her swollen nub, and rubbed it hard on his way back into her.

Abby felt the wave of orgasm rising up from her lower belly. She tightened her legs around him. "Oh, good girl," he said. "Cream for me." She screamed behind the ball gag as her pussy flooded, coating them both. Mark held her close as he came seconds after, jets of hot semen filling her as his cock pulsed inside her, stretching her impossibly more. "My fucking good girl, coming for her Owner," he whispered in her ear.

Abby pulled her jeans back on, wincing a bit as the fabric hit her reddened ass. Mark caught the look. He never missed anything.

"Did I go too hard on you?" he asked.

She shook her head. "No," she said honestly. She'd feel it all the way home, but that, she'd discovered, was never a bad thing.

Not satisfied, Mark pulled the t-shirt down over his head and stalked over to her. He pulled her jeans back down over her hips and gazed at her bare ass. She blushed then. In the harsh light of day (though it was technically night now) the things they did seemed slightly embarrassing. Or maybe she was just embarrassed to admit she liked it so much. She had a pretty high threshold for pain and if she told Mark it wasn't bad, it was the truth. Possibly he even believed her, but he still never failed to mentally catalogue all her bruises and welts, checking for significant damage. When he was finished, he pulled her jeans back up for her.

"I'll give you a bath when we get home," he told her, picking up the crop from the bench.

Abby loved that part just as much as the sex. She suspected Mark enjoyed it, too. He'd wash her hair and then rub lotion over her welts to soothe them. He might have even made her dessert. She smiled at the prospect. She couldn't have imagined that being 'owned' by a man would ever be something she'd want, but she couldn't deny the way it made her feel: loved and cared for. And wasn't that what everyone wanted?

Mark bent slightly to kiss her. As his lips brushed softly over hers, his hands skillfully removed the leather collar at her throat. She felt a strange sense of loss when the cool air hit her neck. She wore it nearly all the time now when they were alone. It had become part of her afternoon routine. Come home, ditch the work clothes and put on the collar. She reached for her shirt draped over the workbench, but froze at the sound of tires crunching the gravel outside.

"Oh, God!" she hissed, snatching at her clothes.

Mark chuckled. "Relax," he told her. "It's just a customer dropping off their ride so we can get to it in first thing in the morning.

Abby tugged her shirt down over her head and held her breath as the key drop box opened on the other side of the cement wall. It was ridiculous. No one could see in unless they came around to the side door and looked through the small rectangle of glass. Still, she swallowed hard and pressed her shirt tightly against herself. Mark appeared behind her, running his hands down her arms. "You're going to have to get over this," he told her.

Abby shook her head. "What if they saw?"

"What if they did?" She turned to gape at him. Before she could argue, he said, "What would they see?"

"Us!"

"I don't think it's me you're worried about."

She blushed and looked away. Mark took hold of her chin and drew her gaze back to his. "You're beautiful, Abby. I tell you every day."

She made a face but didn't say anything. She might be pretty, she'd give him that much, but she had a few more pounds on her than other women; less Kate Moss and more Marilyn Monroe. Mark liked it, loved it in fact, but his acceptance of her had not been her usual experience with men.

"I would never lie to you, Abby. And I'm getting tired of you basically accusing me of it."

"I'm not!" she protested.

"And if I asked you to wear that little red dress to Maria's Friday night?"

She bit her lip.

"Thought so."

"Mark-" she began, but he put his hand up to stop her.

"It's fine," he told her calmly. Then she saw his eyes glitter even in the dim light of the garage bay and she sucked in her breath. "I guess we know what the next part of your training will be."

She dutifully stepped outside as he held the door for her, waiting while he locked it behind them. She had no idea what kind of training Mark had in mind, but she knew it wouldn't be easy. None of his training had ever been easy; but Mark had molded her into the perfect submissive, well, *his* perfect submissive anyway. And in exchange she'd gotten the perfect boyfriend, one who cared for her and cared *about* her. Even just having someone ask her how her day was had been a new and unusual experience. One she found she liked along with the gourmet dinners, over-the-knee spankings, and bike rides to the Badlands at night when the stars were out and the summer breeze felt like Heaven.

Mark slid onto the Harley and she climbed on behind him. She'd given up her own bike for the chance to ride his and smiled to herself yet again as she slid her arms around him. As she held on she thought about *holding on* -to him- and decided that it was about time she did.

CHAPTER TWO

Abby threaded through mid-morning traffic. Instead of turning into the parking garage of the Custer, she sailed past and out of town. Past the outskirts of the city, she drove past rolling fields and the Black Hills forest off into the distance. She wound her Camaro up a steep hill until she reached the last house at the end of the secluded lane. She got out and strode toward the log cabin's front porch. She climbed the steps and entered the front door without knocking. She would have called out, but she didn't want to risk disturbing the baby if she were napping. She turned the corner of the living room and found Sarah at the kitchen table, laptop open, and baby Hope asleep in a bassinet beside her. "Hey," she whispered. Sarah smiled at her. Abby gave Hope's single lock of brown hair a slight tousle as she passed by and slid into a seat next to her friend. "School stuff?" she asked, nodded at the computer.

"Yeah," Sarah said, rolling her eyes. "Online classes are good, but I forgot what college was like."

Abby smirked. "It's a pain the ass, if I remember."

Sarah groaned. "I've got an exam on Monday that I'll have to drive to school for."

"Is Tildy watching Hope then?"

Sarah nodded and blew out a harsh breath. Her sable hair fluttered out of her eyes. "Are you sure you want to hire me?"

Abby laughed. "Too late. The ink's dry. I own your soul."

Hope stirred beside them and opened her eyes. She smiled at Abby and giggled at the two woman. Sarah reached for her but Abby swooped in. "I've got her," she said. She scooped the girl into her arms and settled her on her lap. Hope snatched a handful of Abby's red hair and tugged.

"Hope! Sarah scolded.

Abby laughed. "It doesn't hurt," she assured her as she grinned at Hope and bounced her.

Between growing up in a Las Vegas hotel, working full time since she was a teenager and graduating college early, Abby hadn't spent that much time with children, or any time at all really. She knew she liked them, had a vague feeling of warmth and comfort when she held Hope, but until she'd met Mark having kids had seemed like a nebulous, ill-formed plan that seemed like it might be a good idea, but without someone to share parenthood with, it was an idea that had remained mostly at the back of her mind.

Holding the baby now, she knew she was at least on the path to domestic bliss. Abby had a lot to learn about parenting, but Mark would make a great father. In a few years when the hotel was running at optimal capacity and the restaurant she and Sarah were starting was humming along, Abby thought she might be able to find a whipsmart Assistant manager to help her with her workload. Abby didn't know how babies fit in around play collars and bondage ropes, but she'd never felt more confident that she and Mark could make it work. Mark had told her that he only demanded obedience in the bedroom, which had turned out to be more of a general philosophy than an actual statement of facts.

In truth Mark demanded her obedience in the bedroom, the bathroom, the living room, the kitchen, and once or twice on the weight bench in his 'torture chamber'. What he'd meant was: her finances remained under her control, her hobbies were her own, and her career was all hers. In a few years when they started having kids, they'd have to actually restrict their playtime to the bedroom. Abby remembered fondly being strapped to Mark's weight bench and vowed they'd have to work that in at least a few dozen more times before that room became a nursery.

"But executive chef..." Sarah interrupted.

"Is totally within your ability. Anyway, I'll handle the numbers, you just build me a fabulous menu that'll make us the best restaurant in town."

"You promise there's a light at the end of this tunnel?"

"Only if you promise desserts to die for. This is the hard part," she said, gesturing to the computer. "The rest will be easy. Promise. And gee," she said with a grin, "if only you had a great boss who would let you do most of that from home."

"I love you."

"Well, good because I need a favor."

Sarah looked up from the laptop. "What?"

"I need something catered. Something special for Mark's birthday. I booked the ballroom, just the two of us."

Sarah brightened. "I can totally do that!"

Abby nodded. "I need a kickass ribeye," she told Sarah, because it was Mark's favorite. "And some sinfully decadent dessert," she looked at Sarah with a sly grin, "that maybe we want to take back to the room with us."

Sarah's face flushed deep red, likely remembering the time she and Chris had taken their own dessert to the bedroom. On an alcohol soaked girl's night out long ago Sarah had told them all about it, mortified the next day that she'd revealed so much. Abby laughed as she watched her friend turned red from embarrassment.

"I'm never drinking again," Sarah grumbled.

Abby passed up the Custer for the second time that day. This time she turned the corner and parallel parked four blocks away on a tree-lined avenue. She straightened her blazer, tugged at the collar of her silk blouse, and ducked under the awning of a jewelry store that Daisy had told her about a few weeks ago. She pressed the buzzer and waited for the store's receptionist to visually assess her. A longer buzz sounded in reply and she grasped the handle of the door and pulled. She stepped into the air-conditioning store as the heavy security door. The receptionist smiled and greeted her warmly. Abby returned the nod.

"May I help you?" asked another, older woman as she moved

away from the front desk and out to meet Abby. Her shrewd eyes took in Abby's pressed linen suit and Jimmy Choos. Abby swore the woman almost nodded appreciatively. As she got even closer, the woman's eyes sparkled as she caught sight of Abby's vintage necklace. The snakeskin chain was gold, a small jeweled flower made of rubies and diamonds sat nestled in the hollow of Abby's throat.

"On, my! What a beautiful piece!" she said, indicating the necklace.

Abby absentmindedly touch the metal that had been warmed by her skin. "Thank you," she replied. "It was a gift. And I'd like to get something in return for him."

The saleswoman nodded and swept her arm toward a glass display case behind her. "Of course. What did you have in mind, dear? Perhaps cuff links or a watch. We have some beautiful Piagets or-"

Abby smiled as she tried to picture Mark wearing cuff links or a designer watch. The man had good taste when he shopped for her, but he kept his own appearance low-key. She shook her head. "Oh, no," she told the woman. "I need something more personal."

"Personal? An engraved-"

"Wedding band," Abby finished. "A man's wedding band. And yes, I'll need it engraved."

The woman's eyes flitted to Abby's left hand and she frowned. She was probably attempting to gauge Abby's budget based on her engagement ring, but she came up befuddled after realizing Abby wasn't wearing one.

"That's next on the list," Abby assured her.

The woman pressed her lips together obviously hiding a frown. Abby got the impression that she didn't quite know what to make of a woman who put the cart before the horse, so-to-speak. Perhaps she thought the younger generation had no understanding of the proper order of things. Whatever the saleswoman thought, the hint that Abby would at some point be needing a second ring to accompany the first appeared to be all the encouragement she needed to try and close the sale.

"A wedding ring," she declared. "Yes." She led Abby to a different display case. "And if I may inquire, when is the happy occasion?" She was no doubt wondering if both commissions could be collected anytime soon.

"I don't know," Abby said peering into the case. "He hasn't said yes yet."

The woman's eyes few wide as she stared at Abby. "Right. And…" She seemed to be searching for just the right response. She settled on, "Budget?" She winced as though asking the question so directly was painful to her, but given that conversation up to this point had so completely derailed the woman, Abby didn't blame her.

"No budget," she replied. "But it has to be perfect."

"Oh, absolutely!" she agreed, enthusiastically now that she found herself on more familiar ground and with a fat commission looming large. "Diamonds?" she suggested. "Channel set?"

Abby shook her head. Mark wouldn't care for stones. "No," she said. "Nothing flashy."

The salesclerk's hopes appeared to be a little dashed as the corners of her mouth slid down, but she soldiered on. "What kind of man is he? Refined, elegant?" she asked no doubt looking at Abby and trying to guess who a woman in a pressed linen suit would be dating.

"Ex-military," Abby told her. "He's a mechanic now."

Abby suppressed a grin as she watched the woman desperately trying to sort out the puzzle that was Mark and Abby's relationship.

Keep trying, lady, Abby thought. *I've been trying for months and I don't have it all figured out yet.* Abby may not have had their relationship completely figured out, but she knew she wanted it forever. Her eyes settled on a band on the top shelf of the glass case. "I'd like to see that one."

The woman unlocked the case, slid the glass to the side, and plucked out the dark gray box housing the gold ring. She handed it over and Abby took it out of the box and held it in fingers. It was polished gold on the inside but the outside was hammered. As she twirled it in her fingers, she realized that it reminded her of Mark, polished and shiny but with so many angles that you never knew which direction he'd head next. It looked rough but smooth, beautiful but masculine, everything Mark was when she thought about him.

"It's a treasure," said the saleswoman as Abby rubbed the pad of her finger along the outside. Abby assumed that meant it was designer and expensive, neither of which mattered to her.

"I'll take it," she nearly whispered. When she looked up the woman was smiling at her. "And I'll need it engraved," Abby reminded her.

The woman reached for a small pad and pen. "And the inscription?"

"Love, Honor, Obey."

The woman's smile widened. "Well," she said. "It's so nice to see young people with such traditional values."

CHAPTER THREE

Abby sat at her desk going over expense reports when there was a knock on her office door.

"It's open," she called.

Susan, one of The Custer's full-time front desk receptionists, stepped in with a flat, cardboard box tucked under her arm. "Delivery," Susan told her. "Addressed to you."

The brunette looked puzzled. Abby understood why. She never received personal correspondence at work. This break from the norm had the woman's interest piqued.

"Thanks, Susan," Abby replied, standing to take it from her.

"Is it for your private party? Because Lucas says the champagne you specially ordered will be on tomorrow's delivery truck." She handed Abby a yellow post-it note confirming the message from The Custer's head bartender. This no doubt confused Susan further because The Custer already offered champagne service to its more distinguished guests. Though not too long ago, before Abby had… bought… the historic hotel, "champagne service" had meant something far different.

Abby was certain that the slightly older woman didn't suspect her of any particularly shady business dealings, but Susan was always keenly aware of anything out of the ordinary. Just to dispel any concerns, and because she was so excited, Abby picked up the silver letter opener on her desk and laid the package down. She slit the tape and opened it.

Several yards of lace tumbled from the box as Abby gently lifted it out. Susan gasped. "Venetian lace," Abby told her. "It's a tablecloth. And, yes, it's for the party I booked in the ballroom."

It was beautiful, more intricate and exquisite than it had even appeared in the catalog she'd ordered it from.

"It's gorgeous!" Susan proclaimed. "God, you must be celebrating something really important."

Abby simply nodded. She wanted their dinner to be perfect. She normally didn't splurge on big-ticket items, especially not Venetian lace tablecloths, but afterward she could use it at the house for a formal place setting in their own dining room if they ever needed it. It was really just one more small way she'd transform Mark's home into *their* home. So far Mark had been one hundred percent supportive of Abby adding her own personal touch to the place. She'd picked a few pieces of furniture and had hung several of her favorite photos of the Nevada desert. She carefully folded the fabric and gently placed it back in the box. As she was re-placing the lid, the phone began to ring. Susan excused herself as Abby rounded the corner of her desk and picked up the receiver.

"Hello?"

"Pet."

Abby's pussy instinctively contracted as if begging for the smooth, beautiful cock that belonged to that smooth, beautiful voice.

"Sir," she whispered, already breathless. She was keenly aware of the plug in her ass as she waited. Mark only called her 'pet' during playtime and in the ensuing months since they'd started dating, as if that was even the right word, just hearing it on his lips meant dark and fascinating things were going to happen. The man had more tricks up his sleeve than Houdini. All of them were sexual and nearly all of them ended with Abby having an earth-shattering orgasm. Then again, sometimes the orgasm was the foreplay.

"We have plans tonight," he informed her.

Abby licked her lips nervously. Sometimes the plan for Friday night was simply hanging out at Maria's. Sometimes, however, Tex wanted to stay home and play. She could guess which he had in mind.

"And tomorrow," he said surprising her. "So pack an overnight bag."

Abby listened as he told her to go home and shower and put on a pair of jeans and a t-shirt. "Be comfortable," he said.

She sighed in relief. She didn't know what Mark had in mind, but if he wanted her comfortable then that was a good sign. It meant nothing too scary or nerve wracking.

"You don't have to pack your play collar," he said, surprising her yet again as well as disappointing her a bit too, honestly. "But pet?"

There was silence over the line as he waited… patiently… always patiently, sometimes maddeningly so.

"Yes, Sir?"

"Don't forget the red dress."

Abby's stomach knotted. She swallowed hard. "Yes, Sir."

"I'll be home on time."

She replaced the receiver and took ten deep breaths, in through the nose and out through the mouth, just the way he'd taught her to do when she was on the verge of being overwhelmed. She didn't need him to tell her that she was in for another intense training weekend. The first one had nearly ended their relationship just as it was getting started, but they were both comfortable and more familiar with each other now. Mark would push her, always, but not too far.

Abby arrived home on time as well. She laid her purse on the hallway table and made her way into the bedroom where she slipped out of her business suit. Naked, she headed to the bathroom door down the hall. Before she'd met Mark, Abby would never have wandered nude outside the bathroom of her own apartment, even when she was alone. She'd never been all that comfortable with nudity, which was one the first things Mark observed about her and set about changing.

When Abby had her play collar on she was nude at all times, unless Mark had some special lingerie picked out for her. The fact that he usually kept his own clothes on until they were ready for sex constantly reinforced their respective roles. It had taken a while for her to get comfortable with it as she'd always been curvier than she would have liked, however, Mark's constant interest in her went a long way to dispel most of the doubt that had overshadowed her. She had no problem disrobing at his request, but this compliance had never been tested outside their home. Which was not to say that Abby and Mark never played away from home. They did, often. She'd lost count of the number of blow jobs she'd given him in darkened store parking lots or the times he'd fingered her to orgasm while they were at the movies, but none of that had involved actual nudity. Abby wasn't certain what this weekend would bring, but she knew Mark was growing tired of Abby's poor body image and lack of self-esteem.

She fought back the urge to speculate and instead simply focused on getting ready for their weekend. She let the water heat up in the shower as she laid out her bathroom essentials. In addition to Mark's rules concerning her behavior, Abby also had a grooming regiment. Any time she was home she needed to be ready for play, even though they didn't have sessions every night. Abby needed to keep her pussy smooth, along with her legs. She had a standing wax appointment, but occasionally Mark shaved her himself. He told her it deepened their bond and Abby could see that it did. It took a lot of faith to expose your most sensitive areas to someone with a sharp object. At first she'd been overwhelmed at having him do that to her, but now she preferred it.

Mark took his time, gingerly stretching and manipulating her folds. His hard thumb protecting her clit always drove her crazy. Looking back, Abby nearly laughed at how unimportant being shaved by a man was, compared to the other things he could, and would, do to her. She laid out her self-enema kit and decided that, yes, there were other, more difficult things to overcome. As part of his ownership of her, he demanded use of all her holes at a moment's notice. Abby soon realized it was just part of Mark's psychological makeup. No part of her was denied to him and therefore he possessed her completely.

She cleaned herself thoroughly, outside as well as in, and stepped out of the shower to towel off. Before slipping on a clean pair of lace panties, she thoroughly washed and lubed her stainless steel plug in the sink and re-inserted it. She'd grown accustomed to wearing it several times a week and now had no trouble with it. It was not the largest of the set that Mark had bought solely for her, but Abby had no fear that he would ever use that one on her. Mark liked her tight and responsive, the plug she wore almost daily was purely for her benefit so that penetration wouldn't hurt her.

She had just stepped into her panties and was pulling them up over her hips when the bathroom door opened. Mark stepped in and assessed her shrewdly. Without a word he crossed the room and drew her to him. Her back was to him and her damp hair pressed against his shirt. He took hold of her hip with one hand and dipped his other hand into her panties. Abby leaned against him and closed her eyes. His fingers swept over her tingling skin and her heartbeat quickened, but only from arousal. Mark knew she was a good girl. She always kept herself bare. He would find nothing displeasing down there. She had a feeling he knew, too. He just liked touching her. He slid his hand around the back and felt for the plug. Abby gasped as he tugged on it.

"Good girl," he said quietly as he nuzzled her ear.

He took hold of both her breasts and squeezed gently, his fingers plucking her nipples into hard points. "I want these pierced, Abby."

He used her name deliberately. It wasn't an order. It was just a statement of what he desired. Her body was ultimately her own, he'd told her. Any permanent modifications were up to her.

It wasn't the first time they'd discussed it. She'd been researching it for a few weeks and rolling the idea around in her mind. Now that she'd had a few weeks to mull it over, she was comfortable with the idea. "Okay."

Mark paused. "Yeah?"

She nodded and met his eyes in the mirror. "But not the clit," she said. "It's too risky." Abby was willing to take a chance with her nipples. She thought the jewelry options were beautiful and strangely erotic, but there was a risk of losing sensation and she refused to take the chance that she might lose her ability to orgasm as exquisitely as she could and often did with Mark.

He smiled at her. "Fair enough. Thank you."

He released her after a hug and stripped down out of his work clothes. Abby leaned against the counter to watch. Mark was gorgeous with sandy blonde hair and piercing blue eyes. His body was chiseled and hard, the US Special Forces tattoo on his forearm standing out against his bronzed skin. Abby sucked her bottom lip into her mouth and chewed on it as he lowered his briefs. She caught sight of the curve of his ass and let out a sigh.

He smirked at her over his shoulder. "Down girl," he ordered and she laughed. "You'll get an eyeful soon enough," he told her. "Now go pack while I shower."

"Where are we going?"

He lifted an eyebrow at her.

Abby raised her hands in a warding off gesture. "I'm not asking what we're doing," she clarified. "I'm just asking where we're doing it. For strategic packing purposes."

"We're driving to Sioux Falls and spending the night at the Blakemore."

"Ooh, swanky."

Mark shrugged and opened the shower door. "Yeah, but we won't be in the hotel much," he said cryptically.

Abby tamped down on her desire to ask why. She didn't want to spend the whole four hour drive to Sioux Falls sitting on a red ass. She left the bathroom and headed toward the bedroom wondering what there was to do in Sioux Falls, anyway.

CHAPTER FOUR

They checked into the hotel and headed up to their room. Abby grinned at the large Jacuzzi that took up most of their bathroom. She looked at Mark, but he shook his head. She pouted. "I didn't pick the hotel for the Jacuzzi, pet," he informed her. "We might get in it later, but we have more interesting things to do tonight." She watched as he unzipped their garment bag and he took out the red dress. She tried to hide her scowl. The dress was tight. It clung to her hips and Abby thought it made her ass look too big. It didn't help that her cleavage was on display, either. If she bent over in it, something would pop out, most likely on both ends. Mark loved the dress though and she knew there was no getting out of wearing it.

As she took it from him and laid it across the bed, she wondered for perhaps the tenth time where they were going. Before they had met, Mark had often visited a fetish club here in South Dakota's largest city. Abby was equally curious and terrified at the imagined goings on at a place like that. Mark had assured her early on in their relationship that the club wasn't really a place for a sub like Abby. She was likely to be too distracted, too nervous, and it would be a disaster for both of them. She wouldn't be able to concentrate on his instructions in a place like that and he'd be obligated to punish her. Abby had been secretly glad he had no plans to take her there, though where they were going tonight was anyone's guess.

She fastened the straps to her black high heels and looked at herself in the mirror. She tugged at her hair, strategically placing it over bare cleavage. Mark came up behind her and swept it all back over her shoulders, giving her a pointed look. She opened her mouth to argue, but closed it again after looking at his expression. This was a training weekend and he expected her to obey, even without the collar. He took her hand and led her out of the relative safety of the hotel room and out into a darkened city she'd never visited before. Once in the Hummer, he drove them through downtown, past the small financial district and into an area with alternating late night bars that were open and industrial buildings that were closed. He parked in a parking lot that was filled with other cars, but Abby could find no sign on the door of the building.

Mark opened her door for her, took her by the hand, and led her away from the street and toward the darkened building. Her heels clicked sharply on the blacktop as she kept pace with him.

"What is this place?" she asked him, glancing around nervously. They were more than half a block from the busier commercial street with outdoor patios filled with people drinking microbrews.

Mark didn't answer her as they approached a very large man, larger than Mark himself, wearing jeans and a black button down shirt. Clearly he was a bouncer, though to what kind of club Abby couldn't tell. There were only two doors behind him, both of them were solid steel, and there were no windows all along the length of place.

Mark pulled out his wallet and paid the man. Abby waited to see if there would be a secret handshake as well. The man's gaze turned from Mark to herself and she felt herself shrink just a bit as he looked her over. Her cheeks pinkened and stung. She glanced at Mark to see what he had to say about this man so obviously leering at her. Surely Mark would step in and punch him in the throat or something, but Mark remained silent as Abby was inspected like meat on a rack. She shivered as though she were really in an industrial refrigerator.

"Watching or playing?" the man finally asked as he grinned at her. Abby started at his question, not understanding what he was asking. She glanced again to Mark.

"Watching," Mark informed him.

The man frowned deeply. Apparently this was the wrong answer.

Apparently there was a password, not a secret handshake, and Mark had obviously gotten it wrong. After a moment the man stepped aside, swiping a card into a reader to the left of the door before jerking it open.

"That's a damn shame," he said as Mark ushered Abby inside. "Just a damn shame. I get off in twenty. Woulda been nice to get off in *her*."

Abby's eyes darted back to him, shocked. She gasped, but Mark continued to push her inside. When the door closed behind them firmly, she turned back to face the direction she was being led. Along the right hand side was a series of doors. These weren't steel; they were solid wood with no peepholes or windows. Above each one was a single light fixture. The lights above some doors were lit while others were dark. Mark stopped at an unlit door and turned the knob. With one hand on her back, he guided her inside and closed it behind them. Abby trembled a bit as her eyes adjusted to the darkened room. There were two large upholstered chairs facing a large window. As she stepped closer she realized it wasn't a window, but one-way glass. She stopped short as she stared at the scene in front of her. Beyond the tinted glass was a large room. It was carpeted, with heavy drapes cordoning off small private areas on either side. A bar was tucked into the corner, gleaming lights reflected off the glass liquor shelves providing quite a bit of light compared to the rest of the mood-lit room.

Several couples were occupying every seat, couch, and otherwise flat surface made available to them. Some were fully dressed and seated at tables, laughing and flirting with small groups of people. Others had apparently moved on from social interaction and were now in various stages of sexual play. A small brunette in a short skirt sat on an older man's lap. Her legs were spread and Abby could see that she'd forgone underwear for the occasion. She had the man's trousers unzipped and was sensuously giving him a handjob while he dipped his hands down the front of her dress.

On a nearby couch, another man was fingering a similarly disrobed woman. She was slightly older than Abby while the man was about the same age. One of her legs was slung over his to give him better access. Her silver high heels sparkled even in the dimmed light, but it was not so dark that it wasn't easy to see what others were doing. Even though Abby herself had never been to a place like this, she assumed being able to see and be seen was part of the point.

She pressed her lips together as she moved in between the two chairs and got closer to the glass. "Have..." she began, clearing her throat nervously. "Have you been here before?"

"No," Mark said from behind her. "I've heard about it, but I never had a lot of interest. Or anyone worth bringing." His large hand slid across her hip and down over her ass.

"I can't believe people do this," she whispered.

Mark pressed his lips to her bare shoulder. "Yes, you can."

As Abby watched the various combinations of couples pleasuring each other, it seemed to her that not only did people do this, but also they clearly really enjoyed it. The showpiece was a very large, round ottoman that sat directly in the center of the room. It was dove grey with several square black pillows tossed onto it. Only a few people were using the pillows. In the middle was a blonde, young and lithe, with shoulder length hair. If Abby had to guess, she'd say they were the same age, which baffled Abby because, despite all the things she and Mark had done together since they'd met, she couldn't imagine having the courage to perform the way this woman was doing. And performance seemed to be exactly the right word. The blonde appeared to know very well that she was the center of attention and was enjoying every minute of it. A dark haired, well-toned man was between her legs, licking her slit intently and Abby wondered how the woman could concentrate on the blow job she was giving to a second man who was kneeling beside her.

The blonde didn't miss a beat though, opening her ruby red lips and sliding the man's cock into her mouth. Abby was impressed when the woman managed to take in the full length of him. Mark wanted her to learn to do that and they were slowly working up to it. So far he hadn't seemed to mind that Abby hadn't yet mastered the skill the way this woman had. The blonde lifted her hips, pressing her pussy directly into the face of the man servicing *her*. It was then that Abby knew this woman wasn't just a piece of meat, not just a vapid three holes for horny men of all ages to masturbate into. This woman was clearly directing the show and she had obviously decided that she was going to get as much pleasure as she gave.

As she watched, Abby could feel the heat from Mark's body behind hers. His fingertips skimmed along her bare arms and down to her hips. She gasped as she felt the tug of the hem of her dress. "Which one do you like?" he whispered in her ear.

The room felt hot and Abby felt a little dizzy. She reached out to steady herself against the glass with one hand as one of Tex's hands disappeared up her dress. She swallowed hard. "The blonde," she replied, wetting her dry lips.

"She loves it," said Mark, sliding his hand between her thighs. Abby's legs instinctively parted for him. His fingers found her clit and rubbed gently. She felt her nipples harden in response. "All these people watching her," Mark continued quietly. "She knows she's a star. She can't get enough."

His strong fingers penetrated her, first one and then another. He pushed in and out of her rhythmically, at the same pace as the largest of the men fucking the blonde on the bed. Slow but relentless, pressure building steadily.

"I want you, pet," Mark informed her. She heard his zipper sliding down. She waited with razor sharp anticipation as she felt him pull his fingers out of her dripping slit. She felt a tug on the large silver plug at her rear entrance and gasped as he pulled it from her. As soon as it was out, she felt Mark's slippery fingers coating her puckered entrance. He spread her cheeks wide and she felt the familiar pressure of his cock, just barely softer and more forgiving than the hard steel which had been in her moments ago. As his cockhead breached her, she pushed out the way she was supposed to, opening herself up for him. Once he was fully seated inside her, his hand returned to the front of her, sliding into her wet folds again.

Abby moaned at the feeling of being penetrated by both his cock and his fingers.

"Think this is close to what she feels, pet? Being taken in both holes?"

She whimpered a bit at his words and the suggestion that she feared might be behind them.

"Pet," he admonished softly. "You think I'd ever let another man fuck what's mine? You still love this, though." His fingers sank deeper and she gripped his arms for support. Mark's mouth found her ear again. "You're more beautiful," he told her. "No one would even glance at her if they had you to look at."

Abby felt her heart pounding and somehow she knew that while Mark would never share her with another man, being watched was what he expected of her.

"Tomorrow night, pet," he promised as if he read her thoughts. "Tomorrow night it's you on the ottoman with me inside you and everyone wishing they could have a turn."

CHAPTER FIVE

Abby stirred when she heard the click of the hotel room door. She opened her eyes and glanced at the clock on the nightstand. It was nearly 10:30 in the morning. Mark had let her sleep gloriously late and she was grateful. She stretched, sitting up as she tugged the bathrobe tighter around herself. A bellhop entered the room pushing a room service cart. Mark was close behind him. "I would've let you sleep longer," he told her as the man positioned the cart by the small, round table in the corner. "But you have a busy day and you don't want to be late."

The bellhop thanked Mark for the tip and shuffled out of the room. Abby raised a hand to smooth out her hair. She wondered what she looked like to the other man. Like a woman who'd had anal sex in a swingers' club the night before? Very enjoyable anal sex? Abby accepted that deep down she was that kind of girl, but did she *look* like it?

She crossed the room to the table and sat down in one of the chairs. Tucking her leg underneath her, she reached for the plate Mark handed her.

"Busy day?" she asked.

Mark nodded. As they ate, he reached for a folder on the desk beside him. Abby craned her neck to see what it was. All she could make out was "Spa" embossed on the front. She let out a little squeal of happiness. "Are we getting a couple's massage?" she asked. "You know that doesn't have a happy ending in a place like this, right?"

He laughed and shook his head. "*I'm* not getting anything," he told her. "*You* are getting a day package."

Abby flipped open the folder and read the details of her reservation: massage, mineral sea salt body scrub, and a facial. It sounded like heaven, but Mark wouldn't want any part of that. She glanced up at him. "So we're on a mini-vacation, but we aren't spending it together?" She tried to hide the depth of her disappointment so as not to seem ungrateful.

"Believe me," he said, pouring himself a cup of coffee, "we'll be together tonight."

Abby pressed her lips together firmly. She hadn't exactly forgotten about tonight, but she had been trying to put it out of her mind.

"You're too nervous, pet. Always worried who will see and what they'll think. You're so worried you can barely come half the time. Since you can't seem to let go and enjoy yourself on your own, I'll make you."

Abby took a steadying breath and picked at her scrambled eggs. This was what she'd signed on for. Mark had never lied to her about how difficult it would be to submit to him, but each time she'd let herself go and allowed him to lead her, her mind and her body soared to heights she'd never even considered out of reach because she hadn't known they existed in the first place.

Mark was worth pain, humiliation, and degradation, though it was never like that. The goal tonight was clear: to enjoy herself. She just had to trust Mark that she could. "Yes, Sir."

The masseuse he'd booked was female. No surprise there. True to his word, Mark had never allowed another man's hands on her, which was just how Abby preferred it. Under the woman's expert hands, Abby felt the knots in her shoulders melt away. Not all her tension was bound up in the idea of Mark putting her on display; some of it was just plain work-related stress. Abby loved her historic hotel, but running it was no simple task. The Custer, like an engine, had a thousand and one moving parts and Abby oversaw the performance of every single one of them. She wasn't one to whine or complain about her workload, but leave it to Mark to see beyond her strong façade to the stretched-thin woman underneath. She closed her eyes and imagined his hands on her, his tongue, his piercing gaze.

What would he do to her tonight? And how much would she like it?

After her facial she wasn't surprised to find out Mark had not only paid for the service, but had also covered the tip. She was, however, surprised when she turned to head toward the elevators and back to her room only to be told she had another "appointment." Abby flushed a bit as she thought about her smooth pussy. She didn't need another wax right now. The attendant took her to the hotel's salon, but instead of a private room, Abby was directed to one of the chairs. It appeared as though Mark had also booked her a wash and a styling. She didn't need to wonder why.

A well-groomed pet is a beautiful pet.

She was finally finished at a little past five in the afternoon. As she walked past the row of mirrors leading toward the bank of elevators, Abby had to admit that the stylist hadn't done half-bad. Her red, wavy locks shined as they cascaded over her shoulders and down her back. She wasn't always certain if what Mark saw when he looked at her and what she saw in the mirror were the same thing, but tonight she thought perhaps she was inching a bit closer.

The elevator doors slid open and she stepped inside. As they closed, Abby caught one last glimpse of herself and thought that maybe she wasn't all the way there, but she could maybe pretend that she was - for tonight anyway.

Back in the suite, Mark had ordered dinner for them. Abby feigned disinterest in the large white box on the bed. "After dinner, pet," Mark admonished when he caught her glancing at it.

Abby clicked her tongue nervously. "Is it see-through?" she asked, wrinkling her nose.

Instead of punishing her curiosity, Mark laughed. "God, no.

Sexy, pet. Not slutty."

Abby relaxed a bit more, but only picked at her chicken breast.

"You can't skip a meal," he told her.

"I know," she sighed. "But I'm nervous." In truth she was more than nervous. As the clocked ticked away toward nightfall, Abby's body felt like a live wire.

Mark wiped his mouth with his napkin and stood up, moving toward her. "Stand up," he ordered.

Abby surged to her feet. He unbuttoned her jeans and slid is hand into her panties. His fingers brushed past her clit, making her gasp. He parted her and pushed in a finger. With his free hand he pressed her head to his chest and stroke her hair in rhythm with the hand that was stroking her pussy. "I know you're nervous, pet. It's okay," he crooned. He pushed in a second finger. "But we talked about this. What I want from my good little pet." Abby groaned and swiveled her hips against his hand. He allowed it. "You," he said, rasping his thumb against her clit as his fingers penetrated her, "are mine. You are beautiful," he told her. Abby whimpered and clutched at his arms. "And you will obey me." His lips found her ear. "Come for me," he whispered. "Now, pet."

Abby clenched around his fingers, feeling herself soaking his hand. He took his hand out of her jeans and wrapped his arms around her waist. "Better, pet?" he asked. "Less tense?" Unable to answer, she nodded into his chest. "Good girl," he told her. When she finally stopped struggling for breath, he tugged up her jeans and patted her lightly on the ass. "Now go get dressed for me."

CHAPTER SIX

Abby steeled herself against the bouncer's solicitous gaze, although the dress Mark had bought for her was bound to draw attention. It was black, strapless, and barely hung at mid-thigh length. The bodice was fitted, but the skirt flared out a bit. If she twirled, her thong would no doubt draw even more attention. She hoped Mark wouldn't order her to twirl.

Mark guided her to the door on the right this time. Abby's heart hammered in her chest as they emerged from the small lobby into the play area. She purposely kept her gaze from the wall lined with one-way glass. It was difficult enough to think about the people in the room, there was no sense in worrying about the faceless people watching as well. Abby tugged on Mark's sleeve. "Can I get a drink?" she asked.

Mark nodded. "One."

They headed to the small bar in the corner where Abby climbed onto a leather stool and ordered a drink. She surveyed the room as she took a huge gulp of her filthy martini. There were even more people here than the night before. She supposed that made sense for a Saturday night. Couples younger and older were paired, sometimes grouped, off at tables and seating areas throughout the room. A man and a woman were on the famous ottoman, making out, though they were both fully clothed. It seemed things didn't start getting serious until late into the night.

Abby was lifting her glass for another shot of liquid courage when a hand came down on her bare shoulder. She turned, narrowly avoiding spilling her drink. She was surprised to find the blonde from last night smiling down at her. "We haven't seen you here before," she declared, glancing between Abby and Mark. A man stood slightly behind her, dressed in a pair of pressed khakis and a polo shirt. Abby hadn't known what kind of people frequented swingers' clubs, but this pair was attractive and roughly the same age.

Abby shook her head. "We've... never been here," she replied. "Well, last night... we watched." She sheepishly indicated the bank of mirrors.

The blonde grinned at her. "Did you see me?" she asked in a put-upon, sultry tone, laughing as Abby's face turned scarlet.

"Yes," Abby told her.

The blonde leaned down, giving Abby a full view of her perky tits inside her strappy sundress. "Did you like what you saw?" she whispered. Before Abby could answer, she stood back up and reached for a lock of Abby's curled hair. "So you're here to play?" she asked them.

Abby took a deep breath and nodded. The blonde laughed again. "Don't be shy!" she said, putting a hand on Abby's knee. Abby had to admit she hadn't even considered moving away. The woman's ease and light demeanor were almost infectious. She was the kind of girl you'd look at even if she never got naked.

"I'm Lilah," she said. "This is Sean."

"I'm Abby. This is Mark."

Sean reached for Mark's hand. Mark was gracious but firm. "I don't let her play with other men."

Abby was a bit startled at Mark's abruptness, but that kind of thing must have been par for the course at a place like this because Sean didn't appear to be offended. He simply nodded. "Fair enough."

"What about me?" Lilah asked, still stroking Abby's hair. She let her fingertips glide down Abby's bare shoulder. "Will you play with me, Abby?"

Abby's eyes flicked to Mark who, not surprisingly, remained passive. She understood his expectation of her was to let loose and perform for a room full of people, but like before, anything that happened with anyone else was strictly Abby's call.

"Have you been with a woman before?" Lilah whispered.

Abby looked into her pale green eyes and nodded.

Lilah beamed at her. "Can your man play, too?"

Abby's eyes widened.

"I'll watch," Sean declared with a shrug. Clearly it made little difference to him.

Abby nearly laughed. She couldn't quite picture Mark and Lilah together. Well, she could picture Lilah with a red ass after she attempted to order Mark to eat her pussy. Mark ate pussy, very, very well, but only on his terms. Mark and Lilah together would be like the clash of the titans. Abby wondered if Mark would be able to control his inner dom long enough to come. Mark and Lilah together was a bad idea; however....

Mark shook his head. "I don't-"

"I watched you last night," Abby said, interrupting.

Lilah raised an eyebrow. "Any part in particular you really liked?"

Abby nodded. "Can... can you teach me to deep throat? I can't do it." She glanced at Mark. "Not properly."

Lilah handed Abby her own martini glass. "Drink up, dear Abby, and I'll show you exactly how to please that fine hunk of man you brought with you tonight."

She took Abby by the hand and crossed the room. Peripherally, everyone seemed aware of them as they made their way toward the ottoman. The couple on it vacated quickly without Lilah even having to say anything. She sat on the edge and pulled Abby down with her. When Mark approached, Lilah grinned up at him and reached for his zipper. "Let's get a good look," the blonde announced, unbuttoning Mark's trousers and tugging them down to his hips. As his cock sprang out, Lilah let out a dreamy sigh. "Gorgeous," she said.

"Okay, honey, stick your tongue out flat and guide him in. Not much, just the head." Abby flattened her tongue and sealed her lips around Mark's now erect cock. "A little deeper," Lilah coaxed. "Just to the middle. Not too far, not too fast. Nice and slow." Abby pushed her head forward and felt him slide in her mouth. "Now back out." This time Lilah pulled gently on her hair, pulling her back, "and in just a little bit farther this time. Almost to the back of the throat." Abby tensed a little, but moved forward, slicking his cock with her saliva.

"Now all the way, slowly. Breathe out as it's hitting the back. If you start to gag, swallow hard." Abby slowly inched forward, feeling his smooth shaft caressing her tongue. She let out the breath she was holding through her nose and as he hit her gag spot, she swallowed furiously. She had to pull back quickly, however. "It's all right," Lilah crooned. "Don't take him all the way out, though, just move back slowly until you stop gagging and try again." Abby nodded and tried again, this time when she gagged she swallowed. She made a slurping noise as she tried to keep swallowing over and over again. She felt the swollen head at the back, nudging its way down her throat. She pulled back and gasped for air.

Lilah undid the top of her dress, allowing it to fall to her waist, and gently cupped Abby's tits. "Try again," she murmured in Abby's ear. "Go on. Nice and slow. You know how."

Abby ignored the people that were gravitating toward their little group. Instead she focused on Marks cock and took it in her mouth again. She started with the head; moving down the shaft in a slow and steady up and down motion, taking in another inch every time she slid her mouth back down. Lilah pinched her nipples and she moaned. She took more and more in until she swallowed the last few inches. She breathed in very, very slowly. He smelled like musk, male and powerful.

"Tongue out, breathe through your mouth," Lilah instructed. Abby forced her tongue out while the cock was still lodged in her throat and found she could breathe easily that way. His pre-cum, mixed with her saliva, dribbled down her chin. It didn't feel sloppy; it felt wanton. She moaned loudly. Lilah moved beside her, leaning forward and taking Abby's nipple in her mouth. Abby whimpered softly in her throat as Lilah swirled her tongue around the tight bud.

Abby slid Mark's cock halfway out and then worked it slowly back in, giving him some friction. Her throat muscles worked diligently to take in every inch, gagging only occasionally and forcing her to start over from the middle. She wanted to do better, make this better for him. She'd wished she'd had more time to practice. It wasn't working quite like she'd envisioned when she would surprise him on his birthday with the face fucking he wanted.

She reached up and gently took hold of the back of Lilah's head. The other girl paused from her diligent suckling of Abby's distended nipple. Abby urged Lilah up. Understanding immediately, Lilah rose up and latched her mouth on Mark's heavy sac. He groaned loudly. Abby couldn't deep throat him with Lilah needing room for her task, but she hoped that maybe this would be just as good for him. She slid the cock out to just the head, giving Lilah room to lick and suck Mark's balls, which she did enthusiastically. Abby set herself to nursing his prick and sucking out all the cum he had for her.

She knew it was time when he put both hands on the side of her head in the heat of the moment. She took his cock out of her mouth, extending her tongue so his head lay on it. She looked up at him and watched him watching himself unload into her hungry mouth. The look on his face told her she'd done the right thing. Abby swirled the thick cream around in her mouth, giving him a good show. Then she loudly gulped it down and opened her mouth again for inspection. Now the look on his face told her if he'd had another load in him, he'd be filling her mouth again immediately.

CHAPTER SEVEN

Mark zipped up his pants, pulled Abby up by her shoulders, and kissed her deeply. Abby melted in his arms.

He pulled back, smiling down at her before leaning in. "Play with your friend," he whispered.

Still dazed, Abby didn't respond, but Lilah took her hand and pulled her gently toward the ottoman. She slowly unzipped the rest of Abby's dress, pulling it down over her hips and to the floor. Abby's first instinct was to cover herself, but she fought valiantly to keep her hands at her sides. Lilah wiggled out of her own sundress, giving everyone a good show. She wasn't wearing anything underneath. She coaxed Abby to the bed, kneeling beside her and picking up an extra pillow. She directed Abby to lift her hips and Lilah slid the pillow underneath. She spread Abby's legs wide, giving the crowd an excellent view. It was clear that from club play, Lilah knew a thing or two about performing for an audience.

She slid her hand between Abby's spread legs and rubbed sensuously. When Lilah's thumb grazed her clit, Abby began panting. Instinctively she reached up, rubbing her own aching, swollen breasts. Lilah pressed a second finger against Abby's slick hole and she instinctively spread her legs even further. Lilah's rhythmic push/pull inside her had her insides pooling with liquid heat. She raised her gaze to see Mark studying her intently, as always. It felt so seductive, having his gaze on her. As with the blow job, she tuned everyone else out and concentrated solely on him. She knew what he liked, what he wanted to see. Mark could see every part of her, inside and out, and knew her deepest, darkest secrets without asking. His eyes glittered with the intensity of his scrutiny.

By this time Lilah was fucking her cunt steadily with several of her fingers. It felt so good against the plug inside her ass.

"Has she ever been fisted?" Lilah asked Mark.

"No," he replied.

Lilah turned back to Abby, grinning at her. "You'd love it. I have lube in my purse."

Mark looked at Abby. "It's your body, Abby. Your call. I know you don't want me to do it, but Lilah has much smaller hands. She's right, you might enjoy it." Abby bit her lower lip and considered it. Mark said, "I'll take the plug out so it doesn't interfere."

"I love it," Lilah told her. "Sean does it to me all the time. It took a lot of work to get it right, but it was so worth it in the end. You won't stay loose, it'll tighten right back up. I promise."

Abby nodded slowly. "O- okay. We can try."

Sean brought Lilah her purse as Mark leaned down over the edge of the ottoman. Pressing one hand to Abby's stomach, Mark slid out the plug with his other one. Abby closed her eyes as she heard several whispers all around her. "I'd like to get in that ass," someone murmured. Several other men enthusiastically agreed. Mark laid down beside her, propping himself up on his elbow. As he brushed her hair away from her face, he whispered, "Remember your safe-word, pet."

Abby nodded while reaching out and taking hold of Mark's hand. He squeezed it reassuringly.

Lilah lubed up her neatly manicured hand and inserted two fingers into Abby's cunt. Abby sighed happily. Even the insertion of a third finger only left her feeling full. When Lilah inserted a fourth though, Abby started stretching and she grunted a little. Lilah added more lube with her free hand. Slowly, working in and out of her, Lilah murmured words of encouragement to Abby. "There you go, sweetie," she coaxed. "Just open right up for me."

Lilah worked her thumb in. Abby had the overwhelming urge to spread her legs as far apart as they would go. The sensations were strange. There was a bit of a sting as she stretched, but at the same time, being opened that wide caused her clit hood to spread and the cool air on her exposed nub made her horny as hell.

"Oh yeah," someone said encouragingly. "Get it right up in there. Oh fuck yes."

Abby took a deep breath and spread her legs further.

"Try and fuck it into you," Lilah advised. "At your own pace."

Abby pushed her hips into the hand. The stretch was tough, but it wasn't nearly as bad as the anal plug training had been, she thought. Mark kissed her forehead. "You're doing so well, pet. I'm so proud of you."

Lilah poured on even more lube and then the stretch became a burn. "Oh!" Abby cried out.

"Easy, it's okay," Lilah told her.

Abby whimpered again.

"It's gonna be okay. This is the hard part", Lilah said. "My thumb. It gets so much easier after that. Just relax and fuck Abby. Just like you're fucking your man's cock. Take it all into you, an inch at a time."

Abby spread her legs more. She closed her eyes. "Sir!" she cried out. Mark squeezed her hand. "It's almost there, pet. Just relax and get filled up. I'm here. Be a good girl and take it all for me."

At his words her pussy contracted and released, allowing Lilah's hand to slide all the way in. Abby cried out loudly.

"Damn!" a woman's voice called out.

"God that's sweet," someone replied.

"Mmm," Mark said into her ear. "So good, pet, so good. It's in now. You've got it. So full baby. My little pet is all filled up."

Abby kept rocking her hips into Lilah's hand. Part of the reason she didn't want to be fisted was that it sounded, to her, like being punched in the cunt. But Lilah wasn't punching. When her hand was fully inserted, she slowly flexed it, opening and closing. "Sir, Sir!" she panted. Mark leaned in and kissed her deeply, reaching down and squeezing her clit at the same time. Abby came suddenly, screaming into his mouth. She felt dizzy and full and satisfied and, of all things, triumphant. She winced a little as Lilah slowly slid her hand back out, but Mark was grinning at her. "You did it, pet."

"It was so good," she said hoarsely as the onlookers actually applauded her.

Lilah grinned, too. "I know. There's nothing else like it. Not even a dildo." Lilah crawled up beside Abby and kissed her fully on the lips. "I'm soaked just from watching you enjoy it so much," the girl whispered.

Abby reached out and pulled Lilah to her, kissing her again. She rubbed her friend's breasts and belly. "Lilah?" she whispered. "Do you want Mark to do it to you? He knows how."

Lilah pulled back, looking at Mark and then back at Abby. "If that's okay."

"Abby are you sure?" Mark asked. She nodded. Mark looked at Lilah. "And your boyfriend? He's okay with this?" Mark glanced at Sean who'd taken back his seat. The other man nodded.

"I'm willing," Mark declared. "It might be good for you to see someone do it, Abby. But we need to discuss it. You need to remember your safe-word."

Abby's eyebrows knitted together. "Why do I need my safe-word?"

Lilah stroked Abby's hair. "Have you ever seen your man play with someone else before?"

Abby shook her head.

"The first time can be strange. You feel like you're ready, but you can change your mind quickly. If you start to feel upset or jealous, or it just doesn't feel right, then you say so and we stop, okay? Trust me. I've been playing a long time and all kinds of people can get upset, newbies, lifestylers. Sometimes people who've been playing for years just suddenly don't feel right about a certain person or a certain situation. It's okay to say no, Abby. He's your man. It's your relationship. Protect it."

Abby thought she would be okay. Mark had watched her get fingered before by Sabrina and tonight with Lilah. It might be different with opposite sex partners, though. She had no way of knowing for sure. Mark wasn't interested sexually in Lilah and that made her feel comfortable. He was more interested in Abby watching and learning from it. And Lilah loved fisting and she'd helped Abby with the deep throat blow job.

"I think it'll be okay," she told them both.

Abby and Lilah traded places. "Thanks for helping with the blow job," Abby said, tracing her fingers over Lilah's tummy. "I wanted it to be special for him."

Lilah grinned. "No problem. Watching you two was hot." She kissed Abby playfully as Mark settled himself between her legs.

"I'm assuming you've done this enough to know what feels normal and what doesn't," he said to Lilah. She nodded. "Do you like cervical stimulation?"

"Only if I'm really, really turned on," Lilah replied.

Mark nodded his understanding and slid one hand along Lilah's thigh. She shuddered in anticipation. Abby knelt next to Mark and watched him slowly rub Lilah's lower belly, working his way down to her clit. He rubbed it with the heel of his hand and Lilah wiggled her hips appreciatively. He slid a finger in her, then two, and with his free hand added lube. Abby watched as he pushed in three fingers, working them in and out in a slow, deliberate motion. He then added his pinky before folding his thumb in. More lube was applied and then Abby was amazed. After just a few attempts, the whole fist slid right in. Lilah gasped and moaned, moving her hips. Mark's hand seemed huge to Abby, but Lilah was loving it. It must go back to normal size, Abby thought, because she'd fingered Lilah herself before and she hadn't been loose or sloppy.

Mark twisted his hand in a way Lilah hadn't done to Abby and the lithe blonde thrashed and groaned with passion. He twisted again, in both directions, rather than moving it in and out of her. "Abby, your friend isn't ready for more. Help her."

Abby crawled up and slanted her mouth over Lilah's. She licked her pretty friend's bottom lip before sliding her tongue into her hot, wet mouth. She pinched one nipple, then the other. Lilah cried out loudly, but Abby knew it couldn't have been from anything she'd done. She looked back at Mark. "What are you doing to her?"

"Rubbing her cervix with my finger. It has thousands of nerve endings, more than the clit. Some women can't take it because it's too much stimulation. Others love it."

"Oh God, more!" Lilah demanded. Obviously she was in the latter category, Abby thought.

Mark must have provided the 'more', because Lilah started screeching from a powerful orgasm. Abby pressed her mouth over the impassioned woman's to muffle her sounds.

As Lilah came down from her endorphin rush, Abby cuddled against her.

"*He is amazing,*" Lilah panted.

Abby smiled. "He's good at everything."

Mark pulled Abby up off the ottoman so Sean could join his girlfriend. While Lilah was ready for more, Abby was totally spent. She robotically stepped into her dress for Mark, allowing him to tug it up over her hips. As he pulled up the zipper, a middle aged man with salt and pepper hair appeared before her. He grinned down at her. "You need to come back and see us, Red." The enthusiastic nods of the people behind him told her he wasn't the only who felt that way.

Mark put his arm around Abby's shoulders and guided her toward the door. "Good night," he told the older man. Abby leaned against him heavily as they walked. When the door opened, the blast of summer heat made her forehead bead with sweat.

The bouncer grinned at them. "Must have been a good night," he remarked as they made their way to their car.

Mark lifted her into the passenger seat of the Hummer, kissing her fiercely as he snapped the seat belt at her hip. "I fucking love you," he told her. His fingers on her cheek were soft and gentle and at odds with his rough tone. "Now do you believe me?" he demanded.

Abby had to think what he meant before she could answer. Finally, she nodded.

Mark's lips brushed over hers. "You're beautiful. You're sexy. *And you belong to me.*"

CHAPTER EIGHT

Abby turned into the gravel lot of Burnout and pulled up directly in front of the garage bay instead of parking in one of the spaces to the side. She climbed out of the Camaro and stepped up onto the solid concrete of the work area. Shooter was closest to the open door and nodded curiously at her as she ventured inside.

"Need some parts for your car?" he asked.

Before Abby could reply, Emilio came up just behind him and said, "I got a part for you, Abby. It's big and hard and goes all night as long as its got lube." He grinned at her. "And you don't gotta call me 'Sir' or nothing," he said suavely before attempting to lean against the tool cart next to him. His hand slid off the surface, causing his hip to crash into it sending stainless steel hardware scattering everywhere. "Damn it!" he barked.

Everyone, including Abby, laughed. "I think I'll pass, Emilio," she said. "I like a man who knows what to do with his hands."

Mark crossed the garage bay, smirking at the teenager. "Forget it, Emilio. She's too much woman for you."

Emilio grunted dismissively. "I can handle those curves," he declared. "They don't look that dangerous."

Mark's impossibly blue eyes sparkled as he looked at her. "It's not the curves you've got to watch out for," he told the boy. "It's the mouth. And she's about to give me a heaping helping of sass."

Emilio frowned at Abby. "How can you tell?"

Mark's head tilted to one side as he smiled at her. "I know my girl."

Abby ignored the look he was giving her and put her hands on her hips. "Come to the hotel when you finish up here."

The corner of Mark's mouth lifted. "Is that an order?"

"Yes."

Easy laughed, but Mark just grinned down at her. "Well, now," he said, "should I bother to bring clothes? Or will you keep me pretty much naked all night?"

"Dress for dinner," Abby replied. "After that, neither one of us is putting on any clothes until tomorrow." She put a finger to her lips and pretended to think it over. "Maybe not even then."

"*There's* a birthday present," Hawk declared.

Mark dipped his head toward her. "Yes, ma'am," he replied in his Texas drawl, laying it on extra thick because he was amused. He loved her sass outside the bedroom. Abby suspected it heightened his own experience when he set about taming his little filly in private. She gave him a nod and turned back to her Camaro. She was still a little nervous as the entire afternoon loomed before her, but she thought she hid it well. She headed back to The Custer for the next stage of her plan.

An hour later she was pacing back and forth inside the lobby of the hotel. Despite all her meticulous preparations, she still couldn't seem to calm her nerves. She tugged at the hem of her light blue dress, smoothing the fabric over and over. Before she'd met Mark, she wouldn't have looked twice at a dress like this. Its mid-thigh length and spaghetti straps revealed more skin than she'd ever been comfortable showing. Now, after having been naked in a room full of people, the dress seemed tame by comparison.

Sarah, arms laden with bags, approached the hotel's revolving door. Abby surged forward and grasped the handle of one of the bags as her friend entered the building. "Oh, thanks!" Sarah huffed, rearranging her grip on the other bag. "It's not much, but it's so heavy!"

A few months from now the hotel's kitchen would be fully

functional and available for Sarah to prep meals on special occasions, but Abby didn't want to wait any longer. She led Sarah to the elevators and they rode up to the second floor rather than struggling with the bags. "The steaks are perfect," Sarah gushed. "They're seared with pink peppercorns and Kona Coffee grounds. And the dessert is chocolate mousse with red chili pepper." She winked at Abby. "Like you two need any spicing up."

Abby laughed as the doors slid open. She swiped the keycard to unlock the large ballroom, pulled open the door, and ushered the woman inside. Sarah gasped, stopping short and apparently forgetting all about the heavy bag she was shouldering. "Oh my God, Abby! It looks just like Tildy's wedding!"

Abby nodded. It did look quite a bit similar, minus the flowers that had been festooned on every available surface for Tildy and Hawk's ceremony. This time only a small bouquet of freshly cut white and pink lilies sat as a centerpiece for the only decorated table. The white fairy lights still glowed from the arch at the back of the room. The overhead lights were dimmed and the candles on the table flickered softly.

"It's beautiful, Abby," Sarah said cautiously.

Abby froze as she set her bag down on a nearby empty table. "But... but what?"

"Well," Sarah said sheepishly, "I don't know. It's just, he would have liked beer and pool at Maria's, you know? Tex has never gotten all fancy on his birthday. It's just... it's a lot of effort for a birthday."

Abby ran her hand nervously through her hair and cleared her throat. "Well... see... that's the thing. It's not just his birthday."

Sarah turned to face her.

"It's... I..." Abby sputtered. She had everything she wanted to say to Mark worked out, but she hadn't considered attempting to explain it to anyone else. By way of explanation, she plucked the gray box out from underneath the flower arrangement and handed it to Sarah. The woman's eyes widened as she opened it. "Oh. My. God. Oh, Abby. It's... it's *amazing!*" she said as she turned it over between her fingers.

"I want him," Abby said firmly. "He's mine. It's time."

She knew Sarah could relate. The tiny brunette had decided the same thing not so long ago. She'd told Shooter (and everyone else) when and where to be because she wasn't going to wait any longer for her life to start. Abby was ready, too. She only hoped Mark felt the same.

"I want it to be now," she told Sarah. "And I want it here."

The Custer now felt as much a friend as the woman standing in front of her. Abby couldn't imagine having her wedding anywhere else. She'd come to South Dakota looking for a job and instead she'd found a home.

Sarah replaced the ring and hugged Abby fiercely. "I always wanted a sister," she whispered. Abby returned the hug, and the sentiment, just as strongly.

She'd found a family, too.

CHAPTER NINE

Abby's stomach knotted as Mark stepped into the ballroom. He looked gorgeous in his blue silk shirt and black trousers. No one looking at him would guess how dirty he'd been just a few hours earlier. Abby shivered as she thought about just how dirty this man could get in general. She'd never met anyone like him, capable of doing anything in his life except decide to do what he truly wanted, with the people he truly loved.

"You look beautiful," he told her as he took her into his arms.

"Thank you."

A year ago she would have dismissed his compliment, made excuses for why he'd said it. Now she accepted it as readily as if he'd told her the sky was blue. He took in the dimly lit room, the flowers on the table, and smiled at her. "This is nice, Abby. Is it just us?" he asked, seeing that only one table had been set. She nodded. His lips brushed hers as he gently squeezed her. "Thank you."

"Happy birthday."

He led her to the table, pulling out her chair for her. Mark was always thoughtful. If, like Sarah, he thought she'd gone overboard, he'd never say it. He'd never dash her efforts so carelessly.

"I haven't been in this room since Hawk and Tildy's wedding."

Abby blushed and quickly snatched the stainless steel lid off his plate. Mark grinned. "Now that is a birthday dinner," he declared.

"There's dessert, too."

He gave her a dark look. "Oh, I know what I'm having for dessert."

Abby suppressed a grin and lifted her own plate's lid. She set them aside and ran a hand absent-mindedly over the tablecloth. Perfect. Everything was perfect.

She could barely touch her steak though. Instead, she nervously glanced at the small box tucked under the centerpiece. Only she could see it, looming before her and distracting her from everything else.

"Abby?" Mark said and she realized it was the second time he'd called her name. "Are you alright?"

She nodded, pushing her plate away. Mark grinned at her. "Are we skipping through to dessert? Do I get to lay you out on this table and get my birthday spanking?"

She squirmed in her seat at the thought. "After," she told him breathlessly.

"After. After what?"

"Your gift."

"Oh, boy," Mark sighed. "Did you get another tattoo?" His gaze sharpened as he glanced at her breasts. "You better not have gotten pierced. *You know* I want to be there for that."

She shook her head, stood up, and reached for the box. Stepping around the table, she got down on both knees beside his chair and opened her hand to fully reveal the box.

"Abby-"

She ignored him and lifted the lid. "I love you," she said, aware of the slight waver in her voice.

"Abby-"

"I love you," she insisted. "And I want you to belong to me the way I belong to you. I don't want to be just your pet. It's not enough. Not anymore. I want to be your wife."

Mark laid his napkin down on the table, slid down to the floor, and knelt in front of her cupping her face in his hands. "Abby listen to me."

All of Abby's raw nerves snapped and she choked back a sob. "Oh, God. Don't say no," she whispered. "I love you so, so much."

Mark wiped a fat tear off her cheek with his thumb. "Abby, I love you. You know that."

She pressed her lips together, trying not to cry.

"I want this, too," he told her, "but I was going to wait another year."

Abby shook her head. "I don't want to wait. This is what I want, Mark. *You* are what I want."

He tilted her face so their eyes met. "There are rules in a marriage, Abby," he told her. "Just like in the bedroom. There are only two people in a marriage. You and me and that's it. No Lilah, no Sabrina, no one else for either of us."

Abby swallowed hard and nodded vigorously. "I understand. That's what I want, too. Just you and me and our family."

"Are you sure? You're young," he reminded her. "You haven't lived much. You haven't seen everything."

"I've seen what I want," she insisted. "It's this. Us. Forever."

Mark plucked the ring out of the box. He smiled when the light caught the inscription. "I lived for years never knowing if I'd find the right woman. Part of me thought I never would. And I for damn sure didn't expect to get on my knees for her." He handed her back the ring and extended his hand. "You know, you set a pretty high standard," he told her. "*My* proposal's going to have to top this."

"Your proposal?"

He caught her with a sharp look that thrilled her and made her shiver. "I'm still a *man*, Abby."

She sighed happily. "I know."

He ducked his head to indicate his outstretched hand. She noticed it was rock steady while hers were shaking. She met his piercing blue gaze. "Will you marry me?" she whispered.

"Yes, ma'am."

THE END

ABOUT THE AUTHOR

I live in North Carolina with so many pets that every time it rains I consider building an ark. I majored in English Education, though most of my jobs have involved using my hands: framing art, grooming dogs, stocking shelves. I started writing about seven years ago to avoid going back to a real job.

I've recently taken up roller derby just to test my health insurance coverage.

DahliaMWest@gmail.com

www.dahliawest.com

29952445R10139

Made in the USA
San Bernardino, CA
02 February 2016